Runway COLLISION

...CLIMB ABOARD AND ENJOY THE RIDE!!!

LAMARLO G. WILLIAMS

Mustard Seed Publishing Company

ISBN: 978-0-615-35228-2

Library of Congress Control Number: 2010921977

PRINTED IN THE UNITED STATES OF AMERICA

I would like to dedicate this novel to my beloved children,
Christian K. and Crystal J. Williams

Acknowledgments

First and foremost, I would like to thank God the Father, God the Son, and God the Holy Spirit for placing all the necessary people in my life who supported and encouraged me to write this book.

A special thank you goes out to Paris Cumberlander, Ameera Joe, Judi Lindgren, Latiya Oshidi, Christina Owens, Dena Newberg, Adreine Weathers, Yolanda O'Quinn, and Jasmine White, to whom I had given the grueling task of reading and critiquing the very first edition of this book. I cannot thank you all enough for the special attention that you gave to this book, as well as your encouraging words.

I also would like to thank Michelle Johnson, my daughter's teacher, for cleaning up the first copy for me before I mailed it out to the professional editors: Dr. Maxine Thompson, Darlene Miller, and Alanna Boutin. To you all, I would like to say a big thank you for ensuring that my work was clear, correct, consistent, and concise.

Finally, I would like to thank my wonderful family, who supported me relentlessly and allowed me to go forth and do this work that the Lord has called me to do. To my very patient and loving husband, Lennox F. Williams, and my gifted and beautiful children, Christian Kahnai and Crystal Janae, I sincerely love and appreciate you all. To my brothers, Eddie Lee Collins, Anthony, and James Ohnemus, thank you for hanging in there through all the storms. To my lovely sisters, Yolanda, Gela, Tina, Paris, and Twannita Collins, you know I'm not the only writer in the family (there are too many stories still untold). To my phenomenal and wise sisters in Christ: Stephanie Huff, Chrissy Owens, Lisa Laude-Raymond, Alana Amaker, Adreine Weathers, Michelle Judon, Felicia Harlow, Melody Quinn, Stacy Thomas, Rae Ann White, and Rena B. Ranger, I love you all soooooo much, and I thank God each and every day for allowing our pathways to cross. To my nieces and nephews: Rodney Jr., Felicia, Cornie, Dontae, Kelly, Naz, Stanley Jr., Kylah, Catoni, William Jr., Paris, Sabrina, and Jahari, I love you all more than you will ever know. I do what I do because of You—Our Youth, Our Future.

—*Lamarlo G. Williams*

Prologue
New York, New York, Big City Of Dreams New York

A m I making the right decision? Diane contemplated while she stared out the window of the small-town bus station while both of her parents continued to rant and rave about how she was making the "biggest mistake" of her life. She was moving from their hometown of Macon, Georgia to New York City, to pursue a modeling career.

Attempting to tune them out, Diane walked toward the ticket counter where the desk clerk was busily devouring a Krispy Kreme donut and reading his morning newspaper. Straining to read one of the articles, Diane noticed the date. It was Saturday, June 5, 1984, a week after Diane's high-school graduation. This was the exact day she had planned to leave town to fulfill her lifelong dream. Even though her mind was now flooded with doubt, she quickly decided that she wasn't going to allow her parents to convince her to stay in Georgia any longer.

Thinking back, they had done it once before when Diane was sixteen. A man who worked for a well-known modeling agency walked right up to Diane when she was shopping with a few of her friends at the mall. He took out one of his business cards and placed it in her hand. He told her that she definitely had a future in the modeling industry and when she was ready, to give him a call.

When she told her parents about what had occurred at the mall that day, they quickly dismissed the idea, insisting that she was too young and the stranger was probably not the real deal. A year later, another opportunity emerged yet again when a photographer who worked for a department store approached Diane's mother and asked her if he could develop a portfolio of her daughter to send off to different modeling agencies in New York. Diane remembered that day vividly—because she had cried all night when her mother told the gentleman: "No, thank you."

Diane understood her parents very well, turning her head around to look at them. Mr. and Mrs. LaRue, formerly known as Deacon LaRue and Mother LaRue, were well respected people in their community and attended church regularly. They taught Diane and her two older siblings many lessons, but the two that stayed in the forefront of Diane's mind were: always trust in God and respect yourself—and they especially emphasized respecting the elderly. They also wanted their children to receive a formal and, if possible, a higher education. Diane's older brother joined the army, and her sister went directly into the workforce after graduating from high school. Her parents envisioned Diane, their last child, going off to college to become a teacher or a lawyer—not going off to New York doing, as they would often tell her, "the devil's work." However, after much persuasion—and yet another agent who offered Diane a modeling contract—her parents reluctantly agreed, but not until after she had graduated from high school.

"Time will tell ..." Diane finally told herself when she noticed a bus that appeared down the street with a New York sign glaring distinctively on its front. She walked back over to where her parents were sitting.

"Momma, please don't worry," Diane pleaded as she noticed a tear rolling down her mother's cheek. "I'll be just fine." Diane kissed both of her parents good-bye.

"God, please watch over my baby," Mother LaRue prayed out loud, clinging tightly to Diane's coat.

"Momma, please stop it. I'm eighteen. I'm not a little child anymore," Diane stated firmly, untangling herself from her mother's strong grip. "You'll see. After I have signed my modeling contract, I will not only be able to take care of myself, but I'm going to come back here to Georgia and take care of you and Daddy also."

"That's my girl," Mr. LaRue said, attempting to ease the tension in the air. "I knew there was a reason why we called you our favorite child."

"This is not the time for jokes," Mother LaRue said

sternly. She rolled her eyes at her husband and then turned her attention back to Diane.

"Momma, I promise I won't go to New York and forget everything you all have taught me. For I know ... *with God, all things are possible.* This is why I know everything will work out all right."

"Diane, I know you're right," Mother LaRue sighed. "It's just hard for us to accept that our youngest child is going to such a big city like New York by herself."

After the bus driver loaded the last baggage below the bus, he walked over to the crowd and yelled, "Last call for all riders heading towards Columbia, Raleigh, Richmond, Baltimore, and the final destination, New York, New York."

Struggling to keep her composure, Diane hugged her parents and then quickly disappeared onto the bus.

Many years passed before Diane would actually return home to make good on the promise that she made to her parents on that somber day. For when Diane arrived in New York, she didn't foresee the modeling agency reneging on its promise to sign her. She also didn't factor in all the bumps and bruises that she would soon endure trying to make her dream of becoming a high-fashion model come true. Unfortunately, Diane learned, like many other newcomers who ventured into town hoping to strike gold, that everything in the Big Apple is not always what it seems.

Reality finally set in when Diane found herself working, not as a model, but as an assistant at a law firm. After a few months, her situation began to look up when she received a promotion to be a personal assistant to one of the partners in the firm. This, too, however, was a dream deferred, as Diane found herself entangled in a secret love affair. She hoped and prayed that her wealthy suitor would keep his promise—terminate his miserable marriage and make her his wife. Two years later, Diane, instead, found herself six months pregnant and all alone. Not knowing what to do, she finally found the courage to call her parents. She knew they would be very disappointed. However, Diane desperately needed to hear a warm and consoling voice.

"Momma, I'm so sorry," Diane said as she sobbed un-controllably. "I know I have let you all down."

"Don't worry about us, Diane," Mother LaRue replied. "No matter what situation you find yourself in, you know we will always love you. Please, just come home. We miss you so much."

"I still haven't told you everything."

"Sweetie, it doesn't matter."

"Please, don't tell Daddy. At least, not right away."

"Whatever you have to say … just say it."

"Momma, I'm six months pregnant."

"Oh, my Lord, no! Diane, please say that isn't so."

"It's true. Unfortunately, that's not the worst part of the

story. The baby's father doesn't want to have anything to do with us."

"What?!"

"When I told him that I was expecting his child, he kindly told me that our relationship was over and that I would never see him again."

"Lord, have mercy. No, this can't be true!"

"Yes, it's all true. So, there won't be any wedding bells or matching wedding rings. Nor will there be a marriage, a house with a white picket fence, or a happily-ever-after song."

"How in the world …" Mother LaRue began to ask but stopped midway in her sentence. "You know what? It really doesn't matter now. Just come home, sweetie … just come home."

"No. I just can't," Diane sighed. "I feel so ashamed."

"Would you please put your pride aside? You need your family's support right now."

"Actually, I decided even before I called you that I would stay here in New York. This town will *not* get the best of me."

"You've always been so stubborn," Mother LaRue exclaimed.

"You know what they say …" Diane replied. She began to feel a little better "if a person can make it in New York, then they can make it anywhere. I know my situation doesn't look good, but I still plan to make it in this town."

"Well, do you know if you are having a boy or a girl?" Mother LaRue asked, changing the subject.

"I'm having a baby girl," Diane returned. "I have decided to name her Taylor Ann LaRue."

"I agree with you. Your father will definitely be furious when he hears the news. His anger, however, will quickly diminish when he finds out that you're naming your first child after his mother."

"Daddy has every right to be angry. I've broken all of our family traditions. How am I ever going to be able to look this child in the eyes and tell her about her father, or even give her any advice about life?"

"Chile, please. You're not the first person in our family who has decided to raise a child alone. The way the world is heading in these perilous times, I suspect you won't be the last."

"What's going to become of my child's life? I mean, the odds are already stacked against her," Diane sniffled. She began to tear up again and rub her stomach all at the same time.

"Diane, where is your faith?" Mother LaRue's voice became stern. "Now don't go beating yourself over the head about this situation. You have acknowledged your mistake. You have decided to keep this child and raise her on your own. The past is that—the past—and the future can be whatever you want it to be. Taylor Ann LaRue will be just fine. As a matter of fact, I want you to place your hand on your belly right now. I will start her life off right by praying for our precious angel."

"Thank you, Momma. You always know exactly what to

say." Diane continued to rub her belly.

"Heavenly Father, we thank you today because you alone are worthy to be praised ... we come before you, Father God, with repentance in our hearts for we know your mercy and your grace endureth forever ... we ask, Father God, that you look on this situation and bless my daughter and her unborn child's life ..."

As her mother prayed, Diane sat on her bed. Some of her doubts were beginning to subside. She wanted to sound optimistic as she talked to her mother. Diane was, however, completely petrified. She looked around her small studio apartment, knowing fully well that she did not have money to pay next month's rent. Nonetheless, she was going to muster up a few cheerful words to appease her mother after she finished praying.

"Yes, Momma, I believe ... I know everything is going to be all right," Diane lied. She was now lying on her bed *in the dark*. As her mother ended the prayer, Diane's apartment lights had gone out. Diane wouldn't dare mention this to her mother, but she knew it had to happen sooner or later because she hadn't paid her electric bills in months. After she said good-bye to her mother, Diane rolled over on her side and cried herself to sleep.

Chapter One

The Runway
Paris

Twenty-one years later, Taylor Ann LaRue, better known as "The Bronze Bombshell," stood behind the stage eagerly waiting to rip the runway. It was Fashion Week in Paris. Taylor's agent called her a month ago to inform her that the Jean Paul brothers, two newly emerging fashion designers who were taking the international fashion industry by storm, wanted to book her exclusively as their lead model for this prestigious yet galvanizing event. Without hesitation, Taylor accepted the job. This was primarily due to the fact that she knew David and François Jean Paul personally.

Plus, she adored and was a big fan of their fashion shows as they were highly theatrical and futuristic. This was one of the reasons why Taylor was always a hit on the runway—she loved drama. Even now, her anxiety level was increasing by the seconds. She was ready to spew out her performance and work her magic on the audience. As she waited for the stage director to cue her onto the platform, she looked back to check out the line of models behind her.

"Look alive, ladies," shouted the stage director. "Taylor, you're on in five, four, three, two …"

On "one," Taylor trotted out on the runway. Just like a prize show horse, she stopped, posed, and then strutted down the runway. A bolt of raw adrenaline shot through her entire body as she audaciously sashayed in a shimmery metallic gown that delicately draped her entire body like a glove. She overflowed with confidence as she strutted her sexy, long legs down the runway.

Taylor looked too fierce. She paused midway down the runway and turned around to reveal the draping backdrop of the gown.

"Magnificent!" shouted a gentleman in the audience. Taylor flashed her pearly whites at the crowd and continued to prance down the runway. At the end of the runway, she hit another pose, much like a roaring lion after it has conquered its prey. The audience went wild. They chanted her industry name, "Vive la Bronze Bombshell!"

Outwardly, Taylor looked like she was totally in the zone as she strutted back down the runway. On the inside, she was frantically thinking about her fiancé who still had not arrived at the show. She continued to scan the crowd, wearing her supermodel game face.

"Fabulous, darling … simply fabulous," were the words that continuously echoed from the crowd. Taylor attempted to focus her thoughts back on the fashion show as the audience continued to praise her performance.

"I have done it again," she said proudly to herself. "I have successfully mesmerized the crowd." The designers absolutely adored Taylor. Paris and the modeling industry as a whole had completely embraced her sexy, exotic image. She was recently given the covetous title of the new "IT GIRL"; Miss Supermodel and Diva Extraordinaire ... that was her all right. Taylor decided that she was going to take full advantage of the moment, receiving whatever accolades, campaign endorsements, and contract deals that she could possibly manage during this royal rock star treatment, because this new title would last only a fashion season, *if that long.*

Taylor struck another pose at the entrance of the runway, waited another second, and then exited the stage.

Chapter Two

Backstage Drama
Paris

The backstage action was a complete madhouse. As Taylor raced to change into the next outfit, her mind immediately wandered back to her fiancé, Stephen William Blake III.

"Where in the hell is he?" she whispered while she located the rack of clothes and other items that were neatly laid out for her next run. A backstage assistant began the tedious task of unraveling the garment from her slender frame. Taylor tugged at the material. She was becoming more irritated by the minute. The assistant sighed, rolling his eyes at her.

"If the world only knew the real deal about models and the backstage drama that we have to endure ..." Taylor scolded. She bent down to make eye contact with the assistant. "I'm sure many of those young women who are just dying to fill my shoes would think twice before they sign their names on the dotted line. Wouldn't you agree?"

"Mademoiselle, please hold still," demanded the assistant. He continued to pull and tug at the gown.

Taylor looked at the assistant and thought, *No, he didn't just ignore me* ... Before she could agitate him further, one of the stage coordinators walked over to her.

"Taylor, darling ... there has been a slight change in the next run."

"What now?" she barked. At this point, Taylor was past being annoyed.

"Instead of walking out first, midway in the run, you and another model will come out together—"

"Midway? Another model?" Taylor interrupted. "You know fully well that I was hired to lead this event and as the designers' muse, they're not paying me top dollar to pop in and out of this show to suit your spontaneous inclinations ... should I go on?"

"I understand all that, but this is not about me. We have another outfit that's similar to the one you're about to put on. François wanted to showcase the outfit at this event as well, but we weren't sure if it would fit any of the models, especially at this late date. One of the models tried the outfit on, and it fits perfectly."

"Keep going," Taylor said, as one of her brows went up.

"Don't give me a hard time. It's already a done deal. You and another model will have to walk the runway at the same time." He looked directly at Taylor. "*Improvise* is the key word for today." Before he could finish his last word,

Brenda Starr, Taylor's nemesis, strolled up to them wearing a smirk on her face.

"Perfect timing. Taylor, here's your better half ... Brenda, the beautiful Blonde Bombshell."

A fake polite smile formed on Taylor's face and then quickly disappeared.

"You were right, Brenda," he said. He then kissed her on each cheek. "The crowd is going to love the two of you. You're both powerhouses, and you both have a very strong stage presence. It's perfect. I wish I would've thought of the idea myself."

"This is not going to work ..." Taylor told him. She hadn't shared the spotlight since ... she couldn't even remember the last time.

"Enough of the rhetoric," he replied, walking away. "You're both professionals ... make it work!"

"If it would make you feel better—" Brenda began.

"Look," Taylor said, "I'll be fine, just stay out of my way."

"Pouting won't get the job done," Brenda tossed back.

"Okay," Taylor said, not wanting to admit that she was correct. "Let's do the typical cross after we walk out. On our way back, we'll do a few swirls just after we pass each other, and for the finale, let's end with a dramatic pose. Like I said earlier, stay on your side and we'll be just fine."

Brenda walked away just as she had arrived, like a slithering snake waiting for the opportune time to strike her opponent.

Taylor decided that she had better think about something else ... something positive, because at that moment, she had thoughts of hitting the assistant who was still in the process of unraveling her garment. She knew anger displacement was not the answer, but Brenda's competitive nature always aggravated her.

The assistant had finally removed the entire gown from Taylor's body and begun to help her change into her next outfit. By this time, Taylor had calmed down and her thoughts soon drifted back to Stephen.

Maybe he's actually out there somewhere, but I just didn't see him, she thought. *After all, it's very difficult to see anyone's face in that dark and misty atmosphere. Wishful thinking ...* Taylor finally told herself for she knew Stephen wasn't in the audience, or anywhere in the vicinity for that matter. *He promised that he would at least come and mingle a bit before and after the show,* she thought sadly. Taylor knew that several of Stephen's clients would be at this event. She thought he would attend the show for that reason alone, since making money has always been his first priority. Taylor was becoming more and more frustrated as she continued to think about Stephen.

"Whatever," Taylor mumbled. She pulled the blouse over her head. "I'm sure Stephen will think of some excuse to tell me tonight about why he did not attend this event."

"Oh, well, it's his loss and not mine," she said inwardly, trying desperately to boost her confidence. "He not only missed out on being mesmerized by the one and only *moi* — he has also missed out on increasing his cash flow. I must make a point to remind him of this fact tomorrow ... on second thought, maybe I won't do that."

Taylor thought about the last time she had tried to advise Stephen on building his clientele and wealth. He kindly informed her that he did not need her assistance in that area of his life. He was at the point in his life where he made money while he slept.

"What an arrogant bastard," Taylor huffed pulling the tight-fitting skirt over her slim hips. She had forgotten just that quick that Stephen being an arrogant bastard was one of the many reasons why she fell in love with him in the first place.

"Why isn't he here?" Taylor said aloud.

"*Excusez-moi?*" the assistant asked as he stared strangely at her.

Continuing to put her outfit on, Taylor did not realize that she was talking out loud.

"Were you saying something ... mademoiselle?" asked the assistant. He handed her the shoes that she needed to wear for the next run.

"No ... no," Taylor replied embarrassed, realizing that she must have spoken those words out loud. "I wasn't speaking to you, I was ... I was just doing what they call in America, thinking out loud.

"Sorry," Taylor smiled and then blew a kiss at him. He ducked to avoid her "air" kiss. They both chuckled because even though Taylor stood half-naked in front of this man just a few seconds ago, they both knew that a woman's kiss was the last thing he wanted or desired.

"You look like you can handle the rest. I'll be back to look you over when you're completely dressed." The assistant waved his hand while he walked away and told Taylor to carry on with her American customs. Taylor laughed. She slipped on the five-inch stilettos he handed to her just a second ago.

"Thank God," Taylor cheered silently. The pumps fit perfectly.

She decided to focus on the fashion show as she rehearsed how she would perform with *Miss Thang* in their matching outfits. Finally satisfied with her walk, Taylor began to put on the accessories. It didn't take her long to start thinking about Stephen again. This time, however, her thoughts began to drift into what she called the DANGER ZONE, or as her mother would say, "when your man has a chick-on-the-side."

"Don't even go there, girl." Taylor tried to convince herself that this was not the time or the place to start obsessing about Stephen and another woman.

"You're in the middle of a show," she reminded herself. "This is Fashion Week in Paris, for God's sake. Control your emotions." It was, however, too late, because before Taylor knew it, her mind had already begun to analyze the fact that Stephen had started to act strange—again.

They had been engaged for the past eight months. Prior to their engagement, Stephen was less committed to their relationship and completely devoted to his family law firm.

When he asked her to marry him, he began to spend more time with her at home. However, for the past few months, he had been coming home later and later. This made Taylor suspect that he may be having an affair.

"It's really time for Stephen to settle down," Taylor sighed. "In just three short months, we will be married and I cannot tolerate this type of behavior in our marriage."

Taylor walked over to a mirror that was hanging nearby and examined herself from head to toe. She had to make sure every piece of fabric and hair strand was in its proper place since the assistance reneged on his promise to come back to look her over.

"What are you going to do about this situation?" she asked herself. Several options popped in her head. However, the only viable one was to speak with Stephen's father, Stephen William Blake II. Taylor felt that this was the best option because it was, after all, his bright idea that his son settle down and get married. Plus, Stephen worshiped the ground his father walked on, and he would do exactly what his father instructed him to do.

He asked me to marry him, Taylor reminisced. *And like a love-sick fool, I frantically said yes.*

"What was I thinking?" Taylor said out loud. She quickly looked around to see if anyone noticed her babbling to herself. Everyone was pretty much engrossed in their own conversations, too busy to notice Taylor reacting.

"Okay, ladies, the first run will be over momentarily," shouted the backstage director. "The models that are ready for the second run please line up now."

Taylor snapped out of the Danger Zone and began to get in line with the rest of the models. She located her place fairly easily, as it was right next to Brenda Starr. Periodically, Taylor glanced at Brenda out of the corner of her eye. A weird smile appeared on her face. She envisioned herself brushing past Brenda so harshly that the Blonde Bombshell slipped off the platform and fell right into the crowd.

What a glorious moment that would be, Taylor giggled inwardly. She attempted to refocus her thoughts, for she knew this fashion show wasn't about her or Brenda. It was all about David and François Jean Paul, her beloved friends. This was their day to shine.

Once again, the stage director yelled out, "Ashley go; Pam get ready, you're up next. Please, ladies, try to stay focused."

"Taylor, you're not up yet, but you can go ahead and go to the left entrance of the runway," instructed the lead coordinator. "Brenda will stay here and walk out on this end."

Taylor finally made it to the other side of the stage. As soon as she got into position, it was time for her to rip the runway.

"Taylor, you're on!" instructed another director.

She didn't have time to mentally pump herself up. Instead, she put on her best game face. She knew she looked fabulous, so she decided to go with the flow and feed off the energy of the crowd. The audience instantly confirmed her thoughts as their eyes stared at her with approval.

The two Bombshells executed Taylor's plan perfectly as both models smoothly crossed each other midway down the runway. Taylor looked over at Brenda. Her face was beaming as the overflowing A-list audience wowed their performance. Taylor knew she probably couldn't wait to receive the credit for devising this master plan, having two bombshells on the catwalk rocking the stage and showing the other girls who the bosses were.

As Taylor approached the end of the runway, she noticed a man standing there waiting. She told herself to stay focused. It was probably one of her frantic fans no doubt. However, as she got closer, it was Stephen. He was holding a dozen red, long-stemmed roses under his arm and casually clapping his hands. "Fabulous, simply fabulous, baby," he mouthed.

When Taylor got to the end of the runway, Stephen took one of the roses and threw it on the stage. The rose landed right at Taylor's feet.

"Perfect timing," Taylor said to herself.

Taylor "worked it" while she posed and smoothly picked up the rose at the same time. She gently blew a kiss back at Stephen, turned around, and winked at Brenda. She then strutted back down the runway. The crowd loved it!! Brenda, on the other hand, seemed to be green with envy. She hated to be upstaged.

"Silly me. I'm always overanalyzing everything," Taylor said to herself. "My relationship with Stephen is fine. What more can a woman want or ask for? He could have asked any woman in the world to be his wife. But he asked me.

"I'm a twenty-year-old supermodel with a career that is soaring straight to the sky. I do not, and will not, get out of my bed for less than $20,000. The designers adore me so much that they will never be completely satisfied until the Beautiful Bronze Bombshell has sashayed their creations up and down the runway. I'm engaged and soon to be wed to one of the most desirable multimillionaires in Paris." Taylor secretly gloated and giggled all at the same time as she strolled back down the runway.

Brenda exited the stage first. Taylor turned and hit one last pose before exiting the stage. The crowd exploded as the people in unison applauded and shouted her trade name. Staring back at the audience, she said to herself, "Taylor, darling, pull it together. What woman wouldn't want to be in your shoes right about now?"

Chapter Three

In The Zone
Paris

The paparazzi were on par as dozens of tenacious journalists, TV crews, and photographers jostled one another for position to ask a few quick questions and snap photos of Taylor and Stephen as they arrived at one of the many after-parties going on that night.

The police held back onlookers while they struggled with one another attempting to sneak a peek at the lifestyle of the rich and famous. The entire scene was one of mayhem as dignitaries, celebrities, and high-end fashionistas continued to parade into the club.

Taylor looked at Stephen and smiled. He seemed to enjoy the glamorous night life even more than she did. Before they entered the club, Stephen stopped to answer a few questions that one of the journalists shot at him.

Once inside, Taylor scanned the room to locate any designers she knew. Stephen leaned in close to her.

"I'll be right back," Stephen told her after he noticed one of his previous clients dancing across the room. Taylor nodded her head at him. She knew there was no stopping him. This was Stephen's meet-and-greet time, or as he would say, this was his time to "work the room." Taylor continued to look around the room as she walked in the opposite direction of Stephen. She joined a few of her friends that were sitting at a table nestled in a secluded area in the back.

Twenty minutes later, Taylor noticed Stephen coming their way in haste. *What is he up to now?* He finally made his way to the table.

"You're not going to believe this," Stephen said. He greeted everyone at the table and then sat next to Taylor.

"What? Is something wrong?"

"You're going to kill me."

"What now?"

"My father called, and it's an emergency—"

"Work? At *this* late hour?" Taylor interrupted. "Well, I guess you had better go."

"Hey, that's not fair," Stephen said as he pushed in closer to her. "I don't want to leave, but some important clients unexpectedly came into town—"

"Spare me the details." Taylor turned away from him and looked into the crowd.

"You have every right to be angry," Stephen said, putting his arm around her shoulder. "First, I arrived late to your show and now this." He began to massage her neck. Taylor said nothing as she turned around and looked at him.

"I'll make this up to you tomorrow." Stephen began to nibble on her earlobe. "I promise."

"Okay, just go," Taylor told him. He always made it difficult for her to stay mad at him.

"Are you sure? You're going to be okay here by yourself?"

"Look around, I'm not by myself."

"You know what I mean," Stephen said. He then kissed her on the lips.

"I'll be fine," Taylor replied. She kissed him back on his cheek. "You better go before your father calls you again." Stephen stood up to leave. Taylor's eyes followed him as he weaved in and out of the crowd and out the door. She hoped he was telling her the truth and was not going to meet one of his gal pals for a late-night rendezvous. Before Taylor knew it, she found herself zoning out of the table conversation. She spent the next twenty minutes torturing herself about whether or not Stephen was actually sleeping around on her.

"I guess I will never understand men," Taylor finally told herself. The truth of the matter was that Taylor understood Stephen very well. She just couldn't bring herself to the point of actually admitting that he was, in fact, dating another woman. Taylor felt that she needed some good solid evidence, not just relying on the obsessive thoughts that floated around in her head. She wished she could go back and date the Stephen she had met a few years ago.

At that moment, Taylor's mind drifted back in time … back when she first laid eyes on Stephen.

It was exactly two years ago in New York City at an Alexander McQueen fashion show; she was eighteen years old. Taylor thought she was dreaming when she noticed a well-dressed gentleman standing up in the audience, staring directly at her as she pranced down the runway.

After the show, Stephen immediately came behind the stage to the VIP section and politely introduced himself. Taylor had to admit that she was very impressed with Stephen's chiseled facial features. He was not only good looking, but he was also very intelligent, direct, and charming.

Before long, Stephen was picking her up at her mother's penthouse to go out on their first date. This was a rarity for Taylor as she would normally give guys a hard time when they wanted to take her out on a date. Her mother and mentor, Ms. Diane LaRue, instructed her to always make them wait.

Taylor smiled as she could hear her mother's voice now as she constantly drilled those words into her head. "Men must understand and recognize that you are definitely worth the wait, sweetie."

For the most part, Taylor knew that her mother understood what was best for her and what would enhance her career. However, when Ms. LaRue was not as impressed with Stephen as Taylor was, she felt that her mother was being too protective. Diane, however, felt she knew better. She told Taylor that she did not give Stephen her official stamp of approval because he reminded her of a younger version of Taylor's father. Despite her mother's negative view of Stephen, Taylor decided to go ahead with her plans to go out on one date with him.

LAMARLO G. WILLIAMS

Their first date was simply magnificent as Stephen had swept her off her feet. He started the evening off by taking Taylor to dine at Daniel, a French restaurant on the east side of New York. They were greeted by the maître d', who knew Stephen's father very well. After that, they went to an upscale jazz club in Manhattan and danced for hours. It was apparent by the way they closely held each other all night that neither one of them wanted the night to end. Afterwards, they went to a 24-hour café, sipped coffee and tea, and talked until dawn.

The date finally came to an end when Stephen left Taylor speechless in front of her building door after he had kissed her good night. Taylor knew early that evening when they had left the restaurant that no matter what her mother said, she was going out with Stephen again.

The second date turned into a third, and then a fourth. Taylor felt that she had hit the jackpot. As far as she was concerned, Stephen was absolutely amazing, and he was only twenty-seven years old. Taylor was also impressed by the fact that Stephen had accomplished so much at his young age. He had completed high school by the age of sixteen at a prestigious private school in New York, and received his BS degree in economics in three short years from Howard University in Washington, D.C. He later went on to obtain a law degree and his MBA simultaneously in the next five years at Cornell University. Fortunately for Stephen, Cornell Law School offered the U.S. Juris Doctor/French Master en Droit which is in partnership with the Universite Paris I Pantheon Sorbonne. After Stephen completed the program, he was able to practice law in the United

States and in France. For the past three years, he had been work-
ing with his father in Paris.

Taylor always knew that she would eventually settle down
and marry a distinguished man, but she couldn't believe that she
had actually connected with someone at her age. Stephen was the
perfect gentleman, and Taylor knew that he was the one. She felt
it in her heart, mind, and soul that she would eventually marry
this man.

Yes, Mr. Stephen William Blake III was definitely different
from the other guys Taylor had dated. She gave him her personal
mobile number within the first month. Before that time, only
three people had that number: her mother who was her agent;
K.T., her publicist; and her best friend, Candace, whom she had
known since childhood. Taylor stayed on cloud nine for months to
come, and despite her mother's many warnings, she found herself
each day falling deeper and deeper in love with Stephen.

Even after dating Stephen for a year, her mother never
warmed up to the idea that they were actually a couple. To
this day, Taylor can still envision her mother's stern face
when she told her in the JFK Airport that she was moving
to Paris to live with Stephen permanently. Her mother later
confided that she had wanted to snatch her head off of her
skinny little neck after she made that announcement. She,
however, knew that it was time to let go and let Taylor live
her own life.

"So foolish, so young, and so innocent ..." were the
words that always flashed in Taylor's head when she
thought about that gloomy day. Her mother said these

words to her right before she kissed her on the cheek and walked away.

Taylor noticed that a tear droplet had formed in the corner of her eye. Not wanting to draw attention to herself, she quickly patted it with her finger before it had a chance to roll down her cheek and ruin her makeup. Goose bumps began to cover her arms as she thought about her mother, her father, and her move to Paris to live with Stephen. Her mother's words had lingered in her mind for many months after that day. Taylor never said anything to her mother, but she slowly began to understand what her mother was trying to tell her. Only fools rush in and fall in love with someone they genuinely do not know.

After living in Paris with Stephen for six months, the "honeymoon" period ended abruptly when he informed Taylor that his first priority was to his family's business. Shortly after that announcement, Stephen began to spend more and more time away from their villa.

During those days, Stephen never gave an account of his whereabouts. His mobile phone rang at all hours of the night, and then there was the jewelry. It seemed as if Taylor was always finding another woman's jewelry in their home. Of course, Stephen would insist that Taylor was forgetful of his many gifts to her.

"Taylor, sweetie, don't you remember? I bought you that piece last month in Milan." For a while that tactic actually worked. Taylor would rack her brain for hours trying to figure out which store Stephen purchased the jewelry from.

What a fool I was, Taylor thought. *Love was truly blinding for me during those days.* Taylor finally began to use some of her mother's advice as she decided not to confront Stephen about his behavior.

Diane would always tell Taylor, and her best friend, Candace, that a woman should never confront a man about an alleged affair, especially if the woman is not prepared to leave the relationship immediately. Diane's theory was that when the woman confronts the man and the man doesn't readily admit his mistakes or continues to lie, the woman simply makes matters worse if she forgives the man and stays in the relationship.

Diane knew from experience and from the many dreadful *"love-gone-wrong"* stories from her girlfriends that the man will only disrespect the woman even more. Plus, Diane believed that the man would, more often than not, remember the woman who walked out on him. He would respect the woman who held him accountable and refused to accept his lies.

Taylor knew at this point in their relationship that she was not prepared to leave Stephen. She was hoping and praying that one day soon he would change. After all, don't all men play these silly games during the dating stage?

During those days, Taylor remembered that she had to devise her own game plan. She kept herself looking fierce and busy. She accepted most of the modeling gigs that were offered to her. She had worked so much that she didn't know how her body endured those grueling days. That was, however, how she chose to deal with Stephen and his shady behavior. But Taylor felt desperate. She knew she had to do something because Ms. Diane LaRue did not raise a fool ... even though Taylor knew that she had become one.

"Would you like another drink?"

"Excuse me?" Taylor said as she snapped out of the zone.

"Would you like to order another drink?" the waiter repeated.

"Sure, I would like another Coke," she replied. She attempted to come back to reality and join in the conversation that was going on at the table.

"Did y'all see the outfit Andrea had on tonight?"

"It was a dreadful mess!"

"I know. Did she get dressed in the dark or what?"

"I think she hired a stylist for this event," Taylor finally chimed in.

"Taylor, please. You will never get me to believe that lie."

"Someone better tell her to get her money back!"

Giggle ... giggle ... giggle

Before long, Taylor's mind drifted off yet again, this time to the day Stephen's father stepped in and told him it was time he settled down and got married.

Mr. Blake told his son he believed Taylor would be a suitable partner for him. He also told Stephen she fit their family's image perfectly.

Sure enough, the next month, Stephen flew Taylor to Cairo,

Egypt, where they stayed in the majestic Le Meriden Cairo Pyramids Hotel, offering a breathtaking view from the balcony. Taylor remembered that the desert sands stretched on and on for miles, and the pyramids looked so majestic. Stephen wanted the time they spent in Cairo to be unforgettable. They checked into the most extravagant, luxurious room the hotel had to offer.

As Stephen unlocked the door, nothing could have prepared Taylor for what lay behind it. It simply took her breath away as the golden carpets flowed beneath their feet through the suite. It looked as if the golden sands that surrounded the great pyramids had visited their royal suite. The furnishings were extravagant. Each piece was handcrafted and carefully selected, adding to the magic of the atmosphere.

As they stepped inside, Taylor noticed a fire crackling in the fireplace to her right. Positioned cozily in front of it was an over-stuffed white velvet sofa adorned with oversized burgundy pillows. The golden glow of the embers was accentuated by the abundance of vases of yellow roses intertwined with the sweet fragrance of jasmine, Taylor's favorite flower. Her delight in what she saw was only heightened as she walked into the master bedroom. It was magnificent. The round king-size bed was enclosed by burgundy drapes trimmed in gold and held back on each side with golden cords. It was blanketed in yellow rose petals and jasmine. The golden embers of yet another fireplace cast a warm, gentle glow in the room.

Taylor stepped from the room onto the adjoining balcony. The sun was beginning to set. She stood there and watched the sun disappear below the horizon.

How perfect! How absolutely, wonderfully perfect! She turned toward the room and Stephen stood there behind her. She fell into his arms and kissed his lips as she expressed her love for him over and over. Stephen gently lifted her into his arms and laid her down among the fragrant flowers that covered their bed. She felt his lips on hers as the last light of day faded and the golden glow of the fireplace stroked their bodies.

The next morning after devouring a scrumptious breakfast, Taylor walked out on the balcony to soak up the magnificent view. Minutes later, Stephen came out, got on one knee, and held out a one-of-a-kind 10 carat pink emerald cut diamond engagement ring. Taylor gasped as tears began to form in her eyes.

Stephen reached out and took her hand to place the ring on her finger. He asked Taylor to marry him. Taylor's entire body was trembling as she looked several times at the enormous ring and then back down at Stephen. She finally came to herself and told him yes, she would marry him. Her response was, of course, followed by a passionate kiss. At that moment, Taylor was on cloud nine all over again.

Stephen promised Taylor that he would be more committed and put more time into building a solid relationship. For a while, he made good on his promise. Now Taylor was actually allowed to contact him directly, as opposed to always going through his assistants or his father. Things were finally looking up for them, and Taylor began to believe in Stephen again. She truly felt he was definitely her soul mate and her lifelong partner, just like when they first began to date in New York.

Yet lately, with just three months before they were to

exchange their wedding vows, here she was questioning herself in the DANGER ZONE. She wasn't sure if Stephen was up to his old games and habits again or not. All she knew was that these thoughts constantly consumed her mind, more frequently now than ever. *I'm sure this is all simply a case of cold feet,* she thought.

"Taylor, would you like another drink?" one of her male friends at the table asked, touching her. Taylor blinked and then picked up her empty glass.

"No, no. I'm done," she said, smiling politely. She then stood up and excused herself. She couldn't believe that she had checked out from the table conversation and for so long. It was definitely time for her to go. She hadn't even noticed when the waiter returned to the table with her drink, nor could she remember when she had gulped it all down. *Enough of this madness! I'm going home to bed.*

Chapter Four

Getting Down To Business
Paris

S tephen had to get up early to prepare for a meeting that had been scheduled at the last minute late last night. His father called him while he and Taylor were at the after-party.

"Son, we have an emergency. The Rosenberg brothers came into town unexpectedly, demanding to meet with all of their stakeholders. You know I like having the home field advantage, so plan to have the meeting at the central office … on our turf. Understood?"

"I'm on it," Stephen confirmed. After he finished his conversation with his father, he knew one way or another he would have to work the Rosenberg brothers into his schedule the very next day.

Stephen moved quietly around the bedroom. He did not want to wake Taylor while looking for the documents he had drafted last night.

"There they are," he whispered. He noticed the papers lying on top of his nightstand. He had forgotten that he had placed them there last night right before he went to sleep.

As Stephen went to retrieve the documents, he glanced over at Taylor. She was sleeping peacefully in their vintage empress canopy bed. He immediately began to feel guilty for arriving late to her fashion show, especially since they had not spent much time together after the event. He had left Taylor there mingling with her friends while he rushed home to make sure he was prepared for his meeting this morning. He wasn't completely certain how Taylor got home last night. Maybe a cab or one of her friends dropped her off. However she got home, Stephen knew she clearly wasn't in the mood for conversation. He heard her slam the front door and walk straight upstairs to their room while he continued to pore over the Rosenbergs' file in his study.

Comparing the time on his watch with their digital clock, he quickly began to gather up the documents. It would take a while before he would arrive in the city limits. After he had collected all the papers, he leaned over and kissed Taylor on the cheek.

At 6:35 a.m., Stephen drove out of his driveway in his 911 Turbo Cabriolet Porsche. His thoughts were still on his fiancée. He had planned to wake her up this morning and serve her breakfast in bed. He knew she would have been thrilled by his thoughtfulness because she loved it when he did what she called "the little things." Stephen decided to have Pierre, his faithful assistant, make her breakfast instead.

As he searched for one of his contemporary jazz CDs, he continued to think about what else he could do for Taylor since his original plan had been derailed. "I could have Pierre take Taylor to that new exclusive day spa and salon that just opened up two weeks ago in Paris's downtown district," he contemplated. *That idea just may work,* he thought. Taylor was infatuated with pampering herself, and also heavily addicted to sampling different bath, body & beauty products.

As Stephen pulled up to his building, the Blake & Blake International Law Firm, he thought about Taylor again. *Hopefully, she wouldn't be too upset about last night.* He then thought about whether or not his backup plan would suffice.

Stepping out of his car and tossing his keys to the parking attendant, Stephen chuckled and said, "Taylor will definitely understand; she always does." This was one of the primary reasons why he decided to ask Taylor to marry him. He felt that she was a complete package, which is why he called her a quadruple threat; she was beautiful, smart, independent, and she had a career. *A very successful career at that*, mused Stephen proudly as he walked in the building toward the elevator.

"Ma petite amie est ultra trés formidable," Stephen exclaimed. He pressed the up button on the elevator panel. "Yes, my girl is only twenty years old and is already at the top of her game." He also thought about the fact that Taylor didn't need to be around him all the time, nor did she have

to know where he was at every waking moment. He really loved that about her.

The women Stephen dated in the past were much too clingy, too demanding, or too needy. Taylor, on the other hand, always presented herself as secure and confident. Stephen found those attributes to be very sexy, and he felt that Taylor embodied them so well.

"She might even be too good for me," he mumbled. His thoughts changed to Dena Anderson, his chick-on-the-side. She was also a lawyer. They had met each other in New York at a business conference eight months ago.

In the past, Stephen wasn't always faithful to Taylor. However, after he had proposed to her last year, he vowed to himself that he would make a conscious effort to be more committed to their relationship. Yet, when Stephen met Dena Anderson, his vow and the effort became null and void.

Just the other day, the two of them finally broke all the rules when they had sex in Milan after a business meeting. Stephen had to admit that when he first met Dena, he figured then that they would eventually become intimate. He, however, did not predict that the aftereffects would have his mind spinning in many different directions.

For one, Stephen couldn't believe that he was actually thinking about Dena last night while he lay in bed next to his soon-to-be-wife. He also knew that Dena was the primary reason why he was late for Taylor's fashion show.

What's going on with you, man? Stephen shook his head in disbelief as he stepped into the elevator.

Thinking back, Stephen remembered his initial conversation with Dena. She presented herself much like an onion. His instincts led him to believe that it was all a façade. He just knew if Dena would allow him to get to know her and pull off some of those layers, she would begin to soften up, and he would eventually conquer her. Stephen decided at the moment he was up for the challenge and Dena was definitely worth the wait.

After their rendezvous ended late that afternoon, the joke was on Stephen. He was running around in a daze looking for his shirt, tie, and black tuxedo because he was five hours late for his plane ride out of Milan heading to Paris.

"Just think," Stephen said to himself, "I'll be a married in a few months." Stephen knew Taylor deserved much more than what he was putting into their relationship. He thought about a few of his best buddies who constantly reminded him of this fact. Stephen chuckled because many of his male friends would kill for the opportunity to go out on a date with Taylor. One of the associates in Stephen's firm actually approached Taylor to find out if she would secretly date him.

"What a fool," said Stephen hilariously. Taylor had quickly phoned Stephen and revealed every detail. To that day, the imbecile still hadn't realized that this was the main reason why he continued to get passed over for promotion to partner.

Stephen began to brush his shoulders off like he had seen some of the American rappers do. He simply loved the idea that his friends wanted something he had—and something they could never get.

Stephen walked off the elevator feeling confident as well as cocky. He knew that although he was the unfaithful one, he never had to worry about Taylor dating one of his friends, or anyone for that matter. He knew his reason for feeling this way wasn't because he was all that. He chuckled as he walked into his department.

"Good morning, Tracey," Stephen said enthusiastically.

"Good morning, Mr. Blake," replied Tracey. She quickly put her coffee down and pushed her morning paper underneath her desk. "Your coffee and the agenda for the meeting are on your desk."

"Thank you, and sorry about all the mix-up. I had to cancel and rearrange a few appointments late last night."

"I figured something important had to have happened, which is why I set up the conference room red-carpet style, just like you would have probably instructed me to do," Tracey stated.

"That's why you are my assistant. You're always a step ahead of the game," he declared.

"Is there anything else?" Tracey inquired.

"No, not at the moment," Stephen replied. He walked away from her desk. Turning back to look at her, Stephen called out, "Continue enjoying your coffee and the morning paper."

Stephen walked into his office and sat behind his massive mahogany desk. He immediately began to do his ritual neck exercises to relax and relieve the stress and tension that was slowly trying to build up. After he had finished his morning routine, he sipped his coffee and began to review his agenda and other documents.

"Everything seems to be in order," he whispered confidently. He opted not to get up and check out the conference room. He knew Tracey had set up the room exactly the way he wanted.

"Tracey is definitely a keeper," Stephen said. He leaned back in his chair to relax some more. He knew he had a few minutes before anyone would arrive for the meeting.

Stephen smiled. He thought about the day Taylor told him that she was a virgin. That news actually made him more attracted to her, and their relationship shifted for the better on that very day.

Stephen was only sixteen when he had sex for the first time, and it was with an older woman who was *definitely* not a virgin. After that experience, he generally slept with older and more experienced women. So, the thought of possibly having sex with Taylor, someone who had never been penetrated by a man before, kept Stephen "on hard" all the time. During those days, Taylor pretty much got what she wanted from Stephen … no questions asked.

After Taylor decided to give up the goods, Stephen knew that it was pretty much a wrap. He had Taylor right where he wanted her—on his arm.

"Green with envy," Stephen confessed devilishly as he thought about his buddies. They could not figure out why

Taylor was so faithful and loyal to him.

"It just comes with the territory," Stephen remembered telling them arrogantly. He then turned around in his chair to look at himself in a mirror that hung behind his desk. As he looked at his reflection, he thought about Mr. William Blake II, his first teacher, his father, and his mentor.

Stephen had to admit that when his father first approached him about settling down and selecting a wife, he was a bit apprehensive about the whole idea. Just the thought of being with one woman for the rest of his life did not resonate well with him, at least not at that time. Stephen loved being a big flirt and dating different women.

Nevertheless, it did not take Stephen long to get with his father's program when they decided that Taylor would be a good choice. Stephen's father felt that she had all the right ingredients: beauty, loyalty, and she appeared to be well-educated.

Now, Stephen's father's definition of being well-educated did not necessarily mean having a degree. Mr. William Blake II informed Stephen that whomever he decided to marry must be well educated to the Blake family customs and traditions. She must understand and accept the fact that their family businesses were the number one priority at all times.

Second, she must also understand and accept that she had to bear at least three or four of Stephen's children. This was for legacy purposes. Stephen's father felt that if any woman had a problem with their golden rules, he should let her go immediately. Stephen knew that his father was right about Taylor. She would be the perfect mate, as she willingly accepted all of their family values.

Stephen couldn't understand why he decided to mess up in the "eleventh hour" of his relationship. An image of Dena began to form in his mind.

Chapter Five
Chick-On-The-Side
Paris

A t that moment, Stephen sat up in his chair and looked out his office window. He thought about their first date. He took her to an upscale restaurant in Manhattan.

Just like Taylor, Dena appeared to have it all: beauty, brains, great conversation. Stephen noticed, however, that Dena was able to hold his attention longer—for hours, in fact. Stephen thought that this was because Dena was a lawyer. Her conversation, for some reason, was more interesting and intriguing than Taylor's. Whatever the fascination was, Stephen told Dena that he would love to see her again.

Stephen decided to be up front with Dena and tell her about his engagement to Taylor. He remembered that Dena was not concerned about Stephen's engagement. She informed him that she had no intention of becoming intimate with him. All she wanted from Stephen was friendship.

For a while, they followed the rules. Their physical

attraction for each other grew stronger, and Stephen soon convinced Dena to move to Paris and work as a consultant for their firm. In Paris, they began to end their long work-days at various cafés, restaurants, and eventually, at Dena's apartment. The big day finally came as Stephen thought about their very first sexual encounter.

"Tracey," Stephen stated while he held the button on the phone intercom down.

"Yes," Tracey replied.

"I'm heading over to the boardroom. When the Rosenberg brothers arrive, please page me over the office intercom."

"Yes sir," Tracey returned.

"Tracey, no other interruptions," Stephen said. He got up and began to walk over to the boardroom.

Perfect location, thought Stephen. He needed a place where he could replay his love affair with Dena in his head. Closing the door behind him, he walked over to the chair that was at the head of the table and sat down. Slowly, he turned the chair towards the giant glass window and his mind drifted to Milan.

Stephen and Dena arrived early for their meeting at the Principe Disavoia Milano Hotel in Italy. Stephen had asked Dena prior to planning the meeting to accompany him because he knew her expert legal advice would definitely come in handy during the negotiation phase. Knowing that they would stay overnight, Dena agreed to accompany him only if he reserved two suites. Although Stephen had a hidden agenda, he complied with

Dena's request and reserved a deluxe family suite. It had two rooms, which connected via bathrooms.

As expected, the meeting was a huge success. Stephen and Dena managed to seal a forty million dollar contract for the firm. As they walked out of the conference room, they agreed that they should celebrate this victory in the city. They were both elated, yet still in awe at the same time.

They had such a great time in the city that they did not return to their hotel rooms until early the next morning. When they approached Dena's door, Stephen noticed that her body language was saying everything but good night, or in their case, good morning.

As he kissed Dena on the forehead and said good-bye, he had only one thing on his mind; the surprise that he had waiting for Dena.

As soon as Stephen went into his room, he turned on the parental monitoring screen that was only in the master suite. He had purposely reserved a family suite so that he would be able to watch Dena's every move.

He sat on his bed and began to remove his clothes. He watched Dena kick off her shoes and walk toward the bathroom.

"Perfect," Stephen said mischievously. He noticed Dena's facial expression when she got into the bathroom. He had an attendant decorate the bathroom with white flowers and candles while they were out celebrating in the city.

Stephen noticed that Dena looked inside the huge oval Jacuzzi and picked up one of the many red and pink rose petals that were floating on top of the water. She then walked over to where the attendant placed the bottle of Dom Pérignon champagne chilling on ice, two crystal champagne glasses, and a crystal bowl of luscious ruby-red strawberries. Watching her every move, Stephen wondered what Dena was thinking when she picked up one of the glasses, looked around, then headed for the bedroom.

"I do believe it's show time," Stephen exclaimed. He quickly pulled off the rest of his clothes and opened the adjoining bathroom door. Just then, his cell phone rang.

I wonder who that could be? Stephen thought sarcastically, knowing very well that it was Dena. He quickly uncorked the champagne bottle in his room, filled his glass up to the rim, and jumped into the Jacuzzi.

"Five, four, three, two," Stephen whispered. He predicted that Dena would be back in the bathroom ready to rumble. Sure enough, just as he predicted, Dena came back into the bathroom with her bathrobe on, carrying her champagne glass in her hand. She almost dropped it when she saw Stephen sitting in the Jacuzzi with his champagne glass in his hand lifted up in the air to salute her entrance.

"Please come and join me," he requested seductively.

"How did you pull all of this off?" Dena asked curiously. She walked toward him as he sat there looking like a king in all his glory.

Noticing the connecting door, which was now wide open, Dena picked up a towel, wet it, and snapped it like a whip at Stephen.

"Do you know what I do to men who behave in this fashion, like naughty little school boys?"

"Please, by all means, tell me," Stephen replied. "Better yet, why don't you come over here and teach me a lesson or two or thrrrrrrreee." Before Stephen could finish counting, Dena was in the Jacuzzi delivering her consequences for Stephen's deviant behavior.

What Stephen thought would last for maybe an hour or two turned into hours and hours of passionate, steamy sex. They did not leave the hotel until that evening.

Stephen could not recall how much he had enjoyed being with ___ he ___ himself ___ nking about her over and ov___ ___ is ___ efinit___ first for Stephen. No other woman ___ ___ or, ___ aptivated him like th___ ___ in s___.

"Lo___ ___," Stephen mumbled shamefully. "When I should be preparing ___ mentally for this meeting, I'm here thinking ab___ Dena, reliving every steamy scene, every erotic ___ of tha___ day. What am I going to do?" Stephen ___ ___founded. With his head hung low, he finally stood up and walked toward the window. At this time, he knew it would be extremely difficult to end his relationship with her.

Chapter Six

Such A Big Ego
Paris

Stephen turned around as he heard a knock at the conference door. He was still at the office waiting for the arrival of others and the meeting to begin.

"Mr. Blake," Tracey exclaimed. "I'm sorry to interrupt you." She slowly opened the doors and walked into the room.

"Yes, Tracey, what do you want?" Stephen replied sharply.

"Your fiancée is on line one."

"Thanks, Tracey; I'll get it in my office." Stephen quickly got up and headed toward the door.

As he walked out of the room, he asked Tracey what time it was.

"It's 8:05 a.m., sir."

"Has any one arrived yet?" he said frantically.

"No sir," Tracey replied calmly.

"Get the Rosenberg brothers on line three," Stephen ordered. He walked quickly toward his office.

Stephen sat down in his chair. He breathed in deeply, exhaled, and then picked up the phone. "Good morning, sweetie. I'm surprised that you're up so early, considering the long night you had."

"I'm surprised, as well, but the smell of freshly baked blueberry muffins and garden-stuffed crepes gets me up and going every time. After I was finished, I decided that I couldn't let another minute go by without saying thank you for your thoughtfulness. Pierre did tell me that you had planned to get up and make it yourself, but I know you had to get up early for your meeting. So I just wanted you to know I loved every bit of my breakfast and I love you even more."

Hearing Taylor's voice made Stephen's heart melt. He felt like such a selfish jerk at times.

"You know I'll do anything for my girl," he said sheepishly. "Hopefully, this meeting will end before noon, and if that happens, I should be home before three."

"Please try, Stephen." Taylor swirled the phone cord around her finger. "I have a surprise for you, but I can't tell you what it is. You will just have to come home at a decent hour to find out."

"Sweetie, you know I don't like surprises, and you know I can't promise you that I'll come directly home," stated Stephen.

"The last time I checked," Taylor returned cynically, "your name was written on the outside of that law firm."

"That is precisely why I can't make you this promise. I will, however, make every effort to be out of this building and driving home by three."

"Mr. Blake," said Tracey over the office intercom, "the Rosenberg brothers are on line three."

"Sweetie, I have to go. I left my platinum card on your bureau. Have Pierre drive you to that new spa and salon that recently opened up downtown, and if that doesn't appease you, please do something special for yourself. You truly deserve it."

"Stephen, you spoil me too much. I love you."

"I love you more," replied Stephen as he felt some of the guilt that had built up easing away. Still, in the back of mind, he was thinking about a reasonable excuse to push their wedding date back three more months.

"No such luck," he said out loud. He pressed line three to find out where his clients were.

Stephen walked out of the boardroom with the Rosenberg brothers and their entourage at one o'clock. After everyone had left the building, he immediately called his father to inform him that they were trying to play hardball by threatening to take their business to another firm.

"Son, don't worry about them," Mr. Blake told him. "I'll take care of them. They are just getting a little greedy. You, on the other hand, should be taking that pretty bride-to-be of yours out to celebrate the deal you made in Milan. I believe I was forty years old when I first secured a deal like that one. You should be very proud of yourself, son. I know I am. Go home, Stephen," demanded Mr. Blake, "and I'll see you next week in New York."

Closing his cell phone, Stephen thought about the fact that his father truly knew what was best for him. He decided to go straight home.

"Cancel any appointments I have scheduled for today. I'm going home."

"Right away," replied Tracey. "Also, Mr. Blake, there is a Dena Anderson who has been waiting on line one for you. Should I tell her—"

"No ... no ..." Stephen interrupted. He tried not to look overly excited. "I'll get that call in my office, and Tracey, you can go home for the day as well."

"Thank you, sir. I'll definitely do that right after I have cleared your schedule."

Feeling completely exhausted, Stephen returned to his office and picked up the phone. "Hello, this is Stephen."

"Well, hello, Mr. Blake. How are you feeling? Are you still on cloud nine?"

"Very much so," Stephen replied. He suddenly felt a boost of energy surge through his body. "I had an unforgettable time yesterday afternoon."

"I'm referring to the meeting," Dena said laughing.

"I am, however, referring to the time we shared together *after* the meeting," Stephen stated. "Is there any chance that we can do an encore?" he inquired.

"You're still acting like a naughty boy, Stephen," Dena teased. "I thought by now you would have settled down."

"Are you busy this afternoon?" Stephen asked. He felt his testosterone building up.

"I think I will be able to work you into my schedule, if you come over to my office right *now*," Dena whispered invitingly.

"I'll see you in about twenty minutes." He frantically hung up the phone and walked out of his office.

Taylor decided to call Stephen at the office after she had come back from her spa treatment. She wanted to make sure he was coming straight home.

"Blake and Blake International Law Firm. This is Stephen Blake's office. May I assist you?" asked Tracey.

"Hello, Tracey, this is Taylor again. Is Stephen available?"

"Ms. LaRue, he just left a few minutes ago. He has cancelled all of his afternoon appointments and his last words to me were that he was going straight home."

"Great!" Taylor exclaimed. "Have a nice evening, Tracey."

"You do the same, Ms. LaRue."

As Taylor hung up the phone, she turned to her mother and said, "Stephen should be home momentarily." Taylor was surprised when her mother arrived at the front door this morning. The excitement quickly wore off as Diane questioned Taylor all morning and afternoon about Stephen and their relationship.

"Wonderful," Diane said. "I would like Stephen to take us out to eat. I'm starving."

"Mother, we just ate an hour ago."

"Sweetie, please. You know I only come to Paris for three things: the clothes, the wine, and the food. My stomach is growling, and I would like to eat again."

"Whatever, Mother!"

Diane went on and on asking such questions like: "Darling, have your lost weight?" "Is everything all right?" "Is Stephen treating you well?" "How is their business doing?" "Where is Stephen, and when will he be home?"

"Mother, please stop asking me questions about Stephen," Taylor politely told her. She could not bear to hear another question.

"Stephen is a wonderful man who treats your daughter very well." She sat down on their sofa to rest and continued to defend Stephen. "Who do you think paid for that three-hour body work-over we just received?"

"Let me guess … Stephen," Diane said sarcastically. "All men should do that—and *more*."

"Mother, I have had enough. I'm going upstairs to rest. When Stephen gets here, please behave appropriately."

"What is going on with us?" Stephen asked. They both came from underneath Dena's bedcovers. "Look at us. We're acting like two teenagers."

"I know, and isn't it wonderful?" Dena laughed. She snuggled up onto Stephen and laid her head on his chest. "I haven't let myself go like this in a while. I feel alive again."

"I'm not sure what word to use to describe this experience, or even how I feel, but whatever 'it' is, I do not want it to stop," Stephen said. He began to massage Dena's back and neck.

"Stephen, I do believe we have both gone mad," Dena exclaimed. "For one, this little rendezvous was not supposed to happen. Second, you haven't been using condoms, which is absolutely insane. Finally, don't forget you are getting married in what, ten or twelve more weeks?" Dena sounded cynical. "This is suicide!" she snapped. She attempted to untangle herself from Stephen's arms.

"Calm down," Stephen whispered. "I'm not going to let you get away that easy." He pulled Dena back down to his chest. "You're overreacting. Let's focus on the positive aspects of this situation."

"Overreacting?" She hit Stephen playfully in the back of his head. "Maybe you have forgotten, but my goals in life never included becoming a home wrecker or the infamous 'other woman.' I mean, the very thought of me lurking around waiting for you to screw me repulses me. And furthermore ..."

Stephen began to kiss Dena all over her face, hoping that this would cause her to close her mouth and stop talking. He had heard the "not wanting to be the other woman" speech a million times before.

Attempting to dodge Stephen's lips, Dena continued to fuss. Stephen, however, being a quick study, had already figured out her vulnerable area and zoomed in on that spot. Sure enough, when he reached that area, Dena closed her mouth and melted like a Popsicle in the hot sun.

They were about to engage in another round when Stephen thought to check his watch, because he knew it was way past three.

"It's six o'clock!" Stephen was shocked. He jumped up out of Dena's bed.

"So what?" Dena moaned seductively. She tried to pull Stephen back into her bed.

"Sorry, Dena, but we are going to have to reschedule this event for another day because I told Taylor I would be home by three."

"This is *precisely* why I cannot continue to do this, Stephen." Dena found herself getting more and more upset. "I want you to stay here with me, but I know you have to go home and be with your bride-to-be. Like I was saying earlier, this situation is insane, and we are crazy for indulging in it."

"There you go again, overreacting," Stephen said. He got up and put his pants and shirt on. After he was fully dressed, he kissed her on the forehead and said, "After you calm down, give me a call. Better yet, just call me tomorrow."

Dena could not believe the arrogance of this man. It almost turned her on, but she knew she couldn't afford to get turned on when he was walking out the door.

As Stephen closed the door, Dena told herself, *That man must be literally out of his mind if he thinks I am going to be okay with this type of lifestyle.* "It's over!" she shouted. Dena got up and went into the bathroom to take a cold shower.

Stephen's thoughts were racing as he began to formulate a viable excuse to explain why he did not come home at three as he had originally planned. He thought that he should probably call her to see what type of mood she was in and then he remembered that she had mentioned something about a surprise this morning. Flipping his cell phone open, Stephen dialed his home phone.

"Hello," Taylor said.

"Hey, babe, what's for dinner?"

"Stephen, where have you been?" Taylor sounded angry.

Okay, wait a minute, Stephen thought, *something is definitely not right. Taylor rarely asks this question.*

"Sweetie, did I not say to you this morning that I could not make a promise that I would be home by three."

"Stephen, I called the office, and Tracey said that you had cancelled all of your afternoon appointments. Your last words to her were that you were coming directly home."

Damn! Stephen thought to himself. *I thought I told Tracey to go home.* Stephen would usually inform Tracey about his paramours, but because his wedding date was quickly approaching, he decided to keep his affair with Dena a complete secret.

"Yes, sweetie, that is true," Stephen admitted calmly. "However, after speaking with my father about what had occurred during the meeting, I decided to meet again with my clients. The meeting did not go well for me."

"Honey, I'm so sorry to hear that. Forgive me for fussing at you."

"No, Taylor, I should apologize to you for not calling and making you aware of my whereabouts."

"Stephen," Taylor's voice cracked, "sometimes I wonder if we are doing the right thing."

"What do you mean, 'doing the right thing'?" asked Stephen curiously.

"I mean by getting married at this time in our lives. I do understand how important the family business is. It just—"

"Is someone getting cold feet?" Stephen interrupted teasingly.

"Maybe you're right. My mother is here, and she has been carrying on all day about how or what she would do if you were not treating me right and—"

"Your mother is here?!" Stephen was shocked.

"Yes, Stephen. This was supposed to be my surprise. I wanted all of us to dine in the city, which would give you two another opportunity to get to know each other better."

Great! Stephen thought in disdain. Mrs. Diane LaRue, his soon-to-be mother-in-law, was here in Paris. She was staying in *his* home, and *this* was supposed to be a pleasant surprise for him? *What is Taylor thinking?* This was more like a nightmare. To him, her mother resembled the Wicked Witch of the West in *The Wizard of Oz.* He knew that Taylor's mother did not care for him. She didn't want Taylor to marry him because she told Taylor that Stephen reminded her of Taylor's father, a man who left Diane and never came back.

I would leave that angry, bitter, crazy old woman too, Stephen mused as he remembered the time she threatened to kill him if he ever hurt her daughter in any way.

"She's a lunatic," Stephen stated. He didn't realize he said it out loud.

"Lunatic? *What?*" Taylor demanded.

"Nothing, nothing, sweetie," Stephen replied. "I'll see you all in a just a second." Stephen felt the tension building up around his neck as he drove his car onto the villa driveway.

"I hope to God she doesn't stay long!" He pulled his car in front of the house and slapped his cell phone closed.

Chapter Seven

Treading On Thin Ice
PARIS

Six weeks later, Stephen sat in his office with a baffled look on his face. He had made another attempt to contact Dena, with no luck. "I guess she was really serious," he mumbled. He thought about their last conversation when he called her the next day to find out if she was still upset with him after he had left her apartment so abruptly to go home to his gruesome mother-in-law-to-be. *What a horrific surprise that was,* he recalled.

When he arrived home that evening, his heart almost jumped out of his chest. As he pushed the door open, Taylor and her mother were standing in the foyer waiting for him. Diane stood right behind Taylor with her hands on her hips wearing a ferocious-looking frown on her face. Stephen began to shiver just thinking about that visit. *Stay focused,* he quickly thought. *I need to get back to the matter at hand ... Dena.*

"How are you?" he remembered asking her. Stephen foolishly assumed because she had picked up the phone that she had forgiven him.

"I'm fine," she returned.

"What are you doing now? Do you feel like going out to get a bite to eat?"

"Stephen!" Dena stated, irritated. "I was serious when I told you that I do not want to see you again. Our little sexual escapade is over."

"I know you're upset. Believe me, I would be upset too."

"If you want me to resign from the firm, I can do that as well ..."

"Don't be silly. I would never ask you to do such a thing," he interrupted.

"Then I have to insist that you call me at the office for business purposes only. Other than that, we have nothing else to discuss."

"Come on, Dena. Don't be so mean—"

Click

The next sound Stephen heard was a dial tone. At that time, he thought Dena's gesture was amusing and assumed, once again, that she probably needed some more time to cool off.

"Boy was I wrong," Stephen said, chuckling. He began to shuffle papers around on his desk, attempting to make a solemn effort to get back to work. After ten minutes had passed, Stephen slapped his file closed and placed it on his desk. He decided to take a break because he couldn't focus.

"Tracey," Stephen said while he held the button down on the phone intercom. "Please bring me a cup of hot black tea."

"Right away, Mr. Blake."

Stephen hoped that drinking the tea would relax him and get his mind back on what mattered—clients and their accounts.

Maybe Taylor was right. Stephen was now wondering if they were doing the right thing by getting married. "In six more weeks, I will be a married man and I'm still thinking about another woman."

He pushed himself away from his desk and walked toward his office windows as his mind drifted to his father.

Stephen's father was considered a ladies' man, especially in his youthful years. Back in those days, he was taught by his father, Stephen's grandfather, that all men should marry a trophy wife but have at least one or even two blue ribbons within their reach at all times. Stephen's grandfather felt that this would keep a young man's mind sharp and strong, especially when he had to make those tough business decisions where no one wins—except the major players, of course. So to ensure that he had plenty of restful nights, he keeps his chick-on-the-side close to whisper sweet nothings in his ear. This method would help any man release his tension and stress, as well as make him feel like a million bucks, all at the same time.

Stephen's father had since retracted this business method.

He was now and had been completely faithful to his wife, Stephen's mother, for years. This was, unfortunately, due to the guilt he felt after one of his blue-ribbon mistresses gave birth to his first son during the second year of their marriage.

Stephen's mother always gave his father a hard time about the affair, as well as having a child out of wedlock. While trying to conceive her own child, Stephen's mother lived in denial and pretended that Stephen's half brother did not exist. After Stephen was born, his mother and father rarely spoke of his half brother. His father didn't want to upset or cause his wife any more pain. Stephen's father would, however, visit his illegitimate son from time to time in his hometown.

Stephen remembered when he was thirteen years old. Their family secret leaked out accidentally while he was at a family reunion. He then demanded that his father take him to meet his half brother. When they finally met, Stephen noticed that they really did not resemble each other at all. While Stephen looked exactly like his mother, Stephen's half brother was a splendid image of their father. After their initial visit, Stephen saw his brother only three or four more times.

As the years passed, Stephen's father told him that he wasn't proud of the fact that he didn't invest as much time into his half brother as he did with Stephen. His father financially supported and provided whatever that son needed, but he knew that money would never satisfy or fill the void in a young man's life who needed wisdom and guidance from his father.

This situation always saddened Stephen. He secretly hated what his father did to their family. More importantly, he hated the fact that he barely knew his brother, and that his brother never had an opportunity to really get to know his father. Stephen couldn't even imagine where he would be right now if his father had not been there for him, every step of the way, strategically mapping out his life.

"Sometimes life just doesn't seem fair," Stephen said. He vowed at that very moment that he would never make the same mistake that his father made years ago. "I will have children only with my wife," Stephen declared. He wiped away a tear.

Even now, as Stephen thought about his dilemma with Dena, he recalled that his father gave him some sensible advice after one of their meetings in New York. As Stephen predicted, his father told him that a man should act out all his secret fantasies *prior* to going to the altar. His father also warned him not to make the same mistake as he had thirty years ago. His mother still had a hard time dealing with the fact that Stephen had a half brother.

When Stephen finally told his father that Dena had ended the relationship, Mr. Blake laughed and asked Stephen what his problem was. Stephen couldn't tell his father that he had fallen in love with Dena, so he said nothing.

Mr. Blake continued on, telling Stephen that Dena Anderson was a smart woman. "She's obviously doing us all a favor by staying away. I suggest — no, I insist — that you do the same."

After that comment, Stephen knew that their conversation was indeed over as his father stood up and signaled for his driver to come pick him up.

Stephen often recalled his father's words to him on that day as he rolled down the window of his Bentley. He said, "Son, try and focus on Taylor, your soon-to-be wife. I'm almost a hundred percent certain that you will not regret marrying that one."

Stephen's mind snapped back to reality as he heard Tracey enter his office.

"Here you are, Mr. Blake." She cheerfully placed the tea on his desk.

"Thank you, Tracey." Stephen walked back toward his desk and reached for the cup.

"Do you need anything else?" Tracey inquired.

"Not at this time." He sat down and sipped his tea. Tracey left the room. He thought again about what his father told him to do.

With that in mind, Stephen decided to call Taylor. He knew his workday was over. Flipping open his cell phone, he dialed his house number.

"Sweetie, how is everything going?"

"I'm okay, just feeling a little overwhelmed," Taylor replied as she looked at their wedding presents piled high in the sitting room.

"I just cannot bring myself to start organizing all of these packages, and then there is the mail. Everything seems to be spinning out of control."

"So hire someone," Stephen barked. The day-to-day preparation for their wedding was irritating him. "Or better yet, I can always ask Tracey to come over one evening and help you out. You know she tells me every day if we need help with anything, she's available."

"Thanks, but no thanks. I really have to do this myself. This is supposed to be an enjoyable experience for both of us. I'll start this task today and later on when you get here we can open a few together as well."

"Suit yourself," Stephen said. He was trying to stay focused and do what his father instructed him to do. "Is there anything you need me to do before I come home?"

"No, I don't think so," Taylor replied.

"Don't forget to remind Pierre to prepare the Jacuzzi by the pool for us around four this afternoon. I would like to spend some RR time with my soon-to-be wife before dinner, and definitely before we organize those gifts."

"Come on, Stephen, it will not be that painful," Taylor teased. "Don't worry about the Jacuzzi being ready for us. I have already mentioned that to Pierre twice today, so I'm sure he won't forget."

"Good." Stephen looked at his watch. "I should be home within the next hour."

Taylor hung up the phone and walked into the sitting

room, looking at the mail piled up in the corner of the room. "I really need to stop procrastinating and start sorting through this mail today." She sat on the floor to begin the tedious task. After a few minutes, she decided that she needed a more secluded place to complete this task so she called Pierre for his assistance.

"Oui, mademoiselle?" Pierre said. He looked down at Taylor sitting on the floor.

"When you get a moment, can you please bring the mail and some of those packages lying over there into Stephen's office?"

"Mais oui, Ms. LaRue." Pierre quickly offered his hand to help her get up off the floor.

"Thank you, sir," Taylor said politely. She stood up straight and brushed her clothes off. "I think I can actually finish this job today if I'm sitting at a desk in a closed room where there would be few distractions." She bent over and picked up a few packages, and then headed toward Stephen's study.

Taylor had not realized that one and a half hours had passed until she looked up at the clock on the desk. "Stephen should be home soon. This may be a good time to take a break." As she pushed herself away from the desk to get up, she noticed a large white envelope that had Principe Disavoia Milano Hotel written on the front. It lay on top of the pile of mail that she had designated to open and organize tomorrow.

"I haven't been there in a while," Taylor commented

curiously. She picked up the envelope and opened it. "An invoice?" Taylor whispered. She wondered why Stephen would have this information sent to their home address. As she examined the invoice closely, she noticed two names written, Stephen and a Dena Anderson.

"Who is Dena Anderson?" Taylor tried to recall if she had met her at the firm or at one of the Blake's office events.

The sound of the phone ringing startled Taylor. She thought she had told Pierre that she did not want anyone to interrupt her while she was in the study. She then heard Pierre's voice piercing through the surround sound speakers in the room.

"Mademoiselle, I'm sorry to interrupt you. Please answer line two. Mr. Blake has requested to speak with you."

"Thank you, Pierre," Taylor returned. She picked up the receiver and pressed line two.

"Yes, Stephen," Taylor said.

"Sorry to bother you, sweetie. However, I'm excited to hear that you have begun the task of organizing our wedding gifts. I know you are busy so I won't keep you long. I just wanted to tell you that I told Pierre to prepare the Jacuzzi for six instead of four. I'm leaving the office as we speak to meet briefly with one of my clients about an important matter."

Taylor wanted to complain but she was much too exhausted, so she opted not to as it would be a sheer waste of time. Instead, she said, "That's fine, Stephen ... Please know that if you are a minute late ... I will be in the bed with a sign that has 'do not wake me up' on my forehead."

"Don't be so mean," Stephen replied.

"Oh yeah, Stephen, before I forget, who is ... Dena Anderson?"

"Dena Anderson?" Stephen repeated. His body began to stiffen up. Not knowing what to say, Stephen stated Dena's name again, like it was his first time saying it.

"A bill from the Principe Disavoia Milano Hotel arrived at our home, and it has your name and a Dena Anderson's name on it as well," Taylor mentioned curtly. "I wonder why this invoice didn't get mailed directly to the firm's accounting department."

"Oh yeah," Stephen replied quickly. He didn't want Taylor to become suspicious. "I had a meeting in Milan, maybe a month or two ago, and Dena Anderson is a lawyer who works as a consultant for the firm."

Taylor didn't respond which made Stephen even more nervous.

"Sweetie, you're right about the fact that this information should have been mailed to the accounting department instead of our home. Maybe this was due to the fact that we reserved only two rooms," Stephen explained. He wanted Taylor to notice that he did, in fact, reserve more than one room.

Taylor quickly glanced at the invoice and noticed that there were two suites reserved which made her feel a little more at ease, but in doing that she realized that the bill was already paid in full.

"You're correct, Stephen. There were only two rooms reserved, and it also looks like you used your personal credit card to pay for the rooms, which explains why the bill was mailed to your home address."

"Something must have happened at the last minute," Stephen offered. He felt his body begin to tense up again. "I really can't remember why I chose to use my card opposed to using the company's card to pay for that bill. Thanks for bringing that to my attention. Just place the envelope at the end of my desk so that I won't forget to give it to Tracey in the morning."

"Stephen, you know you shouldn't have used your personal credit card to pay for items relating to the business," Taylor chided.

"Now you're starting to sound like my father, Taylor. I'm sure there was a viable reason why I paid for the rooms with my credit card."

"Okay, Stephen. I'm done talking about this matter. So, I'll see you at six, and not a minute later."

"Don't worry. I'll be there."

That was a close one. Stephen hopped into his car and flipped his cell phone closed. Thanks to Dena, he had reserved two rooms and because of that brief conversation, Stephen began to think about Dena all over again. At that point, he decided to call her one last time.

"Okay," Stephen mumbled while he dialed her number,

"if Dena doesn't answer the phone this time, I have to come to the painful conclusion that she no longer wants to bother with me and our relationship is truly over."

As Stephen placed the phone to his ear, the phone rang twice. To his surprise, an unfamiliar voice answered. "Is Dena Anderson available?"

"Ms. Anderson is not available at this time."

"May I ask who I'm speaking with?" Stephen inquired curiously.

"This is a nurse at the Saint-Antoine University Hospital. Ms. Anderson requested that I answer her phone. She is currently out of her room and is expecting an important call."

Instantly, Stephen began wondering what happened. "Why is Dena at the hospital?" he asked the nurse. "This is Mr. Anderson, Dena's father, and when I spoke to my daughter last night she was fine. Can you please explain to me exactly what is going on?"

"I'm sorry, Mr. Anderson. We were expecting your wife, Mrs. Anderson, to call. Ms. Anderson arrived at the hospital just about forty-five minutes ago, and she told me to tell you not to worry. She believes that the diagnosis might be food poisoning. When she returns to her room, I will inform her that you called and when she speaks to you herself, she can give you more accurate information," the nurse explained.

Stephen found himself making a U-turn right in the middle of the street, heading toward Saint-Antoine University Hospital before he could close his cell phone properly. He wasn't sure why he was doing what he was doing, but he felt compelled to go the hospital to make sure Dena was, in fact, okay.

Forty-five minutes later, Stephen arrived at the hospital. An attendant escorted him to Dena's room. As Stephen walked into her room, he saw Dena lying in the bed asleep, so he decided to sit down. As soon as he did, Dena opened her eyes.

"What in the world are you doing here?" Dena whispered, shocked. "How did you even know I was here?"

Before Stephen could respond, the nurse walked in to check Dena's vitals. She noticed Stephen and told him that only family members are allowed to visit the patients at this time of the evening.

"I'm Mr. Anderson; I spoke to you on the phone earlier today."

"You're the father?" the nurse stated skeptically. She thought Stephen looked very young for his age.

"No, I'm her brother," Stephen quickly answered, deciding to change his story. "My father was actually the one that you spoke with you earlier today. I, however, decided to come up here and make sure our little angel was okay."

Dena chuckled as she could not believe the words that were coming out of Stephen's mouth.

"Well, Ms. Anderson, let me check your vitals, so that your brother can enjoy his visit," the nurse said. She then looked at Stephen and asked, "Would you like a glass of water or juice to drink?"

"No, I'm fine at the moment," he replied. He wanted

the nurse to leave the room immediately. The nurse, however, decided to take her time as she readjusted the bedding to make sure Dena felt comfortable.

When she finally left the room, Stephen said quickly, "I'm here because I wanted to make sure you were okay."

"I knew something was strange when the nurse told me that she had spoken to my father," Dena said. "I didn't bother to correct her. My father has been dead for the past eight years, so I assumed that she was speaking about my mother."

"I'm sorry, Dena. Please don't be upset with me," Stephen pleaded.

"As you can see, I'm fine. For the past few days, I have been feeling queasy and dizzy. I probably have a bad case of food poisoning. I finally decided to come to the hospital today because the pain in my stomach was just too unbearable, and now for some odd reason, I am feeling fine. If it's not food poisoning, it has to be some type of 48-hour bug or flu virus that eventually worked itself out of my system."

Before Stephen could respond, the doctor entered the room. Collaborating with Stephen's story, Dena introduced Stephen to the doctor as her brother and informed him that he could speak freely about her health condition to both of them.

"As you wish, Ms. Anderson," the doctor complied. "The good news is the symptoms you were experiencing were not due to food poisoning or to the flu. The test results reveal that you are five to six weeks pregnant. When you meet with your own doctor, he or she can provide you with a more accurate account of the baby's conception and due date."

"You're kidding, right?" Dena asked as she stared at the doctor, dumbfounded.

"No, I'm not," the doctor replied firmly. "The test results indicate that you are pregnant. We do encourage all patients to get a second opinion when they disagree in any way with our results."

Dena did not say a word. The doctor continued and told Dena that the pains and other symptoms that she was experiencing earlier in the week were all due to the pregnancy, which were normal. "You might have eaten something that the fetus or your body did not agree with at that time. The embryo's sack is very much intact, and there are currently no threats of a miscarriage. Everything looks good, and if you are no longer experiencing any of the symptoms that you reported earlier today, I can release you from the hospital tonight. My only recommendation, of course, would be for you to schedule an appointment with your obstetrician as soon as possible. Do you have any questions?" the doctor asked.

"No," Dena replied. She sat there still in shock hearing this news.

"Well, in that case," the doctor said, "you are free to go. I will sign your discharge papers, and you can go to the front desk with your health card and other information that is required."

Dena and Stephen looked at each other without saying a word. "Unbelievable," Dena exclaimed, deciding to be the first one to break the silence. "Can you believe this?"

Stephen could not speak. His thoughts about Taylor, their wedding, his father, his half brother, and his mother flooded his mind.

He finally spoke. "We can only blame ourselves, Dena. We knew this was possible when we had sex without protection. Let's face it; we were both behaving like foolish adolescents."

"I plan to terminate this pregnancy as soon as I can," Dena said. "You don't have to worry about this 'incident' being in the news, Stephen."

"Dena, you don't have to do me any favors," he quickly returned. "Yes, my life can, and will, go on without any interruptions if you terminate this pregnancy. However, just for the record, I want you to be clear about this one fact. I do not agree with, nor do I give consent for, you to murder our unborn child."

"Thank goodness I don't need your consent, nor do I need you to agree with my decision to terminate this pregnancy," Dena replied sharply.

"Why don't you think about this some more?" Stephen pleaded. "You're still in shock, for God's sake." Stephen could not believe that these words were coming out of his mouth. He envisioned his father telling him, "Son, what is your problem? Can't you see Dena is doing us all a favor?"

"Yes, Stephen, we acted irresponsibly. However, you

know fully well that being pregnant and delivering a baby were never goals that I wanted to achieve at this time in my life. I don't even want anyone to know that I am pregnant, or that I had registered in this hospital today, for that matter!"

"Dena, please calm down," Stephen said calmly. "I can take care of that situation. My father is very good friends with the person who owns this facility, as well as the chief of staff. My only request for you is to please don't make the decision to terminate this pregnancy tonight. I'll be here to support you, no matter what you choose to do. Just please, wait a few days before you make a decision that could have an adverse affect on the rest of your life."

This man is insane. Dena stared at Stephen in disgust. "Stephen, do you think I attended law school, left my home, my job, and my country to have Stephen Williams Blake III, or anyone else, for that matter, call me 'the other woman'? Or better yet, have all the local newspapers make up stories about us, creating all types of baby momma drama? I'm sorry, but I know *exactly* what I need to do."

"Dena, please know that I wasn't suggesting that you take on the role of 'the other woman.'" Stephen sat next to her on the bed. "This might sound crazy, and I cannot even begin to explain everything to you right now, but there is a way that we can fix all of this so that we can all be happy. Dena, will you marry me?"

"I'm calling security to get you out of here because you have completely lost your mind." Dena had a look of disgust on her face. "Have you forgotten that you are currently engaged to Ms. Taylor LaRue, the supermodel and Ms. Diva Extraordinaire?"

"Just think about it," Stephen sighed. He moved closer to her. "Please keep the baby and marry me."

"This was never in my plan, Stephen, to be a wife ... and a mother," Dena confessed.

"I don't know about you, but the times we spent together were truly amazing," Stephen confessed. "I truly believe that I can make you happy, and I know for sure that we would make a great team at the firm."

"What about Taylor?" Dena asked. "Don't you love her, Stephen?"

"To be honest," Stephen said, "I truly thought I was in love with Taylor—until I met you."

"This cannot be happening to me," Dena exclaimed in amazement. "I cannot marry you, and I cannot have this baby."

Stephen said in a low but firm tone, "I will walk out of here and never look back if you can look me directly in the eyes and tell me that you don't love me and you don't have any feelings for me."

Dena knew she would never be able to look Stephen in his face and tell him a lie. She knew that she had fallen in love with Stephen months ago. She actually had been thinking about him almost every day for the past six weeks.

"So you will at least go home and think about everything I have said to you tonight?"

"Yes, I will."

The doctor came in with the discharge papers and told Dena that she was free to leave. Stephen picked up the papers and asked the doctor if the chief of staff was available at this hour of the night.

It was almost nine when Stephen flagged down a cab to drive Dena home. He kissed her gently on her cheek and told her that he would call her tomorrow.

Stephen's body ached all over when he bent down to get into his sports car. Looking at his watch, he thought about the fact that he missed his meeting with his client. And then there was Taylor. How in the world was he going to tell her about all of this? Stephen was sure that she was fast asleep in bed by now. He put the car in gear and drove home.

Chapter Eight

Something Borrowed & Something Blue Paris

It was one week before the wedding date and Taylor noticed that her anxiety level was building up again. She couldn't seem to sit down and relax.

I still have so much to do, she thought. She had missed her appointment to meet with Susan, her wedding planner, last week. Taylor walked past the rooms that were designated for their wedding presents. She stopped and stood in front of one of them. "Stephen was absolutely correct," she sighed. "I should've hired someone to organize all of this — it's beginning to look like a bunch of plants growing way out of control." She continued to walk down the hallway toward their mahogany spiral staircase. *Just breathe in and out. ... In one more week all of this will be over.*

Taylor picked up her pace down the stairs when she

heard the doorbell ring. She glanced at the camera in the security room, and, of course, it was the postman. *Who else would it be?* Taylor went to open the door.

"I'm looking for a Mr. Blake," the postman stated, holding a large white envelope in his hand.

"I am his fiancée, and I can sign for Mr. Blake's mail," Taylor replied.

"Well, I guess that will be fine," the postman said reluctantly. "Please sign here by the X." He handed her a clipboard.

"Don't worry," Taylor assured the man. "You won't lose your job. I have been doing this all week ... if it will make you feel more comfortable, I can call him right now."

"Your signature is fine."

Taylor reached in her side pocket, pulled out her cell phone, and called Stephen anyway. "Hey, it's me again. The postman is at our door with another envelope. It's probably more wedding information ... I'm signing your name as we speak ... okay?"

"That's fine. Can you call me a little later?" Stephen replied, feeling annoyed. Having this conversation made him remember that he still had not told Taylor about Dena and their plans.

"Sorry sweetie. I won't call you again ... it's just ... all of this wedding stuff ... is becoming so overwhelming ..." Taylor smiled at the postman as she handed back the signed document. He handed her the envelope and walked away.

"Look, when I come home tonight, we gotta sit down

and talk about this very topic … the wedding … but now I have to go."

"Sure, babe. See you soon."

Closing the front door, Taylor thought, *He said that kind of weird … the wedding … what was that all about? I guess I'm not the only one who is feeling overwhelmed.* Taylor continued to hold the envelope as she placed another call. This time she called her wedding planner to find out if there was anything else she had to do today. She wanted to be there that evening when Stephen arrived home. Susan wasn't available. Taylor began to panic. This was her third time calling her today, but she still had not made contact. Still feeling overwhelmed, Taylor decided to call her mother, who had been in town now with Candace, her best friend, for the past two weeks preparing for the big day.

Diane answered the phone after the first ring.

"Mother," Taylor said frantically, "I haven't been able to get in contact with our wedding planner, this house is in complete disarray, packages and gifts are everywhere—"

"Calm down, Taylor. Is there anything that I can do for you?" Diane returned.

"Please come over here to the villa ASAP, and bring Candace with you. I really need some emotional support right now. I still have a ton of last-minute things to do."

"Relax, dear." Diane chuckled. "We're on our way. Just do me a favor and go have a martini by the pool."

"Mother, you know I don't drink," Taylor snapped.

"Oh, darling, you are still so naïve," Diane said teasingly.

"Don't you know in just one short week you will be married? You are bound to start sometime; you might as well start today."

"Just hurry up and get over here," Taylor demanded. She ignored her mother's last comment.

The doorbell rang again. Taylor walked back to the front door. This time it was the FedEx man. She opened the door, signed the paper, and directed the man to the room where he should unload the packages from his truck. *This could take hours*, Taylor thought, leaving the front door wide open. Then she realized that she was still carrying around the large white envelope in her hand. She turned the envelope around and saw *confidential* stamped on the front in big bold letters.

"What is this?" Taylor whispered. She decided to open it. Pulling out the documents, she noticed that it was a hospital statement from Saint-Antoine-University.

Maybe I shouldn't have broken the seal. Taylor realized fairly quickly that this information had nothing to do with her or the wedding. "I could just tape it back up." She attempted to put the papers back into the envelope.

That's when she noticed Dena Anderson's name on the papers. *Now this is weird.* She examined the documents. "Who *IS* this Dena Anderson person?" Taylor wondered as she tried to recall what Stephen had told her the last time she mentioned her name. Then she remembered that Dena was a lawyer and a consultant for the firm.

Okay, but why is this woman's personal information being mailed to our home?

Taylor now understood why the envelope had *confidential* written all over it. She also felt that she should put all this information back into the envelope and reseal it, but for some reason she just couldn't. At this point, she was just too curious to find out more about this Dena Anderson.

Maybe something happened at the firm with this woman, some sort of accident or something. Taylor continued to leaf through the papers.

She noticed that Stephen had paid this woman's hospital bill with his personal credit card. Looking at her chart and discharge paperwork, Taylor soon realized that Dena was hospitalized for having complaints of pain in her stomach and possible food poisoning. However, the final results indicated that she was five to six weeks pregnant.

"What does all this mean?" Taylor exclaimed. She felt the need to sit down and pull all of her thoughts together.

Okay, Taylor said as she thought about the hotel, *where did I put that invoice?* At that very second, Taylor jumped up and went into Stephen's office to look for the other white envelope. Finding it, she thought to herself that Stephen must have forgotten to take this information to Tracey because it was in the exact same place where she had put it.

"Okay, now I need a calendar," Taylor whispered. So many thoughts began to race through her mind. An eerie feeling overcame her. She knew she didn't have to work up any negative thoughts or feelings that would take her down the DANGER ZONE, even though every pulse in her body was indicating that she was already there.

Chapter Nine

Uncloaked

PARIS

Still sitting at Stephen's desk, Taylor looked at the invoice and noticed that the meeting that Stephen had in Milan was about ten weeks ago, which was during the same time as Fashion Week in Paris. *Stephen actually checked out of the hotel the same day that he was late for my fashion performance,* Taylor remembered as she continued to look back and forth at the dates. Attempting to put the dates and events in sequence, Taylor thought, *He was definitely with Dena that night in Milan as well as four weeks later, according to this hospital information. Her name is written all over the test results that indicate she is, in fact, pregnant.*

What else was going on around that time? She began to remember that her mother had come into town, and Stephen, again, arrived home late.

"Stephen could've been with her again that night. Maybe that was when she got pregnant. Who knows?" Taylor sighed.

She felt herself becoming more and more furious. She continued to frantically review the documents, noticing the date when Dena was discharged. "Oh my God!" Taylor shouted. "*THAT* was our Jacuzzi night that never happened because Stephen came home so late. Now I know why he was so exhausted and irritable. It was the night he found out that this Dena woman was pregnant, and it could be his child."

Taylor's entire body was now covered with goose bumps as she thought about Stephen and this woman. "When was he going to tell me about this?" she exclaimed tearfully. "After the wedding?"

"Pull it together, girl." Her next thought was to call the hospital. She was going to pretend to be this Dena Anderson person because she had all of her personal information right in her hands. Taylor picked up Stephen's office phone and began to dial the hospital's number.

"Hello," Taylor said, "can you please direct this call to the Medical Records Department?" Taylor then coughed to clear her voice as she waited for her call to be connected.

"This is Saint-Antoine University Medical Records Department. May I help you?" the representative stated.

"Yes. My name is Dena Anderson, and I would like to know what the procedures are to retrieve my medical records?"

"Madame, what date were you here? That would help me find the information that you are requesting faster."

Taylor quickly found the dates and rattled them off to the lady.

"Madame, I'm still not finding your name. Let's try something else. Do you have your account number in front of you?"

"Yes, I do," Taylor replied. She enunciated each number slowly.

"For some strange reason," the representative said, "I am still not finding any records or any information for a Dena Anderson. I can try one more way to look up your information. What is your birthday or personal identification number?" Taylor quickly rattled off those numbers to the representative.

"This is very unusual. I'm not finding your name anywhere in our system. Are you sure you have the right hospital?"

"Probably not," Taylor replied. She hung up the phone and thought about the fact that Stephen had no intention of telling her about Dena.

Staring at the information in her hand, Taylor now understood that Stephen wanted this problem to disappear. He probably paid someone to have this information transferred out of the hospital's system into the privacy of his home.

"He never thought that this information would end up in my hands," Taylor murmured. She grabbed the documents and began to stuff them back in the envelope.

Looking at the calendar again, Taylor said to herself, "Maybe this Dena Anderson had an abortion, but if she didn't, she is about 1, 2, 3 … 10 weeks pregnant."

Hearing the front doorbell ring, Taylor found herself

unable to move. She thought about who it could be. She knew that she would eventually have to get up because Pierre was gone for the day and no one was home to answer the door. Then she faintly heard familiar voices coming from the foyer. It was her mother and Candace, so she got up to greet them as she remembered she had never closed the door after the FedEx man had finished delivering their packages.

"I'm glad we came right over," Diane said. She reached out to hug her daughter. "What's wrong, sweetie? You look like you've seen a ghost. Look at your face. It looks so pale, almost white, which is definitely odd because you are a black woman. Now you know something is not right about that," Diane chuckled.

"I forgot that I told you all to come over here," Taylor sighed.

"Well, the door was left wide open, so we decided to come in," Candace chimed in. She looked at Taylor suspiciously. "Taylor, girl, are you okay?"

"No, I am *not* okay," Taylor admitted looking at Candace, her best friend. They looked so much alike they could easily pass as biological sisters. Candace, however, was a few inches shorter than Taylor. To further distinguish herself from Taylor, Candace dyed her hair jet-black, and sported a short blunt cut. Taylor preferred wearing long hair extensions. She changed the color and the length of her weave regularly. It mostly depended on her mood or the job she had to do on that day.

Taylor decided as she stood there in the middle of the

foyer that she was not going to try and hide this information from her mother or her best friend. At this point, she didn't know what to do, so she escorted both of them into Stephen's study and told them everything.

"That filthy, sleazy liar," screamed Diane LaRue. She looked at all the documents Taylor had showed them. "All I can say is I'm going to *kill* him! Stephen Blake III is a dead man walking. A week before my only child's wedding day! Is he *crazy*? I am going to kill him, I am going to *kill* him," Diane yelled over and over again.

"Mother, stop saying that and calm down," Taylor said finally. She then sat down at Stephen's desk because she suddenly felt weak. "I personally think Stephen is trying to hide all of this because this Dena woman was probably just a one-night stand and she accidentally got pregnant. Who knows, it might be Stephen's baby, or it just might be someone else's baby. The fact of the matter is she probably had an abortion, which is why the documents are here and her name is no longer in the hospital's records. This has to be the case, or else Stephen would have told me otherwise."

"So, let's just find out," Diane stated.

"What are you talking about Mother?" Taylor asked. "Find out what?"

"Let's call and ask her. We have all of her information here. Look here, her phone number is written right here," Diane returned. She continued to examine the papers.

"Where?" Candace asked.

"Right here," Diane repeated. She pointed at the paper. "Her address is written here also."

"Mother, maybe we should wait for Stephen to come home and explain all of this to us," Taylor hesitated. "I'm sure he has a good explanation."

"Girl, I must have dropped you on your head when you were a baby, because you don't have an ounce of common sense," Diane exclaimed. She walked toward the phone.

"Mother, what are you doing?" Taylor asked.

"What do you think I am doing?" Diane tossed back. "I'm going to call this woman myself."

"Mother, please don't call that woman," Taylor pleaded. "All of this feels weird. Calling the *'other woman'* seems so insane as well as juvenile."

"If you don't want to know what exactly is going on, Candace and I sure do," Diane barked as she picked up the phone and dialed the number. "Count this as a learning experience, girls. If this woman answers her phone, it probably means that she recognizes this house phone number. It also might mean she is still dating Stephen. She may even still be pregnant."

"Mother, I'm-I'm sure this woman had an abortion," Taylor stuttered. Her stomach began to do all types of flips while her mother pressed the speaker button on the phone so that they all could hear the conversation.

"Hello," Dena said.

Diane held the phone in the air. She was shocked herself

that the woman actually answered the phone. She then looked at Taylor and Candace to find out what she should do next.

"Stephen, are you there?" Dena asked.

"Hmmm, did you hear that?" Diane mouthed. She looked directly at Taylor. "Well, hello, Ms. Dena Anderson."

"Excuse me, who is this?" Dena asked with an attitude.

"My name is Diane LaRue. My daughter, Taylor LaRue, is Stephen's fiancée."

At that very moment, the walls seemed to be closing in on Taylor as she listened to her mother talk with Dena Anderson, Stephen's "chick on the side." Taylor began to pray that this was just some terrible joke, or even a bad dream that she hoped she would soon wake up from and instead, find herself in bed cuddled up tightly in Stephen's arms.

"Well, well, well," Diane said loudly. "Dena, the evidence is quite clear."

"Look, Mrs. LaRue, I really don't want to get involved—"

"Dena," Diane snapped, "don't you think that you're *already* heavily involved in this situation?"

Silence

"Well, let me just ask you this. Are you still pregnant?" Diane inquired.

"Again, I really don't think I should be the one—"

"Dena," Diane shouted as she interrupted her, "I don't have time to play games with you. Taylor is my only child.

Put yourself in my shoes ... better yet, put yourself in *her* shoes. Taylor is scheduled to wed Stephen in exactly 6 days, 5 hours, 30 minutes, and 22 ... 21 ... 20 seconds and counting. Now, I'm going to ask you one more time, are you or are you not still pregnant?"

"Yes, I'm still pregnant," Dena confessed.

"Is Stephen the father?" Diane asked. "Even if you don't answer that question, I can safely say by looking at this information that Stephen is certainly a very real possibility."

"For your information, Mrs. LaRue," Dena said firmly, "Stephen is the *only* possibility. He is, in fact, the father of this baby, and we have been seeing each other for several months now. I left it up to Stephen how he chose to break the news to Taylor."

"*BREAK THE NEWS?*" Diane barked. "What do you mean 'break the news'?"

"Stephen and I are engaged to be married next month," Dena confirmed. *Engaged to be married* were the last words Taylor heard coming out of her mother's mouth before everything around her faded to black.

Chapter Ten

Shattered Dreams
PARIS

"What is going on in here?" Stephen shouted. He walked through his front door, wondering why it had been left wide open. He didn't see anyone, but he heard voices coming from the direction of his study.

"What exactly is going on?" he demanded, walking into his study to find Diane and Candace hovering over Taylor, who was laid out cold on the floor.

"You filthy liar," Diane screamed. She then got up and lunged toward Stephen, only to be stopped by Candace. "When were you going to tell Taylor about Dena? When, Stephen? When?" Diane asked furiously.

"What are you talking about?" Stephen was completely stunned by Diane's words. "I think the better question to ask is ... *why is Taylor on the floor?*" Stephen became irritated. "Is she okay?" He walked toward Taylor. "Did anyone call the ambulance?"

"As if *you* really care," Diane said curtly.

At that moment, Taylor began to wake up. Candace and Diane carefully placed their hands behind her. With their support, Taylor tried to get up, but she simply did not have the strength to do so. Stephen moved toward Taylor once again, but Diane stood up and told him to stay away from her daughter.

"She is my fiancée, Diane," Stephen shouted. "If this wedding doesn't happen next week, it will be because of you. You have doomed us from the beginning."

Candace's mouth fell open as she looked at Stephen. Then she turned her attention to Taylor who was still lying on the floor.

"You are absolutely correct about that, Stephen," Diane yelled back. "I just know a good-for-nothing liar when I see him. We have talked to Dena Anderson, Stephen. She told us everything about the affair, the pregnancy, and the engagement. You are so lucky we are not in New York!" Diane lunged at him again, only to be stopped once more by Candace.

Stephen stepped back to avoid any physical contact with Diane and attempted to explain his side of the story. Before he could speak, Diane walked over to his desk, retrieved the documents, and said, "DON'T EVEN ATTEMPT TO LIE OUT OF YOUR FILTHY MOUTH." She then threw all the papers Taylor gave her from the hospital at him.

Stephen began to look at a few of the papers. "Where in the world … How in the world did these documents get in this house?" Stephen murmured.

"Help me, Candace," Diane said. She bent down to lift Taylor up off the floor. "Help me get my child out of this hellhole."

"Mom, please," Taylor moaned. She still had no strength to get up.

"Are you okay, honey?" Diane inquired.

"Yes, I'm okay," Taylor replied. "Just let me lie here for a second. I'll be okay. Is Stephen here yet?"

"Yes, he's here," Diane exclaimed. "He finally decided to come home at a decent hour."

"Sweetie, I'm right here." Stephen moved toward Taylor.

Taylor got up on her elbows and attempted to speak but Stephen stopped her. "Taylor, I will answer all of your questions, but not while your mother is in this house."

"You are sadly mistaken if you think that I would allow my daughter to be in this house with you alone again," Diane roared.

"She has to go if you want any type of explanation from me concerning these papers," Stephen declared coldly glaring at Diane.

"Mother, please, leave us alone," Taylor pleaded. She got up off the floor. "I agree with Stephen. We really need to talk. Trust me, I will be okay. I just need some closure, and that will only happen if I am allowed to speak with him in private."

"That's fine, Taylor," Diane said reluctantly. She and Candace began to walk toward the door. "We will, however, be right here outside this door if you need us," Diane snapped. "Taylor, if you are not out of this study in twenty minutes, we will be back in here." With that, Diane and Candace walked out of the study and closed the door behind them.

"I really don't know where to start," Stephen explained. "I met her in New York, and one thing led to another. We started dating, and … I don't know. I seem to really enjoy being with her."

"Please, Stephen. I don't want to hear the details, only the facts," Taylor huffed. She slowly walked over to Stephen's desk and sat down. "Stephen, that woman said you two have been dating for several months. Is this true?"

"It is, Taylor."

"Is this woman pregnant with your child, Stephen?" Taylor asked disgusted.

"Yes," Stephen returned, hanging his head in shame.

"What about your being engaged to this woman?" Taylor questioned. "Stephen, please tell me that this is not true."

"This entire situation became complicated all of a sudden, Taylor. She got pregnant, and then she wasn't sure if she was going to keep the baby."

"So she decided to keep the baby," Taylor shouted. "WHEN were you going to inform me, your bride-to-be, about all of this, Stephen? AFTER the wedding??"

"Taylor, I wanted to tell you so many times, but I just didn't know how to do it. Every time I tried to do it, you would start talking about *our* wedding plans."

"Please help me understand why you didn't tell me about your engagement to this woman. Did you think this little charade was cute, or what?"

"When I found out she was pregnant, that is when I decided to ask her to marry me. I did not want her to have an abortion, and I did not want to be married to you and have a child out of wedlock."

"How HONORABLE of you," Taylor said sarcastically. "Does your father know about all of this?" She stood up from the desk and walked toward him.

"Yes and no," Stephen returned. "Yes, he knows about my relationship with Dena. He told me to end it. No, he does not know that she is pregnant or that we are engaged to be married."

"*Unbelievable*," Taylor said. She began to pace back and forth in the room. "Stephen, you are an intelligent man. You had to know how this would affect everyone. Why would you participate in such a senseless, cruel, and reckless act?"

"I know this all may seem cruel, even crazy," Stephen admitted. "Believe me, Taylor, the last thing I wanted to do was hurt you."

"A WEEK before our wedding, Stephen? How could you?" Taylor screamed. She then began to cry furiously. "Look at us. Look at me. I would have never guessed in a million years that our relationship, our fairytale story, would end like this. Boy, was I a fool. I really thought you loved me, Stephen. I even went against my mother's wishes. She was right all along. She warned me about you. She told me not to come to Paris with you, and what did I do?"

"Taylor, your mother was wrong about me," Stephen declared. He reached out to hug her. "She's just a bitter old woman."

"You're absolutely right, Stephen," Taylor snapped back. She jerked away from his grip. "My mother was wrong, but only about one thing. She told me that you would end up breaking my heart. She was absolutely wrong about that one, Stephen, because you did even better, like you always do. You didn't just break my heart, YOU SHATTERED IT INTO A MILLION PIECES!"

Tears began to flow down Stephen's face. "You have to believe me, Taylor. I did not plan for it to end like this. You have to believe me!"

Taylor walked past Stephen, opened his office door, and left him.

"Wait, Taylor," Stephen cried. He followed her out of the door into the foyer. "There is so much more you still don't know about me, about this entire situation. I thought I was doing the right thing. I didn't want to make the same mistake as my father did thirty years ago."

Same mistake as his father? What is he talking about? At this point, Taylor kept on walking. She didn't care to listen to any more of Stephen's lies. She was so proud of herself. She was finally able to walk right through the foyer, pass those giant wooded double doors she had grown so accustomed to, and never look back. Taylor began to wonder where her mother and Candace had gone until she noticed them waiting for her by their limousine at the entrance of the villa.

"It's over," Taylor said. She then hopped into the limousine and sat down. Both Diane and Candace tried their best to console her. However, Taylor just stared at them. She could not hear any words that came out of their mouths.

It's amazing how the human body functions. She sat back in her seat and tuned out her mother's and Candace's voices. Her chest was now throbbing with pain. Soon, her entire body felt like an aftereffect of a train wreck.

"Sweetie, are you okay?"

"Mom, please," Taylor pleaded, "you don't have to worry about me. I'll be all right. All I want to do right now is go to sleep."

As Taylor closed her eyes to rest, she thought about the meaning of her mother's wise words. Like so many young women her age, Taylor had also decided to risk it all. Unfortunately, her plans did not pay off as she had envisioned in her dreams. Although she did walk away today with several nuggets of wisdom, Taylor knew she had paid a steep price for them. She knew one thing: if her mother made it when her father walked out on them, she would make it as well. At that very moment, her mind, body, and soul shifted into survival mode and she drifted off to sleep.

Chapter Eleven
Back On The Block
New York

A few days had passed before Taylor arrived in front of her building. She stepped out of the limousine, tilted her head upward, and looked at the elongated skyscraper where she and her mother had lived for years.

"Home Sweet Home," Taylor whispered. She wasn't sure if she was ready to move back in with her mother, but she instantly felt better as soon as those words left her mouth. Taylor knew she should have left Paris months ago, especially since her intuition continued to point to the inevitable ... Dena, Stephen's love interest. Trying to stay positive, Taylor had to give herself credit for walking away before she made an even bigger mistake by marrying the pompous jerk.

"Well, hello, Ms. LaRue," the doorman said with a thick Caribbean accent.

"Hello to you," returned Taylor. She extended her arm out to shake his hand. "And your name is?"

"My name is Franklin McPherson." The doorman pointed to his ID badge. "Your mother informed us that you would be arriving this afternoon."

"What happened to Charles?" Taylor asked curiously. Taylor had been eight years old when Charles, the previous doorman, came to work at their building.

"He moved on to a better position," Franklin answered. "He is now an assistant night supervisor at a five-star hotel in uptown Manhattan."

"Wonderful," Taylor said excitedly. "When you see him again, please give him my best regards."

"I certainly will, Ms. LaRue." Franklin opened the door and ushered her into the entrance of the building.

As Taylor walked through the lobby of the building toward the elevator, the pain in her chest began to ache with insurmountable pain. She finally understood what it felt like to actually have a broken heart.

The pain first started two days ago when she left Stephen's home. It intensified when she boarded the plane at the Paris Charles de Gaulle airport to come home. Although Taylor vowed that she would never drink alcohol, she ordered a cocktail with the hope that the pain would eventually dissipate. Unfortunately, the problem only intensified. She noticed this right after she gulped down the last drop. Taylor rubbed her chest all the way home.

When she got off the plane, she decided to stay in a hotel near JFK. Even though she continued to drink, the pain never subsided. She also was not prepared to be alone with her mother in their penthouse. Taylor knew her mother loved her and would do anything for her, but she was just still so humiliated by all of this mess.

"What am I going to do when the media has figured out that our wedding has been cancelled and we are no longer a couple?" she pondered. "I won't have to worry about hiding from my mother. I will, however, have to find a hole or a cave somewhere to hide from the rest of the world."

Walking onto the elevator, Taylor hung her head low. She wondered if she would ever get over Stephen being with Dena, and the fact that she was pregnant with Stephen's child.

A tear began to form in the corner of her eye. She began to visualize that afternoon again in her mind. As the tears flowed down her face, sharp pains began to bombard her chest. Taylor was relieved that she was the only one on the elevator, because just thinking about Stephen and the breakup made her become emotional all over again.

"God, if you're up there, please help me," Taylor murmured. She looked up toward the ceiling of the elevator. "I certainly cannot start this all over again." She wiped the tears from her eyes.

The elevator doors opened, and Taylor stepped out. She searched through her purse for a tissue. Instead, she noticed the extra set of keys to the penthouse her mother had given her before she and Candace boarded their plane to return to New York.

As Taylor picked up the keys, she found herself laughing as she thought about her mother's gesture. *I guess Mother thought I might change my mind and go back to Stephen's villa. Not in a million years.* Taylor quickly pulled out the set of keys and power walked to the front door. "Stephen will never have the pleasure of being with me again."

Taylor opened the door and walked into the living room. She took off her coat and threw her purse on the coffee table, then sat down on the sofa. As she looked around, she noticed that everything was still pretty much in the same place when she left almost a year ago.

"Mother is so predictable," Taylor said. "I guess she will never change." She picked up the TV remote off the coffee table and turned on the television.

"Great!" She quickly pressed the power button to turn off the television as the first image that popped up on the screen was a young couple kissing passionately.

Taylor gently lay back on the sofa. She was still experiencing sharp pains throughout her body so she began to cry once again.

"What am I going to do with myself?" Taylor began to feel lonely and very frustrated. She decided to go look in her mother's makeshift closet wine cellar. Taylor knew now that drinking alcohol wouldn't take the pain away but for the present moment, it definitely made her blues go away. When she had found a suitable bottle, Merlot red wine, she went into the kitchen to look for a corkscrew and the biggest wine glass she could find.

"What in the world did I do in my life to receive the type of treatment I got from that man? I tried not to be an evil, overbearing witch. I was always the nice one," Taylor said. She sat down at the kitchen table and poured herself a drink. After finishing the glass, Taylor noticed that she was unsuccessful in drowning her sorrows, as thoughts about Stephen continued to flood her mind. She wanted to call Candace, but she knew from here on out that she could tell Candace, and her mother, for that matter, only bits and pieces of the truth, but not all of the truth. Taylor felt they were too judgmental and simply wouldn't understand. So, she decided to do the next best thing — she called K.T., her publicist, the only person she could genuinely talk to about this situation.

"Where are you? I have been so worried about you. Did you finally make it to your mother's place?"

"Yes, I'm at my mother's. When I got off the plane, I checked into a hotel first, though."

"What for?"

"I was too tipsy to make it home."

"Too tipsy? Don't tell me you're drinking now."

"I'm pouring another glass as we speak."

"Don't go overboard because I'll have to do damage control for that situation as well."

"Speaking of situations, has Stephen contacted you?"

"No. Does that disappoint you?"

"To be honest, yes. I gave that man everything I thought he wanted in a woman, and more," Taylor sighed. She left the kitchen area and went back to sit down on the sofa in the living room.

"I gave him my body, mind, and soul. I even gave him my innocence. I was such a fool! And what did I get in return? Nothing—absolutely nothing!"

"I know, girl. I know just how you feel."

"Have you heard anything? I mean from the press?"

"Not yet. The notices went out immediately, informing your guests that the wedding has been cancelled. I have been sitting around waiting to hear … anything, good, bad or indifferent. If I hear anything negative, I'm going to be all over the source. You know I got your back."

"I can always count on you." Taylor smiled. She knew K.T. was more than a publicist to her; she was a loyal and good friend. "Just keep me posted … especially if you hear from Stephen."

"Will do."

Click

Taylor walked back into the kitchen to place the receiver back on its jack. As she came back into the living room, she began to cry uncontrollably. She plopped down on the sofa and decided at that very moment that she would never allow another man to get that close to her again. She knew she was young and should count this unfortunate situation as a loss, but the pain she felt in her heart told her she was done. She hoped as she fell fast asleep that her broken heart would someday be mended back together again.

Ring ... ring ... ring.

Taylor was awakened by sound of the phone. She knew that couldn't be anybody else but her mother. She still felt exhausted. The ringing finally stopped, only to start again after two seconds had passed. Taylor made an attempt to reach for the receiver, but her aching body would not allow her to sit up. Then she heard her mother's voice from the answering machine that was on the kitchen's countertop.

"Taylor, Taylor, I know you're there. Please pick up the phone."

The last thing Taylor wanted to do was talk to her mother. Her initial thought was to just continue to lie there and ignore her mother's request. Instead, she mustered up the strength, got up off the couch, and answered the phone.

"Yes, Mother, what do you want?" Taylor asked wearily.

"Still not feeling well, sweetie?" Diane returned.

"Please do not call me sweetie. Do I need to explain why?"

"No, darling. I'm sorry. I just wanted to call to make sure you are okay."

"I'm okay," Taylor lied. "I'm still experiencing some jetlag."

"I won't keep you, because I know you need to rest. I did want to tell you that I have booked you two jobs in Manhattan for next week."

"Sorry, Mom, you'll have to reassign those jobs to another model because you know full well that I'm not feeling good. Plus, I don't feel like working right now. I'm just not in the mood. Surely you, of all people, should understand how I am feeling right about now."

"Trust me, Taylor, the best thing for you to do is keep yourself busy so you won't have to time to even think about … well, you know who."

Taylor had to smile to herself as she thought about her mother's vow that she made in Paris while they drove to the airport. Diane swore that Stephen William Blake's name would never come out of her mouth again. It seemed as if she was sticking to her promise.

"Thanks, but no thanks. I hate to tell you, but your daughter is an emotional wreck. I'm not going to work anytime soon. As a matter of fact, I am officially on vacation starting today until … until … well for at least thirty days."

"Thirty days?" Diane replied, surprised.

"Yes, for at least thirty days. I can't even think straight, let alone get in front of a camera to promote someone's product. All I can think about is Stephen and what he did to me, to us, and to our guests."

"All of that has been taken care of, pumpkin. Your guests have been properly notified."

"Great, so when this mess finally hits all of the newsstands, I will have to relive every moment of our tragic story all over again. I hate Stephen … I just hate him."

"Believe me," Diane said, "I do know exactly how you

are feeling. Given time and the proper rest, you will definitely feel better. One day, you will look up and wonder how in the world you allowed yourself to fall in love with such an idiot."

"Thank you. Thanks for understanding."

"Take your thirty days off and get some rest. I'll be home later on this evening."

Chapter Twelve

Fragile & Fragmented
New York

Weeks later, Diane found herself feeling extremely exhausted. She stood almost comatose, staring out her office window looking unto the vast city of Manhattan. She was worried about several pressing issues, but the primary one was her daughter, Taylor. She continued to stare out the window while the sun slowly descended, bidding its farewell before it set on the west side of the town. This was Diane's cue that it was time for her to snap out of it and get back to work.

She turned around and walked back to her desk. Minutes passed and she still couldn't focus on any of her work. Her mind drifted back to Taylor and how their lives were so similar. Diane hoped Taylor's fate, especially as it related to men, would surpass her substandard choices. She thought about Taylor's father in particular.

Twenty years ago, Diane decided that she would never get

married. It was right after she had her heart broken by Taylor's father. Diane met Taylor's father when she was just eighteen years old. He was a distinguished, middle-aged, African American man. He was also a married man. He told Diane the classic "male in distress" story. He was in a miserable marriage, and he was going to divorce his wife when the time was right. Diane, being so young and from a small town, actually believed him. She noticed after years of dating this man that the time, however, never seemed to be right.

She finally got a reality check on their relationship when Taylor's father immediately ended their two-year relationship after she revealed to him that she was expecting their child. He kindly told Diane that he would financially support the child, but he could never be a part of their lives. After that day, Diane never saw Taylor's father in person again. When she went to work the next day, she was told she no longer had a job. She later learned that Taylor's father and his family had relocated to California.

Diane thought the pain would never end. Eventually it did, and she quickly shifted gears to survival mode. She decided to stay in New York and raise her daughter by herself. Taylor's father did make good on his promise to support Taylor financially until she was eighteen years old. A check arrived faithfully to their apartment every month. Diane invested every penny into Taylor and into making a better life for both of them.

Like Taylor, Diane's beauty was undeniable. Doors began to open up and she was allowed to step into the mercurial world of modeling. Diane had finally made it to the level where she had several modeling contracts in New York and internationally as well. Years later, Diane and another model decided to start their own modeling agency in New York.

At the same time, Diane continued to shape and groom Taylor every step of the way. Taylor was able to attend the most prestigious private schools in New York. On Taylor's thirteen birthday, Diane decided that she could begin to model professionally.

A few years later, Diane's business partner died of breast cancer. In honor of her colleague, Diane continued to expand the business into what it is today, a well-known and respected modeling agency.

"Mrs. LaRue," Diane's assistant called out. She peeked into her office to find out if she was still in there.

"Yes," Diane returned, looking up from her desk.

"Candace is on line three. Should I tell her to call back?"

"No, no. You know Candace is like a daughter to me. I need to speak with her right away." Diane immediately picked up her phone.

"Well, hello, Miss Candace," Diane said excitedly.

"Hello, Ms. Diane," Candace replied. "I got your message so I'm calling you back."

"It has been a while since I've heard from you. That's why I thought I would give you a call to find out how you and your friend are doing. You know she won't tell me anything anymore."

"Well, I'm doing fabulous as usual, but I cannot say the same for Taylor. She won't tell me anything anymore either.

I couldn't even begin to tell you what is really going on in that mind of hers."

"I know," Diane moaned. "Plus, you know she hasn't worked in over a month. It seems as if she doesn't want to come back to work because every time I mention booking her a job, she becomes upset and then isolates herself. I really don't know what to do, which is why I called you. You have to help her get out of this rut."

"I just don't have any great suggestions of how I would go about helping Taylor. She would kill me if she knew I told you that last week we all went out with some of my gal pals."

"I don't know if I can bear another story." Diane folder her arms across her chest and rested back in her chair.

"Should I stop?" Candace asked.

"Just go ahead and tell me. I need to know what Taylor's mind is focusing on."

"Well, as I said a minute ago, I convinced Taylor to come out with some of my friends. I thought being out might give her a fresh perspective on life and on men in general. Diane, by the end of the night, I was asking myself why I brought this girl out with me. All she wanted to do was talk about Stephen."

"What?" Diane said, astounded

"Yes, she did," Candace confirmed. "Finally, we thought it was over because she didn't say Stephen's name for the next thirty minutes. Then, this woman came into the restaurant with her fiancé wearing an engagement ring that resembled the one Stephen had given Taylor."

"Oh my goodness!" Diane slapped her hand across her forehead.

"Once Taylor noticed the ring, it was all over. She would not stop talking about Stephen, even though she knew none of us wanted to hear about it anymore. I tried my best to divert the conversation, but no! Taylor insisted on ruining the night."

"I think she's depressed," Diane stated.

"Now, Mom." Candace always called Taylor's mother by that name when she was about to divulge Taylor's most intimate and personal information. "Are you sitting down? Because you might just faint when I tell you what happened next."

"Oh Lord," Diane murmured. "What did my baby do next?"

"Taylor decided to prove to all of us that the ring that the woman had on looked like the one that Stephen had given her by showing us her ring!"

"She still has the ring?" Diane exclaimed.

"Yes, Mom, she still has the ring, but the sad part of this story is that she is carrying it around in her purse."

"My poor baby. I truly believe Taylor needs some help — I mean, some professional help. I did not have a clue it was this bad."

"I agree, Diane," Candace replied. "I have to say that I have never seen Taylor act like that before. My friends were like, *it's time to go!*"

"I took off work yesterday to treat her to a day at the spa and she flat-out refused to go," Diane said. "She had on those dreadful pajamas that she wears every single day, and I do believe those are you-know-who's, but I refuse to question her about it."

"Good," Candace agreed.

"Plus, she has started drinking, and she thinks I don't know."

"I wasn't going to tell you about that one. I gotta keep a few of our secrets to between us."

"Please, I have found too many empty spaces on my wine rack not to know something was going on." They both chuckled. "Seriously, I'm at a complete loss as to how we can help this child out. What about Brian? Does he have any single male friends? Perhaps you all can go out on a double date or something."

"Yes, Brian does have single male friends, but to be honest, I'm really afraid to introduce anyone to Taylor right now. It simply would not be fair to the guy. Plus, she swears she will not date anyone any time soon."

"Okay," Diane agreed, "maybe double dating is not the answer. Can you please just get her out of the penthouse tonight? She needs to get up and get out of that penthouse and begin to interact with other people."

"I will certainly try," Candace promised. "I'll make a suggestion like going to a place that is low key, possibly to a small jazz club in Harlem."

"Now, that sounds perfect. I'll talk to you later."

Diane smiled as she hung up the phone with Candace. She knew that Taylor was in good hands. Candace was like her second daughter. From the first time Taylor introduced Candace to Diane at one of their dance recitals, Diane knew there was something special about Candace. They were both gifted dancers which was how they became such good friends. For Candace, academics took precedence over dance, and Taylor's main focus was on modeling.

Candace went on to college and after she had graduated, she ended up taking over and upgrading her mother's beauty salon. Taylor, on the other hand, went on to rip the runways internationally. After all these years, they still remained good friends. Diane hoped Candace would be able to convince Taylor to go out tonight.

A few hours later, Taylor got up from her usual spot on the living room sofa when she heard the doorbell ring. She went to look at the camera in their security room to see who in the world would come and visit them at this late hour.

"Candace," Taylor whispered, wondering what in the world she was doing over in this end of town. "Hey, girl! What's up with you?" Taylor said curiously while she stood in the doorway.

"Nothing much," Candace said nonchalantly. "I hope you don't mind me dropping by unannounced."

"Girl, you know you are considered family around here,"

Taylor replied. "Do you want something to drink or eat?"

"No. Actually, I came by to see what you were doing tonight. I'm bored, so I decided to come all the way over here to find out if you wanted to go out for a drink or get something to eat."

"Bored, huh?" Taylor repeated curiously. "Where's Brian?"

"He's out of town," Candace said quickly. "The Knicks are on the road for another week. They are playing in Chicago tonight. You know I don't have satellite, so I can't watch the game at home."

"I just don't feel like going anywhere. Going out takes too much effort."

"What effort?"

"I would have to get in the shower, comb my hair, and get all dolled up. I'm just not in the mood."

"Have you noticed that lately you are *never* in the mood to do anything?"

"Now you are starting to sound like my mother. Did she put you up to this?"

"To do what?" Candace snapped.

"To try and get me to go out," Taylor said. She walked over to the television and turned it on.

"Why are you turning on the television?"

"I *do* have satellite TV and the sports channel," Taylor said with a smirk on her face. "Yeah, you're right." There was Brian just like Candace had told her, running up and down on the court at Chicago's Bulls arena.

"Now, don't you feel stupid," Candace laughed at her friend.

"No, I don't," Taylor returned. "I know my mother, and she is always up to something. She really gets on my nerves."

"On a serious note, Taylor, we are both very worried about you. Just look at you. Have you eaten or even washed up today?"

"I just don't have any inspiration to get up and do much of anything any more. I'm hoping this feeling, or whatever it is that I'm going through, will pass soon. I always seem to feel the same way, every day.

"Don't tell my mother, but look at this." Taylor pulled out an international celebrity gossip magazine from underneath a pillow on the couch.

"What!" Candace exclaimed. She continued to read the front page. "This isn't even true! Where did you get this from?"

"K.T."

"Oh yeah, Kimberly Thomas, your publicist."

"Correct," Taylor said. She then reached for another magazine and began to flip through the pages. "K.T. FedExed all of these to me as soon as they hit the press. I've been here reading this stuff all day. Can you believe I'm still thinking about Stephen? My heart still aches, and my pride is very much bruised. Now that the press has publicized our business, it just seems to be a never-ending story. I feel so stupid. Candace, how could I have been so naïve?"

Tears began to form in Taylor's eyes as she looked at her best friend for answers.

"Honey," Candace reached out to embrace her friend, "you're probably right in regard to everyone knowing about the breakup, but breakups happen. Have you watched *Access Hollywood* or *E News* lately? These types of scandals happen every day."

"I know, but I still won't be able to go to Paris for a long time. I'm even thinking of changing my career."

"Changing your career?" Candace repeated awkwardly.

"I want to work with children. Maybe I should become a teacher, you know, like an art teacher or something that is normal."

"When did you do it?" Candace asked jokingly.

"Do what?" Taylor returned confused.

"When did you fall down and hit that big head of yours? Now, I *know* you have truly gone mad. A teacher! Are you crazy? Do you *know* how much teachers make a year?"

"No, not really."

"A teacher's annual income is what you would make in one day."

"This is not about how much money I can make in a day, Candace," Taylor replied rolling her eyes.

"Hello … Earth to Taylor," Candace teased. "Let's just get out of here because you are truly talking crazy!"

"Okay, I'll go out with you." Taylor had to admit that Candace had a way of making her feel better, even though leaving the modeling business and possibly become a teacher was not crazy talk. Taylor had been modeling since she was a toddler, and modeling internationally since she was thirteen years old. After all those years in this business, she definitely needed a break from it.

"Let's get out of here before you change your mind," Candace said. She attempted to rush Taylor along.

"All right, all right," Taylor replied. But she continued to move at a slow pace.

"Hurry up, already!" Candace declared. "You're moving too slow. You can wash up and get dressed at my house. We're going out on my end of town anyway. You won't have to worry about the media people over in my 'hood."

"Okay, just let me write Mother a note. I don't want her to worry. We're roommates now. I'm trying to be respectful."

"Don't worry about that," Candace snapped. She stopped Taylor while she searched for a pen.

"Candace, you know how Diane is. She'll probably think that I have jumped off the roof of this building if she comes home and I'm not here."

"You're right." A devious smile appeared on Candace's face.

"Right about what?"

"Diane called me as I was closing up the salon—"

"I knew it!" Taylor interrupted. "You are so bad, working together to get me out of the house."

"It's only because we love you," Candace said. She hugged and then pushed Taylor toward the front door.

Chapter Thirteen

The Road To Recovery
New York

Taylor fumbled with her Blackberry, waiting anxiously in the sitting area to speak with the therapist that her mother suggested. To appease her mother, she finally agreed to meet with Dr. Davis, but for one time only. Taylor knew that her life was stagnant at the moment; she was still not convinced that she needed professional help to get her out of this unfortunate rut. When she pulled into the parking space in front of the building, she almost changed her mind. She threw her phone device in her purse, picked up a magazine, and thumbed through the pages unproductively.

"Ms. LaRue, Dr. Davis will see you now," the receptionist said as she stood up from her desk. She escorted Taylor through double doors into a place that looked more like a conference room than an office.

"You can sit down anywhere you like. Dr. Davis will

arrive momentarily to begin the session," the receptionist instructed.

Taylor decided to sit down toward the head of the table. She thought that the view from the window might calm her racing thoughts. Just as Taylor sat down at the huge oval table, Dr. Davis walked into the room.

"Hello, Ms. LaRue." The woman extended her hand out to Taylor. "I'm Dr. Davis."

"Hello, Dr. Davis." Taylor quickly stood up to greet the doctor.

"It's a pleasure to have you here."

"Thank you." Taylor smiled.

"Did you have trouble finding the address?"

"No, I'm very familiar with this area."

"Please, make yourself comfortable."

Taylor looked around the room before sitting down again. It was tastefully decorated. The walls were adorned with several stunning photographs.

"You may wonder why we are beginning the consultation session in this conference room opposed to starting the intro-ductory stage in my office," Dr. Davis stated, as she walked around the room. "I generally like to explain to my potential patients that I usually conduct all of my consultations, as well as a few of my initial sessions, in this room due to its size."

"It does have a calming effect to it," Taylor returned. She continued to look around the room and noticed the overstuffed chairs and couch that were nicely arranged in the corner of the room.

"As you can see, there is plenty of space to walk around or shift your position as often as you feel the need to. The goal here is to create an environment that alleviates and reduces any stress or tension you may feel as you discuss critical information pertaining to why you have sought help. This room is also soundproof, so you don't have to worry about others hearing you. This information is important to know, especially if you feel the need to yell, or scream, or speak in a loud manner. You are welcome to do so."

"Interesting." Taylor wondered if she would appreciate that aspect of the room.

"Before we begin our session, I notice from the questionnaire you completed that this is your first experience with therapy. You must have a lot of questions." Dr. Davis sat down adjacent to Taylor and picked up a pad and pen.

"No, not really." Taylor's mind went blank. She was still a little nervous.

"I'd like to begin by exploring your expectations of our therapeutic relationship and understand what you hope to gain from this relationship. Then we can talk about what it is that brings you to seek the help of a therapist like myself."

Taylor listened attentively and then explained what her expectations and perceptions were of a therapist. Several questions began to emerge in her head. She thought about what would happen if an emergency arose and Dr. Davis was not available, who would be available should they continue this relationship. When Dr. Davis paused, she decided to ask her that question.

"Good question. Generally, questions like that one are answered by the business manager. In case of an emergency, someone is always as close as your phone. If I am unavailable, one of my colleagues will fill in for me and inform me of the situation upon my return."

"That's good to know." Taylor was beginning to feel a bit more at ease as Dr. Davis continued to talk.

"Everything we discuss is confidential. This agreement, however, is always breached if you intentionally plan to harm yourself or someone else. I must also inform you that there are times when I tape my sessions in this room. Of course, this is done with the patient's consent. Please stop me if you have any questions. I know this is a lot of information. Do you have any questions? If not, I will continue."

"I was just thinking about the taping of sessions. Someone would probably get a real kick out of my session. 'Celebrity model still in crisis over recent breakup' Yeah, I do not think it would be a good idea to give consent for any of my sessions to be taped."

"Understood," Dr. Davis returned. "I do, however, like to inform all of our patients about the various services we offer in this practice."

"Thank you," Taylor replied. She now felt the need to walk around and begin talking about why she made this appointment.

"Ms. LaRue, it is important to mention to you that our methods and approaches are all very much client-driven," Dr. Davis explained. "Empowering you as well as providing you with the tools necessary to achieve self-acceptance are the ultimate goal. Do you have any questions that you would like me to answer before we get started?"

"I don't think so," Taylor said apprehensively. "I am, however, feeling a bit overwhelmed for some reason."

"Anxious to get started perhaps?" Dr. Davis inquired.

"I think so."

"Well, in that case, let's get started."

Looking out the window, Taylor glanced back at Dr. Davis as she heard a bell ringing.

"We are at the hour and a half mark," Dr. Davis indicated. She continued to jot down Taylor's last comments.

"I can't believe ninety minutes went by so fast. Initially, I didn't even think I would last ten minutes in here," Taylor said. She moved away from the window and walked toward the clock on the wall.

"Well, Taylor, you have been holding a lot of emotions on the inside. Although you have a good support system in place, you haven't allowed yourself to open up and genuinely talk about your feelings to them."

"I know," Taylor agreed, feeling ashamed. "For some reason, I think they will judge me. Especially my mother! She was, however, correct in that she knew I really needed to talk someone. Actually, I could talk another hour, but don't worry. I won't; at least not right now."

"We can continue on if you like," Dr. Davis stated. "I

generally utilize two hours during the consultation session. Remember, you are in the driver's seat."

"No, this is a good time to stop. I think this was a good start for me, for us." Taylor felt that a real connection had been made between her and Dr. Davis. She was definitely the one that was going to help her get out of this rut; she could feel it. Even though Taylor knew that she would have to do most of the work, she was very proud of herself.

"You're correct in that this was a good start. Your motivational level, as well as your ability to move forward to complete your goals, is very high."

"Dr. Davis, I'm still so fragile right now," Taylor confessed. "As good as I feel about myself and moving forward with my life, I still think about Stephen frequently. One minute I hate him for what he did to me and to my mother. Then, the next minute, I'm wondering what he is doing or if he is even thinking about me."

"The road to recovery won't happen overnight, Taylor," Dr. Davis restated. "Let's practice one of the strategies that I mentioned to you just a few minutes ago."

"Which one?" Taylor asked. She then sat up straight in her chair.

"Replacing old thoughts with new ones." Dr. Davis guided her while she attempted to role play using the suggested strategy.

"I think I finally got it, but I may need reminders to use it from time to time."

"Good job. So, we will pick this up again next week, same day and time?"

"Absolutely," Taylor confirmed. She got up from her chair and walked toward the door. As she walked out of Dr. Davis's office, she felt somewhat empowered. However, when she walked outside of the building, the night air hit her face. And Taylor's thoughts drifted to Stephen once more.

"I'm sure he's with Dena right now. They are probably snuggled up tightly on that huge white sofa that I loved so much, roasting marshmallows in front of the main fireplace. They might be discussing the baby, their wedding plans, or their future. Taylor, stop!!!" She suddenly realized that she was doing it again.

"Replace negative thoughts with positive ones," Taylor repeated out loud. "It's Stephen's loss and my gain." Taylor smiled, attempting to flag down a taxi.

Stephen looked at his watch. He couldn't believe it was 1:45 p.m. already. He knew he was not mentally prepared to meet with his next client, who was due to arrive in his office in thirty minutes. Stephen felt that his entire life was fragmented, broken off in so many pieces.

"Will I ever be able to pull all the pieces back together again?" Stephen murmured.

"Mr. Blake, your two o'clock appointment called to cancel and ask if they could reschedule for another day."

"There is a God." Stephen heaved a deep sigh of relief. "Tracey, please clear my schedule for today. I don't feel well, and I really need to go home."

"Would you like a cup of tea?" Tracey returned.

"No, I'll be leaving here in about fifteen minutes." Stephen began to clear his desk. He opened the bottom desk drawer, a place where he put his files for his high-profile clients. There was a picture of him and Taylor. They looked like a perfect couple, so deeply in love.

"If only Taylor knew." Stephen thought about Dena and put the picture in his suit pocket. He knew he wasn't in love with Taylor, but he missed her a whole lot.

"Mr. Blake?" Tracey peeked into his office door.

"Yes, Tracey?" Stephen looked up.

"Your calendar is cleared, and I have rescheduled the meeting for next week. Hope you feel better."

"Thank you," Stephen said. He scanned his desk one more time, turned off his lights, and walked out his door.

Driving home, Stephen decided to drive past the hospital where he found out Dena was pregnant once again. When he got closer to the hospital, he moved over in the right lane because he knew he wanted to stop and find a parking space. For the past month, this had become a ritual for Stephen. Each time he thought this might make him feel better. However, it always made him feel even worse. Yet, each day, he continued to torture himself. Deep down inside, Stephen felt he deserved every bit of the pain for what he did to both Dena and Taylor.

A week after Taylor had left Paris, Dena moved into Stephen's villa. His father was furious, and Dena was still shaken up by everything. Stephen truly believed that after the residue had settled down, Dena, he, and the baby would have a wonderful life together. But when Dena did not return home after two days had gone by, he started to worry. He decided to go to her apartment to see if she had decided to move back in there. He still had the key to her apartment. When he arrived at her front door, he let himself in and to his surprise, he walked into an empty apartment. Everything was gone. Stephen noticed an envelope taped on Dena's bedroom door with his name written on the front. He read the letter and to his dismay, found that Dena had left him for good.

Stephen,

If you're reading this letter then I know you're in my apartment and have already figured out that I am not coming back. I apologize, for I had no intention of ending our relationship this way. I knew if I had seen you, you probably would've tried to change my mind. You do have a way of making me feel vulnerable where I would get sidetracked and lose myself in you. However, the truth would still remain ... I never wanted this life. Yes, I wanted a friend, maybe even a secret lover. Never would I have thought what had happened to us would have occurred. I feel so guilty ... I never wanted to be a home wrecker, I never wanted to be your wife, and even more importantly ... I never saw myself as a mother. My goal in life was simple, so I thought. I always wanted to make partner at a top law firm. When I met you, I knew you could make that happen. I had no idea that I would actually fall in love with you. I also did not factor in everything that had transpired over the past few months. Your father was correct; I'm the only person who could truly put an end to this tragic love story. I also must tell you that I plan to have an abortion and move back to New York. Please don't hate me. I'm doing what I believe is best for both of us. I'll always remember what we shared.

Dena

Stephen pulled out the documentation from his wallet that Dena later sent in the mail which proved that she did have the abortion two days after he found the letter in her apartment. Every day, he looked at the paper, the date, Dena's blood type, the medical procedure that was performed, and the facility where she had the operation, and finally the cost of the procedure as it was written in Euro and in U.S. currency.

Looking at the hospital, Stephen thought, *Today, all of this ends. I really need to get over this and move on with my life.* Tears began to slowly trickle down his face. Stephen knew this was the last time he would drive to this hospital so he brought along a cigarette lighter with him. He wanted to burn these papers he had been holding on to as well as the picture of him and Taylor which he had placed in his suit pocket.

Stephen stepped out of his car, flicked the top back from lighter, and set the documents and the picture on fire. Tossing the burning items from his hand, he stepped on them repeatedly until the fire went out.

"It's over!" Stephen exclaimed. Both women were out of his life for good. He got back into his car, started up the engine, and slowly pulled away from the curb into the street.

Stephen's next stop was his parents' home. He knew he had to have a conversation with his father because he was shocked and disappointed when he read the letter. After Dena left him, all he could hear was his father's voice saying to him over and over again, "Son, please try to focus on Taylor these next few weeks … I'm almost a hundred percent certain that you will not regret marrying that one." Stephen knew that both women deserved so much more than what he was giving them. He prayed that at least Taylor would find what she truly was searching for … true love.

"So how was it?" Diane asked eagerly. She heard her Taylor come in the front door.

"The great Diane LaRue was right once again," Taylor said as she bowed before her mother.

"Stop it!" Diane chuckled. "I can't help that I'm always correct … I was born this way." Diane walked into her bedroom; Taylor followed and plopped on the bed.

"So how was it?" Diane repeated.

"It was interesting," Taylor confessed. "I now recognize and understand that I do need help to get over this hump, or whatever it is that I'm going through."

"I believe the word you are searching for is called depression."

"For your information, Mother, Dr. Davis did not call 'it' depression. As a matter of fact, she never used that word at all during our entire session. I'm not saying that I am not experiencing some form of depression. I'm just saying that Dr. Davis hasn't diagnosed what I am experiencing as clinical depression."

"I know exactly what it is because I have experienced everything you've been through, and more. And if Dr. Davis never gives 'it' a name, I will, and 'it' is called depression."

"Okay, I give up," Taylor exclaimed. "You think you know everything because you have experienced a few disappointments in your life."

"A *few disappointments?* You better be thanking God right now that you did not have to go through what I have experienced in life. At least you got a ring, a car, and house … no, not a house, a *villa* to live in for twelve months. I got a—"

"Please, spare me the details," Taylor interrupted. "I really can't believe you are even comparing what we have been through, like one was worse than the other. We were both done wrong by no-good men, so let's just leave it at that."

"Fine," Diane fired back. "All I'm saying is that I think you're in a state of depression and you should call 'it' what 'it' is. This is what's wrong with today's generation. They want to make up new words to describe old problems, problems that your grandmother and great-grandmother experienced time and time again.

"If the truth be told, they were all just as depressed going through their situations as the next person. But, maybe you're right, Taylor, because they did not call it depression back in those days either. It was called 'you better stuff those feeling back in your heart and pray to God that *this too will pass*' because there was just no time for crying.

"If it was not for my mother praying for me, I don't know what I would've done."

"I know, I know. I've heard this story all my life. I love you. I really do, but please do not torture me tonight by telling your '*how I made it over*' story again."

"Wisdom, that's another major component your generation lacks today. With that said, I am done." Diane picked up a book from her night table and began to read.

"Good," Taylor teased. She leaned over and kissed her mother on the forehead. "I thought you might want to know that I do plan to attend another session with Dr. Davis. Actually, I plan to go until I have reached my goal. I figured that would make you happy."

"Good night, Taylor." Diane continued to read her book.

"You're not good at acting, Mom," Taylor got off her mother's bed and walked toward her bedroom. "I know what I said made you excited!"

"All I can say is …" Diane shouted from her room, "I

know there is a God, and I pray to Him every day that He helps you get back on track and right back on that runway!"

Taylor walked in her room and quickly closed the bedroom door. After hearing her mother's comment, she knew she would have to find a place of her own soon. After Taylor bathed and put on brand-new pajamas that her mother had bought her, she found herself just lying on the bed. For whatever reason, she could not go to sleep.

After an hour went by, Taylor decided to get up and look out the window. She thought that maybe looking up at the night sky would sooth her to the point that she would be able to fall asleep. She had not had a good night's sleep in a while. She knew this time it was due to being excited about her initial therapy session. Still, her mother's comment about going back on the runway haunted her. She felt in her heart that her modeling career and that entire lifestyle was over.

Taylor wasn't sure why, but she connected dating Stephen with modeling. She met and started dating Stephen at a very significant point in her career. She had just begun to get recognition by all the important players in the modeling industry. She had just made it to the top of her game, and then came Stephen to continue the roller-coaster ride. It was a true fantasy.

Then two years later she was given the crown of a supermodel, and being engaged to Stephen was the icing on the cake. She had it all, and she almost achieved the dream that every diva desires. She was going to marry an A-lister that every woman in the world would kill to have. A fantasy, it was, but now Taylor was ready to move on with her life, leaving all of the bling, glitz, and glamour behind.

At that moment, Taylor felt the urge to dance just like she did as a child. She remembered when she used to dance she always felt a sense of freedom. Taylor knew she would eventually have to have that one-on-one conversation with her mother and let her know just how she truly felt.

After all, she would be twenty-one in a few months; she could go back to modeling anytime. Taylor opened up the window and leaned her head and upper body out of it to soak up the moonlight. She felt the urge to experience the world on a different level. She tried to envision what that might look like. She thought about enrolling in college or working with children. The possibilities were endless. She then thought about her different bank accounts.

When Taylor started to model professionally, her mother opened up a savings account and deposited all of the money that she earned into it. Taylor never needed to use any money from that account because there was always plenty of money leftover from her child support checks. When she started dating Stephen, he never allowed her to spend her own money. He always wanted to pay for everything. So, all the money that she had ever made in her life had been growing and multiplying in savings and investment accounts that her financial advisor developed for her.

She was a bit apprehensive to even look at her financial

portfolio at this point. She knew that she had accrued quite a bit of cash and that she didn't have a clue what to do with it.

Well, one thing is for sure. Taylor stood up, shut the window and climbed into bed again. She knew she didn't have to make any decision about it tonight. As she drifted off to sleep, her thoughts went to Stephen ... *I wonder if he even misses me? I guess I'll never know.*

Chapter Fourteen

After The Storm
New York

Taylor felt like a new woman. She walked out of Dr. Davis's office for the last time. For the past five months, she had been faithfully coming to her office once a week. Taylor exhaled once again when she left the building and walked onto the busy street. She had accomplished her goal of reaching an acceptable level of self-love and confidence. She was now ready to face the world because she felt so free—free to laugh, free to cry, free to love, and live again.

Flipping her cell phone open, Taylor decided that today would be the perfect day to talk with her mother about her modeling career and future plans.

"Hello, Taylor," Diane said. She was in the middle of assigning models for a major campaign ad.

"Hello, Mother," Taylor replied. "What are you doing for lunch today?"

"No time for lunch today," Diane returned. "Why do you ask?"

"I really need to talk with you. It's important."

"Wait one second," Diane stated as she put the receiver down. "John, can you handle this alone? Something has come up with Taylor. You know how it goes with children. They never really leave the nest."

Taylor shook her head as she waited for her mother to finish her conversation.

"You know, you're the best!" Diane placed the phone receiver to her mouth again. "Yes, sweetie, I can meet you for lunch today. Let's meet at our usual spot in front of 212 in an hour. We can eat there or at another location. We'll decide when we get there. See you soon."

"Good-bye, Mother." As Taylor closed her cell phone, she felt excited because she had completed her first task on her "moving forward" list.

Standing in front of 212, Taylor looked at her watch again. Her mother was thirty minutes late.

"Where is she?" Taylor wondered while she looked for her cell phone. When she finally located her phone in her oversized bag, she called Candace to find out if she was available to meet them for lunch. Candace's phone rang and rang until her voice finally pierced through the phone ... *Please leave a brief message after the tone ... beep.*

"Great," Taylor said feeling irritated. Anticipating a

negative reaction from her mother, Taylor needed Candace by her side for support and to act as a buffer. Candace usually played the referee role well.

"Okay," Taylor murmured, "just breathe in and out."

Just as she finished her breathing exercise, her mother's driver pulled the car up to the curb and Diane gracefully disembarked from her limousine, talking on her mobile, of course.

"Sorry, sweetie," Diane mouthed to Taylor. "John, I'm in front of the restaurant with Taylor, I gotta go." Diane ended her call and kissed Taylor on both cheeks. "You know our business motto. Time is money, and money is time."

"No problem. You know I understand," Taylor replied.

"Shall we eat right here, or shall we go further down the street toward Guastavinos, Lenny's, or Unis?" Diane asked.

"It really doesn't matter to me. My main reason for asking you out to lunch is to talk to you. So any atmosphere that's nice and cozy works for me."

"Okay," Diane replied. "Let's eat here."

"That works for me," Taylor replied. They began to walk toward the entrance of the restaurant.

"That was pretty good," Taylor said. She finished the last bite of her pan-seared chicken breast.

"Yes, it was," Diane agreed. She was anxious to hear what Taylor wanted to talk to her about. "So, what did you want to talk to me about?" Diane was done entertaining Taylor with small talk.

"Initially, I wanted to have this discussion after we had dessert, just in case one of us wanted to get up and leave ... I was thinking that we would have at least finished our meal." Taylor noticed that a frown had appeared on her mother's face.

"Okay ... okay ... okay. Mom, this topic will not be an easy topic to discuss because I know how you are when it comes to me going back to work." Taylor began to fumble with her napkin. "To be honest, I really don't know where to start."

"Let me help you out," Diane replied curtly. "Let's just start with the topic. What is it?"

"Modeling," Taylor said apprehensively. "More specifically, my modeling career." Taylor waved at the waiter, attempting to get his attention.

"Your career," Diane exclaimed. "Keep going." Diane stopped talking when the waiter walked over to their table.

"Please bring us two hot caffé lattes," Taylor ordered. The waiter nodded his head and walked away. "What was I saying?" Taylor asked as she was now wishing that she had this conversation with her mother at home.

"Your modeling career," Diane repeated.

"Yes, about my career, Mother. I really need a break."

"*Another* break," Diane said chuckling underneath her breath.

"To be frank, Mother, I need more than a break away

from modeling. Actually, I do not want to model at all. Okay … there … I finally said it, and it felt good releasing those words from my mouth."

Diane stared at Taylor without saying a word.

"Mother, please," Taylor pleaded, "I don't like it when you look at me like that, so say something. Say anything."

"What do you want me to say? You're twenty-one years old, and capable of making your own decisions. I have to remind myself *to let go and let God* handle you and your affairs. I believe I started doing that when you decided to move to Paris."

"Please don't remind me," Taylor returned, annoyed. "I know I'm old enough to make my own decisions. I just wanted to have this conversation with you because I know you wanted me to come back to work, and I knew in my heart that I simply had no desire to model anymore."

"Fine." Diane shifted her position in her seat when the waiter walked over and placed the latte in front of her.

"Are you ladies ready for dessert?" the waiter inquired.

"No thanks," the two women said in unison.

When the waiter walked away, Diane asked, "What do you plan to do with yourself now?"

"I think I want to go to college."

"You *think* …" Diane was now annoyed.

"No, I plan to enroll at New York University as a part-time student. I have not been in a classroom setting in a while. I only intend to register for one or two classes at a time. I prefer evening classes."

"What are you going to study or major in?"

"Business, maybe. I even thought about majoring in education."

"Education?" Diane repeated curiously as she raised an eyebrow.

"Yes, education. I've had thoughts of possibly becoming a teacher. Mother, stop looking at me like that. I happen to like the idea of working with children."

"Forgive me, Taylor." Diane tried hard to keep a straight face. "It's hard for me to picture my daughter working as a teacher in one of the public schools here in New York. I really can't see it, but who am I?"

"Okay. Maybe going to college to become a teacher is not the answer. I do, however, plan to enroll in college as well as work with children some day. It just may not be in a public-school setting."

"Let's stick with majoring in business," Diane declared. "What type of business or businesses would you like to start or learn about?"

"I thought about opening up a boutique and selling a few of my prize possessions. You know all the stuff that is piled up in your storage collecting dust? Clothes I don't need any more, party jewelry, and clothes I have never even worn. I plan to sell it all. Especially everything Stephen bought me over the years."

Diane frowned again as soon as Taylor mentioned Stephen's name.

"Mother, just for the record, I have completely forgiven

Stephen, and I suggest you do the same. He no longer rents space in my head or my heart."

"Thank goodness." Diane continued to sip on her latte.

"I think I can make a pretty penny. You know I have enough clothes to fill up one or even two houses."

"You are definitely right about that," Diane declared.

"I think opening up the boutique coupled with taking a few business courses will help me jump-start my pursuit to become a bona fide entrepreneur."

Diane said nothing.

"What are you thinking right now?" Taylor asked curiously.

"Nothing," Diane sighed.

"Mother!!" Taylor pushed her drink away from her.

"What do you want me to say, Taylor? I believe you were born to be a model. You still have another good six to seven years left before you would have to venture off into another career."

"You're correct; however, I would like to be in control of my life for once, without a mother or even a man directing every step of the way. I want to be the director, the writer, the person who makes all the decisions. If I'm making a mistake doing this, so be it. It was my mistake to make."

Silence

"Mom," Taylor continued, "I just need to find out who Taylor really is … I want to know what my passions are, and this time away from modeling will help me to know if modeling truly is a passion for me. If it is, my heart will direct me right back on the runway."

"I'm proud of you, sweetie, truly I am," Diane admitted. Taylor reminded her of herself when she told her parents that it was time for her to leave her hometown and move to New York.

"Mother, are you okay?" Taylor asked in amazement. She couldn't believe her mother was actually somewhat in agreement with what she was saying.

"Yes, I'm fine. You remind me so much of myself when I was a young woman trying to find my identity and place in this world. I, too, had a conversation just like this one with my parents. Everything in my body was telling me that I had outgrown my little old country town. I knew there was something more out in the world for me. Through the good and the bad, my instincts were correct. There was, in fact, a whole world waiting for me to change and to inspire."

"Thank you, Mother." She got up from the table to hug and kiss her mother. "You don't know how much this means to me for you to at least understand where I am coming from. I love and respect you so much, and I know sometimes you don't think I listen to you, but I do. I'm honored and so very proud that you are my mother."

The waiter came over and placed the check down on the table as they were wiping the tears from each other's eyes. Diane reached over and picked up the check. Taylor quickly grabbed for it, but Diane already had a firm hold of it.

"I'm paying for lunch, Mother," Taylor said firmly. "I invited you to lunch ... remember?"

"By all means, Ms. Taylor," Diane returned. She handed Taylor the check. "Ms. Taylor is all grown up now. Very large and in charge, as the young people would say. So, my next question is when are you moving out of the penthouse?"

"Actually, Mother, that was my next subject, but I thought I should wait until tomorrow to talk about moving out."

"You *really* want to move out too? Taylor, you know I was just teasing you a moment ago ... I really enjoy your company."

"I know you do, which is why I decided not to move too far away from you. Do you remember the O'Connors who live on the 10th floor?"

"Yes, I do."

"Well, I recently found out that they are selling their condo."

"Where have I been?" Diane asked surprised. "Where in the world are they moving to?"

"Florida," Taylor replied. "They are moving in a very exclusive retirement community which I am sure is really nice. They actually let me look inside their place two days ago, and I really like it."

"You're *really* serious, huh?" Diane looked at Taylor with pride.

"Yes, I am. If I decide to purchase it, we can still eat dinner together from time to time — that is, if you don't have some man over instead."

"Okay, now you *really* have gone mad," Diane said chuckling. "All the truly good men who are my age are dead or are already taken. So, that wouldn't be the case for me … maybe for you but certainly not for me."

"Well, it just may be the case for me. I allowed Candace to set me up on a blind date for next week."

"Thank you, Jesus," Diane said. Mimicking some of the women in her church when she was a child, she threw her hands up in praise. "My baby is dating again … hallelujah!!"

"Mother, stop it!! People are beginning to look at us."

"You're right, baby. Let's go home. This is all just too much for me to take in on one day!"

Chapter Fifteen
Ladies' Night
New York

"**I**t's a done deal," Taylor's lawyer confirmed. He came back into the room where they had the closing procedures and placed the keys to her newly purchased condo in her hand.

Three weeks later, Taylor had second thoughts about being that close to her mother so she purchased another condo that was two blocks away from her mother's building.

"Great," Taylor murmured. She felt relieved. "That wasn't as painful as I had envisioned. I thought we were going to be in the closing for hours."

"You should know by now that you'll never have a bad experience with me." The lawyer waved good-bye and went into another office. He mentioned to Taylor earlier that he had to attend yet another closing in the same building after their meeting was over.

A number of months had now passed since the breakup,

and Taylor was on top of the world. She exited the building and walked toward the parking lot to locate her newly purchased HSE, Range Rover. She knew her SUV wouldn't be hard to find as the color was rimini red metallic.

"There you are," Taylor whispered. She then clicked the button which unlocked the doors and started the engine. Jumping into her ride, Taylor felt so elated. She finally felt independent for the very first time.

"Who can I call?" Taylor wondered. Her mind quickly went to her best friend, Candace. She began to dig deep into her purse to locate her phone. She decided to call Candace and invite her and Brian to her new domicile.

"Come on … come on," Taylor repeated impatiently. Her first thought was to hang up when she heard Candace's voice message. But she left a message instead, for she really wanted to invite company over to celebrate with her.

"Candace, call back, ASAP!" Taylor demanded. As she flipped the phone closed, her hand vibrated. It was her phone ringing. "That was fast." Without looking to see who was calling her, Taylor answered the call.

"Hey …" Taylor said.

"Hello, Taylor. This is Kevin."

"Kevin?" Taylor inquired.

"Your blind date from last Friday."

"Oh yeah, Kevin."

"So how are you? Your face … the rash? Hope it's looking better."

"I'm fine. I'm highly allergic to pecans. I don't know

what I was thinking when I ordered that dessert. When I got to my truck, I used an EpiPen injection ... it works every time."

"Glad to hear that you're okay. So ..."

"Can I call you back?" Taylor quickly interrupted. "It's just ... you caught me at a bad time."

"Sure. No problem. I'll call you later ..."

Click

Taylor slapped her phone closed and threw it back into her purse. *How in the world did he get my number?* She tried to remember if she had given him the number prior to their date, but she couldn't recall. Taylor backed up out of the parking space and drove onto the busy street. She couldn't get her mind off of Kevin, her blind date. The one Candace had arranged for the two of them.

"That was a pure waste of time." She chuckled as she recalled the evening.

Taylor had psyched herself up about going out tonight. She looked at her watch again. Her blind date, Kevin Lyle, was now fifteen minutes late. Looking around the restaurant, she had hoped that wasn't a sign of how the night would unfold ... lagging, dragging ... sort of dillydallying along.

This really wasn't an official blind date, she thought as she noticed the hostess direct Kevin to their table. There wouldn't be an initial moment of surprise when they laid eyes on each other. They were already aware of what the other person looked like due to their celebrity status. Taylor didn't know much about him, only that he was an accomplished actor that most women wanted to get to know, and he perceived her to be the typical superficial supermodel. He mentioned that to her when they talked on the phone prior to arranging this meeting date. As he stood up before her, Taylor decided that her primary goal tonight was to change his perception about her. As she looked at him, she thought she had died and gone to heaven. He looked so much better in person. He was tall, dark, and handsome. His skin was flawless, and his cheekbones were chiseled and broad.

"Taylor," he said. Taylor smiled back at him politely. He then nodded at the hostess in gratitude. "It's a pleasure to finally meet you."

"I have to say that the feeling is completely mutual."

The date had officially started. The waiter approached their table and asked if they were ready to order drinks. They both laughed because they had said yes in unison. This broke the ice and scattered away any residue of nervousness that was lingering between the two of them.

After dinner was served and they had a few more drinks, Mr. Kevin Lyle started looking more like all the other guys Taylor had rejected in the past. By then, she was completely turned off. Kevin talked about himself the entire night. She tried to get his attention and possibly change the conversation by yawning directly in his face. Unfortunately for her, the tactic didn't work. He was too full of himself to even notice and continued right on yapping about his callbacks, awards, and his many nominations. Taylor had decided right then and there ... no matter what happened or how much he insisted ... she was not ordering dessert. She wasn't spending another hour with this narcissistic egotist.

"What a loser!" Taylor said, chuckling. She changed her mind and ordered dessert. Pecan pie, the only thing she knew would break her face and neck area out in seconds and would provide an escape from Kevin, all at the same time. And it worked.

Taylor looked around and noticed that she was still driving in the business district. She thought about calling her real estate lawyer again. Her next goal was to locate and purchase the perfect spot for her boutique.

"What would I name it?" she pondered.

"CREATIVE DESIGNS by Taylor LaRue, which is a great idea, but I have not designed anything as of yet. Maybe I will name it, A PIECE OF ME or maybe FROM MY CLOSET TO YOURS." Before she knew it, she was in front of her new residence. Taylor drove into the underground garage and pulled into her personal parking space.

Ring ... ring ... ring.

"That has to be Candace," Taylor mumbled. Reaching for her purse, she began the tedious task of looking for her cell phone again. Moving items quickly around in her purse, she wanted to find her phone before it stopped ringing.

"Hey, girl, what's up?" Taylor said. She knew it was Candace calling her back.

"Congratulations!" Candace exclaimed. "I am so happy for you ... Ms. Independent Woman."

"Thank you, thank you," Taylor replied. "What are you and Brian doing tonight?"

"Brian is in Denver. He has a game tomorrow night. I'm

not doing anything, and my last client is under the dryer as we speak."

"Okay," Taylor replied while she soaked up her new surroundings. She got out of her truck and walked toward the parking lot elevators.

"I'll just have one of the girls close up for me and head toward your area in about two hours. Should I buy food or drinks? I'm sure you haven't gone grocery shopping yet."

"No, not yet. I plan to order us something good and have it delivered over here. There are a lot of really good restaurants in this area."

"Who was that?" Taylor asked. She heard someone yell in the background, *"Can I come?"*

"That was Tasha," Candace replied. "She doesn't even know who I'm talking to … it could be a killer for all she knows. She would like to join us."

"Tell Tasha I said hello, and she is more than welcome to accompany you tonight. The more, the merrier. We can have a small party. Just for us girls … I'm up for it."

"That sounds cool. I can ask Stephanie and Shelly to come too—that's if they're still here. Shelly may have left already, but I can call her later on."

"That's fine," Taylor stated. She knew most of the stylists at Candace's beauty salon. "Maybe we can check out the new club that just opened up a few blocks away."

Taylor finally made it to her door. She anxiously pulled out her key, opened the door, and entered into the palatial space that opened up into a large vestibule leading into a grand gallery. Her place was completely empty. When she had viewed it last, the previous owners still had their boxes in the living room area stacked high on top of one another. Taylor exhaled as she walked further into the open space. She looked up at the high, dramatic ceilings and began walking toward the large, wood-framed windows that provided a stunning 360-degree view of the city in all four directions. She turned around and pranced into the huge state-of-the-art kitchen that was adjoined to a breakfast and family room.

She knew she wouldn't have to upgrade or replace any of the amenities any time soon.

"Hello, Taylor? Are you there?"

"Yeah, I'm here. I'm just in awe right now. I can't believe I have my very own space."

"I can't wait to check it out. In regard to the club, I'm sure everyone will be up for going out," Candace said, changing the subject. "The question to ask is … are *you* going to be ready to go out?"

"Yes, I am," Taylor stated confidently. "Did you forget … it was my idea?"

"You know your mother is going to flip out when she hears about this. She calls me every other day asking about you. I can just hear her now: first you quit modeling, enrolled in college, and bought a SUV. Then you go and purchase a condo, and now you're partying at nightclubs … what next?"

"She wouldn't know anything if you didn't tell her,

Candace. The two of you gossip too much, especially about me."

"And we love every minute of it, too," Candace tossed back. "Speaking of gossip, how was your blind date with Kevin, the actor that I hooked you up with? You know he called me asking for your number."

"And you gave it to him. Thanks a lot!"

"Was it that bad?"

"Bad is *not* the word. Can I tell you that he bored me to death?"

"What!?"

"All he did was talk about himself all night. I almost fell asleep on him."

"You're so silly. Do you know how many women would die to even get close to him?"

"Well, they can have him. Plus, I can't see myself seriously dating anyone any time soon. I know this is sad, but it's true."

"I give up," Candace said, feeling exhausted. "I'll settle with going out tonight. Dealing with you, I forgot that we have to take it slow. I'm still very happy with your progress, though. You're definitely moving in the right direction."

"Thanks, Candace. Hearing you say that means the world me. You still get on my nerves. You and my demanding mother. Speaking of my mother, I better call her now and tell her the good news."

"I have to go too. My client just got out from under the dryer. See you in just a bit."

Looking out her windows, Taylor was beginning to appreciate the city's night skyline.

"Taylor, I had a great time," Tasha exclaimed. She walked toward the front door preparing to leave for the night. "And your place … it's definitely swanky, just like me."

"Thank you," Taylor said.

"Girl, from the balcony to your master bedroom to the beautiful white oak flooring … it's all to die for! I know you just moved in here, but if you ever want to sell this place … please think about me. I could see myself living in this building."

"Thank you," Taylor stated again. "Especially for joining the celebration. You know we'll have to do this again. Are you sure you don't want to come to the club with us?"

"No," Tasha sighed. "Tyrone has been blowing up my phone all night. He just won't stop calling me."

"What's up with him?"

"He usually does this when he wants me to come directly home and put him to sleep … if you know what I mean." Tasha nudged Taylor on the arm.

"Well, I better let you go and take care of your man."

"See ya, Tasha!" everyone yelled in unison. Taylor walked Tasha to the front door.

"Don't forget to call Candace when you get home," Taylor reminded. "Will do," Tasha returned. They quickly hugged each other, and Taylor closed the door.

"Okay, ladies. Are you all ready to go out and get our

party on?" Taylor asked as she walked back into the living-room area and picked up the phone to call a taxi.

"Yes, we are ready!" Candace confirmed. "I just want to mix one more drink for the road. You know I have to get my drink on while Brian is out of town."

Taylor frowned at Candace in amazement.

"What? Why are you looking at me like that?" Candace asked. She folded her arms across her chest and began to look at Taylor dumbfounded. "Did you forget that you just gulped down two drinks yourself?"

"Now, I'm beginning to regret that I started this habit," Taylor said with an attitude. "You know I don't like it when you drink, especially when Brian is out of town."

"Here she goes ..." Candace put her glass down and directed her attention to her other friends. "She never likes me to have any fun."

"That's not true," Taylor laughed. "I just don't like it when you drink *waaay too much*. And you usually do it with me when Brian is out of town."

"Okay ... ladies ... ladies ... we're getting distracted," interrupted Shelly, one of Candace's friends. "We're sup-posed to be celebrating ... not listening to the two of you engaging in another one of y'alls dramatic catfights."

"Hey, I'm all for having fun ..." Taylor continued, at-tempting to make peace.

"Fine with me," Candace relented. "Let's go. I'm ready to get out of here. I can always get another drink when we get to the club."

Taylor shook her head in disbelief while the ladies pranced out of her front door toward the elevator.

"All I have to say is," Taylor shouted back at them "I'm not acting like Brian tonight."

"Brian?" Shelly inquired.

"I'm not nursing your boss back to good health if she drinks too much tonight. That's Brian's job, not mine."

"Yes, she will," Candace stated reassuring her coworkers. "The first round of drinks is on me."

"Stop all your talking and walk." Taylor rolled her eyes at her friend. "The taxi should be arriving soon."

Twenty minutes later, the taxi pulled up in front of Club Oasis. "Wow! This seems to be the happening spot. It's the place," everyone said in unison.

"Look how jam-packed it is in there, and look at the line of people still waiting to get in at this hour," Candace said.

"Too bad for them," Taylor said with a smirk on her face. They got out of the taxi and strolled to the front of the line.

"Excuse me," shouted a lady who was waiting in line. "The end of the line is around the corner back that way." Ignoring the woman as if she had never spoken, Taylor flashed her ID. The bouncer at the door immediately ushered them in the entrance way. It seemed as if all eyes were on them as one of the waiters directed them to the VIP section.

"Let's sit over there," Candace said pointing toward a

certain area in the lounge. "That seems like a good place for us to chill out and relax." Everyone followed Candace as she led them to one of the tables.

"You all came at a good time," the waiter stated as they sat down at a table. "The drinks are free."

"Great!" Candace exclaimed.

"Yeah, a few of the New York Giants players just walked in. Apparently they're in a very good mood because one of them just made the announcement a few minutes ago." The waiter quickly picked up an empty glass and wiped off their table. "Let me take this glass back to the bar, and I'll be right back over here to take your order in just a second."

"Take your time," Taylor hollered while the waiter rushed off. "We're not going anywhere." She began to snap her fingers to TI's monster hit, "Whatever You Like,"... *"stacks on deck ... Patrón on ice ... and we can pop bottles all night ... you could have whatever you like ... whatever you like."*

"Let's go out on the floor. I'm ready to dance."

They followed Taylor as she led the way onto the dance floor.

Taylor couldn't believe that two hours had gone by so quickly. They were all having such a good time drinking, dancing, and chattering with each other.

"What are you drinking?" the waiter asked.

"Excuse me?" Taylor answered, feeling a bit confused.

"That gentleman over there would like to buy your next drink." The waiter pointed toward a table full of football players.

"Tell him thanks, but no thank you," Taylor responded. She looked over at the table and one of the men lifted his glass up in the air. "To be honest, I'm done drinking for the night." The waiter walked over to the table where the guys were sitting.

"You're so mean, Taylor!" Candace remarked. "The man was only trying to be nice, and look at him. He is *fine*, too!"

"I'm not being mean," Taylor said. "Look at me. Do I look like I *need* another drink?"

"You still could have accepted his offer," Candace added. She stuck out her tongue at Taylor. Taylor reached in one of the empty glasses at their table and flicked some of the melted ice water onto Candace. Candace was about to retaliate when her girlfriend Stephanie got in between them.

"Stop acting like children, ladies, and look to your left," Stephanie told them. "Mr. Good-Looking is walking over here."

"Hello, ladies," the gentleman said. "I hope I did not offend anyone, particularly the young lady right there." He pointed in Taylor's direction.

"No, you did not offend us," Taylor said quickly. "I've had enough for the night. But thanks for offering."

"No problem," the gentleman returned. At the moment, the music changed and everyone began to head toward the dance floor.

"Excuse us. We'll be back," Candace said. She and Stephanie trotted to the dance floor.

"Would you like to dance?" the gentleman asked.

"No thanks," Taylor answered. "I've danced enough for the night as well … I'm sorry."

"No need to apologize," the gentleman returned. "What's your name?"

"Taylor." She then covered her mouth and yawned. "Please forgive, I can't believe I just did that … I'm truly exhausted."

"Okay, Taylor, I get the hint," the gentleman said. He got up from the table. "I won't hold you all up any longer."

"I wasn't trying to be rude," Taylor stated. "It's just that I haven't been out in a while, and I'm really tired, and I need to go home, now."

"No need to explain," the gentleman said with a cheerful disposition. "It was nice meeting you, Taylor."

"Thank you," Taylor replied, and they nodded their heads in unison. The man walked away from their table. Shelly grabbed Taylor as soon as he was out of their sight. "Do you know who that man was you just blew off?"

Candace and Stephanie came back and sat down at the table.

"No, I don't, nor do I care," Taylor said boldly. "I'm glad you all are back. I'm ready to go." As they got up to leave, Taylor noticed the man staring directly at them.

"Was that the guy you just blew off?" Candace asked. She noticed him staring at Taylor as well.

"I can't believe you all don't know who that guy is," Stephanie added. "He's been in the salon before. Brian referred him to us for a haircut. Remember, the man who usually cuts his hair was not available that day?"

"I remember him vaguely," Candace replied.

"That's Michael Washington, the New York Giants' new quarterback. He got traded to New York from a team in California. He also made a few appearances on our favorite sitcom. Candace, remember the episodes when he got all wet and had to take his clothes off? Girl, I thought I had died and gone to heaven when I saw that man in his birthday suit. That's when I and every other woman in America fell in love with him. He also just signed a multimillion dollar contract to play for the next five years."

"Now, *that's* my kind of a guy," Candace boasted.

"Your girl here not only turned down a free drink, but she also turned down the opportunity to rub up against his brick-hard abs."

"What!?" Candace mouthed. She looked at Taylor and shook her head with disappointment.

"That is not even the worst part of this story. When he asked Taylor her name, she yawned directly in his face. Taylor, girl, you're crazy."

"I did not!" Taylor laughed.

"Yes, you did."

"Okay, so I did, but I apologized."

"I can't believe you," Candace grumbled. "I have to ask Brian about him. I think Michael is from New York, but I'm not sure."

"Keep walking, ladies," Taylor pleaded.

They continued to walk toward the front door of the club.

"I don't care who he is … let's just get inside one of those waiting taxis."

They walked to one of the taxis at the curb and jumped in. "You all are more than welcome to crash at my crib." Taylor kicked off her five-inch heels, leaned on Candace's shoulder, and closed her eyes. Shortly after the cab pulled away from the curb, Candace looked down at her friend. "Now, look who is nursing who." Taylor was out cold.

Chapter Sixteen

Cackling Hens
New York

"How are my favorite girls?" Diane walked to the table with Kimberly Thomas, Taylor's ex-publicist, and kissed Candace and Taylor on each cheek before sitting down to dine.

"You're in a good mood." Taylor winked at Candace.

"Come on … aren't I *always* in a good mood?" Diane smiled and then picked up a menu.

"I'm not going to get into it with you today." Taylor turned her attention to K.T. "It's been a long time, old friend. What have you been up to these days?"

"Well, it's been kind of slow since my number-one client let me go."

"Has it been that bad?"

"No, I'm just teasing." Kimberly grinned. "Actually, your mother referred not only one but two A-list actors to me."

"And you never told me what happened with those

potential clients," Diane chimed in.

"One of them signed a contract yesterday. So, he is officially on my roster, and the other one is still reviewing my profile. Hopefully, I will hear something soon." K.T. pulled out her blackberry and began to review her text messages.

"Have you heard from ..." Taylor tapped her fingernails on the table. K.T. looked up at her. "You know who?" Taylor mouthed Stephen's name and then opened her menu. She pretended to look through it while waiting for K.T. to respond.

"You'll never believe what I heard ..."

"No ... no ... no. Don't say another word," Diane declared. "We're not going down that road today, especially while I'm sitting here."

"Where is that woman who sat down just a few minutes ago in a good mood?" Candace muttered.

"You can talk about 'that subject' during one of y'all ladies' nights out sessions," Diane returned.

"Speaking of ladies' night out, where was my invite?" K.T. looked back and forth at Candace and Taylor. "You know I got eyes everywhere. I heard you had a good time at your new place and at Club Oasis."

"Everything was planned at the last minute ..." Taylor replied.

"No need to explain," K.T. interrupted. "I probably couldn't have gone out even if I wanted to."

Changing the subject, Diane asked, "So, Taylor, how is the decorating going in your new condo?"

"Actually, it's going quite well. I hired an interior decorator last week."

"Well, of course, you have." Diane chuckled and then winked at Candace.

"Mother, would you stop it?" Taylor said while looking at Candace angrily.

"I'm not getting in between the two of you at all today, so let's just change the subject right now," Candace declared. She noticed the waiter walking over to their table.

"Give us another minute," Diane said. She picked up the menu as the waiter stopped in his tracks.

"For your information, Mother," Taylor continued after the waiter left their area, "I would have decorated the condo myself, but my classes are consuming a lot of my time."

"Beautiful," Diane said nonchalantly. She continued to read the menu. "I agree with Candace, let's move on to a new subject. Taylor, have you found a location for your boutique?"

"Candace and I were talking about the boutique right before you all walked in here. I have narrowed down the search to five different locations in the city. I would be most honored if you could accompany me when I go out to look at them."

"Moi?" Diane teased. "You really want *me* to do something for the great Taylor LaRue?"

"What boutique?" K.T. inquired. "Once again, I have been left out of the loop. I'm not liking that I don't work for you anymore."

"I'm looking for a place to sell some of my old and new clothes. I'm going to sell jewelry as well. I have some really good pieces. After traveling the world for so many years, I've accumulated a lot of stuff ... gifts and clothes from designers that I have worn maybe once, if that ..."

Diane sighed while she continued to look through the menu.

"You have to excuse my mother; she's still adjusting to the new me."

"Which is ...? " Candace said as she exaggerated each word.

"A self-driven entrepreneur who wants to give back and serve others, preferably children, in some unique way."

"Okay, now I understand your new persona," K.T. said. "You need something to do until you come back to your senses, rehire me, and start doing what you do best ... the catwalk on the runways of Paris."

"Makes sense to me," Candace chimed in again.

"Neither one of you are helping me out here ... I'm serious about this."

"We can change the subject now," Diane finally weighed in on the discussion. "I have had this very same conversation with her on several occasions. I have come to the conclusion that she's being stubborn just like her mother. Let Taylor go on and find her passion in life." Diane adjusted her body to look directly into Taylor's eyes. "Whatever it is ... I hope it makes you happy."

"All righty then," Taylor said. She closed her menu. "Is

anyone still hungry?" She was glad the conversation had finally come to an end.

"So, what are y'all eating today?" Diane inquired. She picked up the menu again. "I think I'm going to order my usual."

"Me too," Taylor agreed, nodding her head at the waiter. The waiter came over, jotted down their orders, and disappeared behind the kitchen doors.

Ring ... ring ... ring.

"That's me," K.T. said. She excused herself from the table to answer her phone. Minutes later, she returned. "Hey, a new Boys and Girls Club just opened in Harlem. That was one of the board members."

"Yeah, one of Brian's friends owns the facility," Candace said. "Which reminds me ... Taylor, Brian said they desperately need volunteers to help out in any way. You know, like providing tutoring services, etc. I think that would be right up your alley."

"That does sound like something I would be interested in. What's his name?" Taylor asked.

"I'm not sure," Candace answered. "Brian just mentioned that they were childhood friends. Their friendship drifted apart due to their different interests in sports. Brian played basketball, and he played football, I think."

"Okay. Just tell Brian to give me the address, and I'll do the rest. Maybe I can teach a dance class or something." Looking at her mother, Taylor asked, "What do you all think? Don't laugh."

"Actually, the more you talk about being a dance teacher, the more I think that it would be a great idea," Diane admitted. "Thinking back, the two of you were outstanding dancers. We all know that I'm partially responsible for Taylor not continuing on with her study of dance. I do believe you, Candace, should have joined a dance company. I was surprised that you turned in your shoes to go to college. You two were really just that good."

"Actually, I hated the practices and the productions," Candace confessed. "My mother finally came to grips with the fact that becoming a professional ballerina was her dream and not mine. I was more interested in talking to Taylor every Monday, Wednesday, and Friday since we did not go to the same school. You know, we had to keep each other up to date with what was going on in our pathetic teenage lives."

"It definitely wasn't a passion of mine," Taylor added. "I have to say, though, what we learned definitely prepared me for modeling."

"In what way?" Candace inquired.

"Well, I was much more graceful and dramatic than many of the other girls on the runway. A lot of that was due to our ballet lessons."

"Chile, please," Diane chimed in. "Those traits you possess are innate, and you got them from me." They laughed as the waiter walked over carrying their steaming hot meals.

"Here you are, ladies," the server said. He placed the meals in front of each of them. "Can I get you anything else?"

"Not at this time," Taylor replied. Her thoughts went back to the idea of working with children. She began to get excited all over again. If not tomorrow, she was definitely going to Harlem and check out the center the following the day.

Chapter Seventeen

The Mystery Man
New York

Two days later, Taylor walked into the Boys and Girls Center in Harlem. She still did not know the person's name who actually owned the facility.

This is really nice. Taylor was in awe of the different African American artwork that graced the walls in the main entrance. She continued to walk down the corridor when she noticed a man sitting at the front desk.

"Excuse me." Taylor finally reached the reception area. "Is the director available, or maybe the person who owns this center?"

"Yeah, I think Mike is around here somewhere."

"Mike is the director or the owner?"

"I'm sorry," the young man replied. "Mike is the owner, the director, the coach, the janitor. He is working in every department right now because he's still in the process of hiring people to fill these positions. We haven't officially opened up the center to the public as of yet. My name is Chuck, by the way. I'm one of the five coaches who work here. Right now, I'm acting as the receptionist. We haven't filled that position yet either."

While Chuck was a bit overweight, he didn't look half bad. Taylor could tell by his body shape that he probably played football at one time in his life. Maybe, during his high school years, as his body wasn't as firm or chiseled like a seasoned football player's.

"I'm interested in possibly volunteering here at the center," Taylor told him. "It sounds like Mike is a very busy man. Do you think he'll have time to talk to me today?"

"A volunteer?" the man said. He got up from his chair quickly. "Yeah, he will be more than interested in talking to you. You can wait in the lounge room while I try to locate him."

Taylor walked over to the waiting area and sat down on one of the sofas. She picked up one of the fashion magazines from those that were scattered over a table.

She didn't notice the owner when he walked in and quickly walked right back out of the room as she continued to peruse the pages of one of the gossip magazines.

"What's wrong, boss?" Chuck whispered curiously. "You act like you saw a ghost."

"I know that woman," Mike whispered back. He peeked back into the room. "Well, I don't actually know her, but I met her at a club. Taylor … that's her name. She completely blew me off."

"No, she couldn't have given Big Mike the cold shoulder," Chuck chided. "I thought every woman wanted a piece of you."

"Well, I guess that rumor isn't true. Man, I haven't experienced rejection like that since, since, hell, since high school. She really gave me a hard time. She was yawning as I was trying to spit my A game at her."

"Naw, man, you gotta be kidding," Chuck replied shocked. They both peeked into the room and then moved back out of her eyesight. "I would have loved to see that with my own two eyes."

"It was highly embarrassing, man. I was completely embarrassed. I'm only telling you this right now because you'll have to go in there and tell her that I'm not available to speak with her right now."

"Why not, boss?" Chuck asked looking confused.

"Look at me, dude. I can't let her see me like this." Mike pointed at the sweaty mix-and-match jogging suit he had on. "Tell her to come back tomorrow at one o'clock if she's still interested. By the way, did you tell her my name?"

"Yeah. But don't worry, man. From her response, I really don't think she has a clue who you are."

"Of course she doesn't," Mike stated arrogantly. "She is one fine chick, but she will soon know and recognize who that dude she thought she kicked to the curb really is tomorrow. Don't say my name again. Just tell her to come back tomorrow at this time."

"No problem, boss," Chuck replied. He waited for a

second until Mike was out of sight, then he walked into the room. He found Taylor still looking through the various magazines.

"Excuse me," Chuck said. "What did you say your name was again?"

"I'm sorry," Taylor returned. "I should've introduced myself when I first walked in. My name is Taylor LaRue."

"Ms. LaRue, the owner can't meet with you today. He can meet with you tomorrow, around this same time."

"Great," Taylor stated. She then looked at her watch. "Tomorrow at one o'clock definitely works for me. Thanks again for all your help." Taylor smiled at the young man and walked out of the room.

"Hey, boss," Chuck yelled, "Ms. Taylor LaRue is gone. You can come out now."

"What did she say?" Mike asked anxiously. "Will she be back tomorrow?"

"Relax," Chuck teased. "She'll be back tomorrow. It seems like she really wants to work here."

"I'll have to see about that," Mike declared.

"Now, boss, put your personal feelings aside. We really need a woman looking like Taylor LaRue in this place every day, if you know what I mean."

"I hear you, man," Mike agreed. He walked over to the window and looked at Taylor getting into her sporty SUV. "She's definitely a cutie, but I can't promise you that I will let her work here. However, I will be nice to Ms. Taylor LaRue. That is her name, correct?"

"Yep, Ms. Taylor LaRue."

Checking her watch again, Taylor could not believe that she had been waiting to speak to this man for an hour. She was becoming angrier and angrier as anxious thoughts rambled through her mind. *What in the world is he doing? The center is not open, so he couldn't be that busy. Did he forget that he has an appointment today? What kind of an organization is this anyway? This is completely rude and unprofessional.*

"I should get up and leave," Taylor murmured to herself. However, she continued to wait. The thought of working with children in this community compelled her to sit in her seat a little bit longer.

"The owner is ready to speak with you," Chuck announced with a smirk on his face.

Taylor wondered what he was thinking about.

As she walked in the office and sat down in the chair facing the desk, she noticed a man sitting in a chair with his back turned away from her. He was talking on the phone.

Unbelievable! I can't believe this man is talking on the phone. He should have left me waiting in the lobby. Taylor coughed, attempting to alert him to the fact that she was in the room.

"Just another minute, miss," the man stated. He continued to talk on the phone.

How rude! Taylor seriously thought about walking out of his office at this point. The owner finally said good-bye, hung up the phone, and swung around in his leather office chair to face her.

"Please forgive me," the man offered. "That was actually my mother. If you knew my mother, then you would understand why I had to answer her call. I also apologize for the wait. I just arrived in the building a few minutes ago from a meeting that was scheduled at the last minute. I usually do not come to the center dressed in this sort of attire." He then stood up to show off his perfectly tailored Armani suit.

"No problem," Taylor said shocked. She couldn't believe that this was *the same man* that she blew off at the club a few nights ago. What was she thinking that night as he sat in his chair looking absolutely gorgeous? His skin was an even-toned chocolate brown. He resembled someone Taylor had met before, but her thoughts were now scattered. Her anger had disintegrated as she sat there in shock.

"My name is Mike ... or I'm formally known as Michael Washington." He stood up again to shake her hand.

"My name is Taylor LaRue."

"What brings you to the Harlem Boys and Girls Center?" Mike questioned candidly.

"Well, a friend of yours told me about this center," Taylor replied. "He really felt that your facility would be the perfect place for me to volunteer."

"What friend is this?" Mike inquired. He knew that this could change everything he had planned for the duration of the interview.

"Brian, he plays for the New York Knicks," Taylor confirmed.

"Yes, Brian Johnson and I are very good friends. We actually grew up together in the same neighborhood not too far from this site."

"We met through a mutual friend," Taylor returned. "His girlfriend is my best friend."

Game over. Mike sat up in his chair and cleared his throat. Brian Johnson was one of his homeboys. He knew he couldn't play a trick on one of his friends.

"So, Taylor, what type of services did you want to provide to the children here at the center?"

"I thought about providing tutoring services," Taylor said sheepishly. She knew that wasn't what she really wanted to do.

"I've already hired a coordinator that will be responsible for overseeing various programs, and our comprehensive tutoring program is one of them. She is responsible for interviewing and hiring all of our tutors, and I do believe she mentioned to me when I spoke to her last that she actually had a waiting list of people who wanted to tutor and be a part of that program. I can have her put your name on that list ..."

Taylor interrupted, "I was also thinking about providing free dance lessons to the young girls here at the center."

"Now *that* just might work," Mike replied. He decided he wasn't going to be mean, but he sure wasn't going to make it easy for her. "Where else have you volunteered or worked?"

"This is actually the first time I would be offering myself to do this type of work. I recently changed my professional career."

"So, you don't have a resume or a bio with you today?"

"No, I don't. I didn't think I would need one."

"You didn't think you would need one?" Mike paused and looked at her dumbfounded. "Okay, you mentioned you recently changed your profession. Can you talk a little about that?"

"I've been working as a model for the past eight years."

"A model," Mike repeated. He stared at her, attempting to jog his memory. "Yeah, I have seen you before ... in that hair commercial, right?"

"That's right," Taylor admitted. "I've never danced professionally. However, I had ballet lessons for nine years, starting at the age of three. I can provide you with letters of recommendation from my former teachers."

"Yes, that would be great," Mike returned. "I'll also need you to undergo a criminal background check since you'd be working with children."

"Where does one go to get a criminal background check?"

"You can go to the police station. They will run your record and do fingerprints. You know, the basics."

"Police station, fingerprinting—that sounds so intrusive."

"You're working with kids ..."

Taylor sat up straight and flipped her hair. She wasn't

sure which card to play, the very important person or the damsel in distress. He was too hard to read. "Is there any way to get around …"

"No, it's mandatory." Mike continued to look at her with a blank face. *Sorry, sweetie, you're cute but not that cute!* He was trying to keep it together, but he really wanted to burst out laughing. Looking at her face, he could tell she wasn't used to not getting her way. "There are other places that I could refer you to—"

"No, no. That's fine. I can do a background check."

"So, how often would you offer these ballet classes? Once a week, twice a week, bimonthly?"

"I really haven't thought about how many days I would be available to do this. Maybe two times a week during the after-school hours. Also, I wouldn't just offer ballet lessons. I plan to incorporate a variety of dance styles in my classes, including African traditional dance, tap, as well as some hip hop."

"This all sounds like it's a go," Mike replied. "You can give me your schedule at a later date. Do you think you'd be ready to start in two weeks?"

"Yes," Taylor stated confidently.

"Great. I'll mention all of this to our new director. He'll provide you with all the details."

"Sounds good," Taylor said.

"Do you have any questions?"

"No, not at this time." Taylor wanted to apologize for her rude behavior, but he was acting as if this was their first time meeting each other, so she decided not to take the risk.

"Well, in that case, welcome aboard. I want you to know that we value and appreciate all of our volunteers. You'll definitely see this first-hand as we have already planned several events that will highlight and showcase all of your efforts."

"That's nice," Taylor smiled. "It's always great when an organization acknowledges and appreciates the service their workers provide. I'm sure you know that we do what we do for the children and never for the glory."

"Well, of course, I do," Mike replied. "I must remember to thank Brian for sending you over to us."

"Thank you for giving me this opportunity." Taylor was all smiles as she stood to shake his hand. Minutes later, she was out of the building and walking toward her truck in the parking lot.

"I'm going to kill her," Taylor whispered. She couldn't get to her truck quick enough before she began to dial Candace's cell phone number. Candace's voice message came on. Taylor quickly ended the call and pressed the re-dial button.

"You're talking to me today," Taylor huffed. She jumped in her SUV and drove off the center's parking lot.

"Hey, girl, what's up?" Candace said. She answered her phone on the second ring.

"Guess where I was today?" Taylor stated sharply.

"Where?" Candace asked, sensing a hint of irritation in Taylor's voice.

"The Boys and Girls Center in Harlem."

"Great! How did it go?"

"Stop playing games, Candace," Taylor replied frustrated. "You probably already knew what was going to happen today ... didn't you?"

"What are you talking about?"

"The owner. Did Brian tell you who the owner of the center was when he recommended that I go check this place out?"

"He just said it was an old friend of his," Candace replied. "What is the problem? Did something happen?"

"Are you *sure* you're not playing one of your games with me?"

"What are you taking about, Taylor?"

"Can I tell you how shocked I was when I found out the owner of the center was Michael Washington?"

"The quarterback from the New York Giants?"

"Yes, the guy that I blew off that night at the club."

"Oh, no!" Candace chuckled. "The old folks always said, you reap what you sow. I hope you've learned your lesson. The next time a man or anyone else, for that matter, approaches you, please give him the acknowledgment and respect that any human being deserves."

"Your point is well taken," Taylor admitted. "I'm sorry for accusing you. When Mike turned around in his chair and looked at me, my mind immediately went to you. I just assumed that you had a part in what I would consider a cruel joke."

"Seriously, I had no clue. What happened anyway?"

"He was kind of rude, or maybe I should say he was firm but in a very professional manner. If he remembered me from the club, he gave no hints during the interview."

"Trust me when I tell you, I'm *sure* he remembers you."

"I don't know. He didn't even recognize who I was until I told him I used to model."

"That's probably because he has been living in California for years. He's more familiar with most of the black actors, not models."

"I guess," Taylor replied. "I'll tell you this much, he looked much better in the light than in the dark. Wearing an Armani suit may have helped him as well. He looked super fine."

"So you might indulge him after all, huh?" Candace teased.

"I only said he was fine," Taylor confirmed. "I never said that I would date him."

"Never say never," Candace reminded. "These are words of wisdom that your mother would certainly say."

"Girl, please. Diane would kill me if she knew I was dating the boss. What she would say is … *'As you young people say, dating your boss is not a good look. Been there, done that.'* You know she gets on my nerves dishing out her pearls of wisdom, because she always seems to be right."

"Yeah, that's okay because when you call me and say, *'Girl, what do you think about me and Michael dating each other? It's only one date,'* I'm going to kindly remind you about this conversation. NOT A GOOD LOOK, TAYLOR! I'm just teasing. You know what I really would say ... you *better* work it!"

"You're crazy," Taylor said laughing. "I better let you go."

"Please keep me posted," Candace returned.

"Stop it," Taylor demanded. "Nothing is going to happen between us. To be perfectly honest with you, I really can't see me being intimate with him or anyone. Not yet. This is the only part in my life that I'm still stagnant in. I have built up such a high wall that Superman could not bust through it. But I have noticed that I'm becoming attracted to men again. I mean, I'm actually saying words like, 'he is fine' or 'his tight butt sure looks good.' But to fall in love again, well, that's just not going to happen. The man would have to be near perfect, *he would have to be Jesus."*

"Yeah, yeah, yeah, I've heard those words from many women before. Just when I was giving up hope on finding a decent man, here came Brian. Neither one of us was looking to date anyone. Two years later, here we are engaged and we are still asking ourselves, now how did we get here? It starts with just that ... *being attracted to one another, Ms. Taylor."*

"Whatever," Taylor sighed.

"Now I really have to go. My four o'clock appointment just walked through the door. Just remember *my pearls of wisdom* when you and Mike are sitting across from each other at your favorite café."

"Bye, Candace," Taylor huffed, frustrated. An image of Michael sitting behind his desk popped up in her head. Taylor had to admit that even though he acted like a serious prick, he did look like a scrumptious piece of Fudgy Chocolate Crème Pie, one of her favorite desserts.

Chapter Eighteen

Giving Back New York

Feeling good about recently purchasing the boutique, Taylor jumped out of her Rover, energized and ready to teach another dance class. She decided to incorporate theatrical techniques into the dance lessons this week, so she brought some old clothes, costumes, and other items in boxes that were stacked on top of each other in the rear of her truck.

I'm definitely going to need some help. Taylor opened up the back door of her truck. She walked into the center looking for anyone who would help her. Then she heard voices coming from the gym. When she approached the entrance to the gym, she stopped at the double doors so she wouldn't interrupt the practice session that Mike and Chuck were conducting.

Hopefully, this practice will be over soon. She quickly walked inside the gym and sat down in a chair near the bleacher area where other spectators were gathered.

"Run, Caleb!" Mike shouted. He waited for the boy to get to a yellow line and then he threw him the ball. "Marcus, you're next. Run! I want to see who is concentrating on their 'A' game today." Mike threw the football high in the air, and the boy caught it. "*That's* what I'm talking about," Mike yelled. He gave him a thumbs-up. When the boy returned the ball to Mike, he reached out and gave him a bear hug. The boy's face beamed with excitement.

"That's so sweet," Taylor mumbled underneath her breath. At that moment, she began to develop a new appreciation for Mike. She noticed how easily he engaged and interacted with the boys. He seemed to have such a genuine rapport with not only these boys, but with most of the kids at the center.

Even though Mike was sweaty and grimy-looking, he still looked good to Taylor. She tried not being so obvious while she watched him stroll across the gym floor wearing a torn NFL T-shirt that exposed his perfectly cut abs and a pair of loose-fitting shorts that draped across his buttocks very nicely. Taylor's insides had begun doing their own thing. She continued to follow Mike with her eyes. She couldn't believe she was now attracted to this man.

"Okay," Taylor whispered, as she got up to leave the gym, "it's definitely time for me to get out of here. I do believe it's getting a bit warm in here." As she got up to walk toward the gym door, she heard someone calling her name.

"Taylor," Chuck shouted again. "Do you need someone to open the dance studio?"

"No," Taylor mouthed. She waved her hand, indicating to him to come over to her. Because of the noise, she knew he wouldn't be able to hear what she had to say. Chuck began to jog slowly toward her.

"The maintenance guy cleaned and locked most of the rooms upstairs this afternoon," Chuck explained. "I saw you sitting in here, so I thought maybe the dance studio was locked too."

"I haven't been upstairs yet, so I don't know if the studio is locked or not. I was looking for someone to help me bring in the boxes I have in the back of my truck."

"I'll do that for you," Chuck said. "When Mike ends this practice, which should be in the next ten to fifteen minutes, we'll bring the boxes up."

"Thanks," Taylor said graciously.

"Here's the master key," Chuck said. He took it off his key ring and handed it to Taylor. "If the door is locked, then you won't have to come back down to find someone to open it up for you. Go on upstairs. We should be there shortly." Chuck turned around to jog back to his position.

"Chuck," Taylor quickly yelled, "here are my car keys. Please lock my car when you all are done."

As promised, Mike and Chuck were bringing up the boxes one by one. Trying to stay focused, Taylor continued to do her warm-ups as she prepared herself for the dance class.

"Check out those legs," Chuck said. He nudged Mike on his arm. They were bringing in the last two boxes from the truck.

"I don't have time, man," Mike returned. He tried to sneak a peek out of the corner of his eyes. "You know I have to get back downstairs and redo all the coaches' schedules for tomorrow. This is the last time I want to hear that we couldn't have practice because there was no space available. I know we have several activities going on at the same time, but we have to be more organized so that kids can truly benefit from our programs."

"Man, stop all your rhetoric," Chuck chided. He directed Mike out of the studio so that they could look at Taylor practice through a window that was on the side of the studio. It provided a perfect view that was less intrusive.

"Take a break for moment," Chuck commanded. "Now, just look at that beautiful work of art floating in the air."

"All right, man, I know she looks good," Mike said. Knowing Taylor was in the next room, inches away from him, frustrated him even more. "To be honest, I have been trying to avoid her, and if we didn't have this scheduling problem today, I would have been successful once again."

"Why are you trying to avoid such a pretty young woman like Taylor?" Chuck asked. He continued to look through the window.

"What do you propose that I do, Chuck? She has already given me every indication that she doesn't want to have anything to do with me, except of course, to volunteer here at *my center*."

"That was two months ago, man," Chuck said attempting to lift Mike's confidence. "She could have completely different feelings toward you right now. Man, if I was you, I would go in there right now and ask her out to dinner tonight. You know you're still dying to go out with her."

"Chuck, because you're so lame," Mike teased, "you, of course, wouldn't understand that there is an art to charming a woman like Taylor to go out on a date with a dude like me. You can't just go up to her and say, 'Would you go out with me?'"

"Whatever, man. It's your loss." Chuck walked back into the room to give Taylor her car keys.

"No way," Mike murmured.

Taylor gave Chuck a big hug and a kiss on his cheek. Mike moved away from the window and waited for Chuck near the top of the staircase.

"Who's lame now?" Chuck pointed at the place on his face where Taylor planted a kiss.

"I have to admit, I'm a bit envious of you right about now."

"You better be. I just secured a hug and a kiss from your lady."

"She's not my lady," Mike returned. "Well, at least, not yet."

"Now *that* is the Big Mike I know," Chuck said, patting Mike on his back. "Take your own advice. Stop avoiding her and come with your 'A' game."

"Whatever, man," Mike replied.

"Okay, whatever," Chuck repeated. "All I want to hear you say right about now is, '*Chuck, you're the man.*'"

"Chuck, you are the man," Mike said reluctantly.

Taylor was completely exhausted. She finally finished putting the rest of the costumes back into the individual boxes. Then she plopped down on the floor and thought about how well the lesson had gone that day. The girls thoroughly enjoyed putting everything that they had learned thus far into a dramatization. This must have put them into a talkative mood because everyone participated during their rap session, which was definitely a first. To develop a better rapport with the girls, Taylor decided to have a rap session at the end of every dance lesson.

Today, LaTonya, who was a thirteen-year-old eighth-grader, opened up and revealed to the group that she was thinking about giving in to her boyfriend, who has been pressing her to have sex with him. Taylor and the other girls weighed in on the conversation and were able to convince her to not only wait until she was physically and mentally ready to be intimate with the opposite sex, but to also talk to her mother who was a registered nurse.

Taylor sighed as she thought about how her day started, and how it was not even close to being over. She knew she had to stop by the boutique tonight and interview Paul Harris, a potential interior designer that she might hire to give the boutique the facelift it truly needed. A friend referred this person to Taylor, but she really didn't know much about his work, so if she didn't like his presentation tonight, she would be right back at square one.

As she gathered up all of her belongings, Taylor noticed that she still had the master key that Chuck had given to her earlier that evening.

I'm sure he will definitely need this tomorrow. She left the room and walked down the stairs to the first floor.

As she walked into the administrative area of the center, she noticed Mike in his office working diligently at the computer.

"Excuse me," Taylor said, tapping on his door.

"Yes," Mike returned. He looked up at her and thought *Damn, she looks good.*

"I'm sorry to interrupt you, but do you know where Chuck is right now? I forgot to give him this key back."

"He's still here." Mike got up from behind his chair. "He should be in his office in the back. Wait here; I'll get him for you." Mike walked around his desk and out the door. Taylor's eyes followed his buttocks all the way down the corridor.

"Hey, Chuck," Mike yelled, walking down the hallway.

"What's up, boss?" Chuck replied. He quickly appeared from around the corner.

"Taylor wanted to give you back your key." Mike pointed to where Taylor stood waiting for him. Chuck quickly jogged to her with Mike following.

"Here you are," Taylor said. She handed Chuck the key. "Thanks again for bringing the boxes in for me."

"Anytime," Chuck replied. "If you need anything else, just ask."

"Well, there is something else." She thought about the boutique. "Since you offered, does either one of you know of anyone that is really good at remodeling, especially with plastering or painting walls?"

"Why do you ask?" Chuck inquired.

"I just purchased a piece of property which will be a boutique that I plan to open soon. I got it for a great price, but it needs a lot of work."

"Well, you know Mike practically did all the work here at the center," Chuck stated. He looked directly at Mike, raising his eyebrows.

"Impressive," Taylor replied. She began to walk around the outside of the offices.

"I did some of the work when I had the time," Mike explained. "My guy, Todd Scotland, is the true professional. He deserves most, if not all, of the credit. I can give you his card; I know I have one of them somewhere around here."

"Where is your place located?" Chuck looked at Mike, irritated. "We can also come and check out the place and give you a few pointers. I say 'we,' because I helped out around here also."

"It's in the city," Taylor replied. "It's actually not too far from here. I'm going there right now to meet with a designer that I'm not really comfortable with because I have never seen his work."

"That's not good," Chuck commented. "Tell you what, Taylor. We'll come and check out your place tonight — that is, if we are all done here. Are we all done here, boss?" Chuck smiled at Mike.

"Yeah, we're all done," Mike replied, looking at Taylor. "We'll follow you in my car into the city." He was kind of curious to see what else she had going on in her life.

"This is great!" Taylor exclaimed. She started walking toward the front door.

"This is not bad," Mike and Chuck stated in unison. Taylor quickly turned on every light switch in the store.

"It definitely needs a face-lift, but I like it," Mike confirmed.

"Thanks," Taylor replied. "I want the designer to create a Euro chic environment." Taylor began to search for the floor plans.

"The location is perfect, and Euro chic should fit right with the people in the neighborhood," Mike said. He continued to walk around her place. "If you're not happy with the designer's work, my friend Todd will definitely help you out. Chuck and I will also help out as much as our time will allow."

"Thank you so much," Taylor said, excited. "I completely understand about your time. Please know that whatever time you all can offer me will be very much appreciated, and of course, generously compensated."

"Whatever time Chuck and I put into this project will be at no cost to you."

"I can't accept that."

Mike quickly interrupted her. "Just consider us helping you out as a favor. Taylor, you must remember that I don't remodel or paint for a living. It's truly a passion of mine, and I don't know about Chuck, but I only do it for myself and my close friends. Because you're volunteering your time at the center, I do consider you a friend and not just a person who happens to work at my center."

"Okay," Taylor agreed reluctantly.

"When is this person supposed to arrive?" Chuck questioned. He checked his watch. "Isn't he late?"

"Yes, he is late," Taylor confirmed. "He should have been here twenty minutes ago. That's not a good indicator … huh??"

"I know Todd will agree to do this job," Mike stated. "I can give him a call tomorrow."

"I'm going to wait here just a little bit longer," Taylor said. "I'll call you first thing in the morning to let you know what I have decided. This is great. Everything seems to be working itself out. I'm getting excited all over again."

Taylor escorted the men back to the front door. She hugged and thanked them once again, then locked the door as she watched them walk toward Mike's car.

"Thank you," Chuck said sarcastically.

They hopped in the car.

"Thank you for what?" Mike turned the ignition.

"Did you or did you not finally get that hug you've been waiting for?"

"Yes, I got the hug, but I didn't get the kiss. Did you see me try to lean my face into hers? As you can see, she didn't pick up on my gesture."

"Next time," Chuck said, chuckling.

"There had *better be* a next time," Mike stated, as they drove onto the boulevard. "I'm truly impressed with Taylor. Not only is she cute, but she seems to have an intelligent mind behind those alluring, smoky, sexy eyes. She's a lady who knows exactly what she wants. I like that about her. She reminds me of my mother."

"What? I've never heard you say that before," Chuck exclaimed. "Oh no! Could Taylor be *the one*? I mean, you're already comparing her to your mother. That's definitely a first."

"Taylor is definitely a challenge, and you know how I like a challenge. My philosophy has always been … if it comes easy, then it's probably not worth keeping. Plus, if I even remotely think that a woman reminds me of my mother, the only woman that I truly love, then you gotta know that's *definitely* a good look for the little lady."

"Well, you got in the door tonight," Chuck said. He hit Mike on the shoulder.

"Not quite," Mike replied. "I do believe that I made up some serious ground tonight. Good looking out for a brother."

"I was smooth, wasn't I?"

"I owe you one," Mike said. "She really has a nice place. After we put a little work in, it should really look cool, or Euro chic, as she would say."

"I bet you get that kiss you've been waiting for," Chuck said grinning.

"I better get more than a kiss."

"Now *that's* the Big Mike I know."

"Get the dirty porno flick out of your mind," Mike said. "I told you that I like Taylor." Smiling on the inside, Mike knew Taylor was definitely a woman he could see himself hanging out with for a while.

Chapter Nineteen

Vulnerable & Guarded
New York

Three weeks later, Taylor decided to go to the boutique after her dance session was over. It was now six o'clock. She was sure no one would be there by the time she would arrive. This would give her an opportunity to conduct a more detailed inspection of the place. She had hoped to have the grand opening in two more weeks.

As she parked her truck, she noticed that the lights were still on inside of the boutique. Taylor's initial thought was to leave, but curiosity won her over as she got out of her truck and walked toward the door.

"Hello! Hello!" Taylor shouted. She entered into the boutique. No one responded, so she continued to look around the place.

So far so good. Taylor was very impressed. Most of the walls and countertops were up and installed. She heard voices in the back area, so she proceeded to walk to that section in the store.

"Are you leaving?" a man yelled. Taylor continued to walk toward the voices.

"Yeah, man, I'm done for the night. I'll lock the front door when I leave." Just as he finished his last word, Mike's friend Todd whirled around and almost rammed right into Taylor.

"Well, hello," Taylor said, stepping back to avoid a collision.

"Sorry, I didn't realize you were here," Todd replied. "I hope you like what you've seen so far."

"Everything looks great," Taylor returned.

"As you can see, we pretty much followed your floor plan, and the layout is practically done." He pointed toward her office area. "You did have some extra space in your office area, so I decided to turn the half bath into a full bathroom. Come check it out."

They walked back in that direction.

"This is amazing!" Taylor exclaimed. "It looks like you'll be done soon."

"Don't worry, everything will be fixed and in working order for the grand opening."

"I hope you don't mind," Mike said. He walked up on them from behind. "I utilized your shower yesterday. I looked like I do right now, only worse. My entire body was covered with paint."

"Oh my," Taylor said as a big grin appeared on her face.

Her insides were doing their own thing again. Mike looked sexy as ever, even though his body had paint sprinkled all over it. "Now, how long have you been here?"

"I decided to come over just about an hour and a half ago. I wanted to finish the painting I started yesterday. It's a surprise, so you're not allowed in that part of the store until it's finished." Mike pointed to the area in the store that was off limits.

"Okay, I like surprises," Taylor agreed.

"Well, I'm out of here, good people," Todd announced again.

"See you tomorrow, man," Mike replied. As Todd walked toward the front entrance of the boutique, Mike turned to Taylor.

"It's time for a break. I brought a light snack and some soda. Would you like to join me?"

"No, I better not. I might get in your way."

"No. Actually, I would appreciate the company," Mike confirmed. "I'll bring you back a soda."

"That's fine." Taylor decided to look around the place again while Mike went to get her a soda.

"Everything seems to be coming together quite nicely," Taylor proclaimed loudly. "You were right about Todd. I like what he has done so far."

"I knew you would love his work," Mike said. He returned and handed her the soda. "I'll be right back. My sandwich should be warmed up by now."

Taylor continued to walk around and noticed a half-painted picture of a woman on the wall.

"This is stunning!" she gasped. Taylor had accidentally walked into the area that Mike said was off limits. The woman's skin was a silky jet-black, and her eyes arrested Taylor as they sent chills up her spine. *Breathtaking ... this is simply breathtaking.* The entire picture looked vivaciously authentic. Taylor heard Mike walk up behind her. "You know you're talented?" She continued to stare at the unfinished mural.

"You spoiled the surprise," Mike sighed. They decided to sit down in front of the painting.

"I'm sorry, but I wasn't aware that this was the area that I wasn't allowed to walk in."

"It's okay. When it's finished, you're *really* going to be in awe."

"What art school did you attend?"

"Actually, I didn't perfect this gift at an art school. Initially, I started drawing pictures to release my frustrations. I had no idea that I was good at it until my mother, teachers, and other people finally helped me realize that this was, in fact, one of my innate gifts from God. I didn't pursue any further training because I also enjoyed playing football, and I was exceptional at that as well."

"So do you have paintings similar to this one just lying around your house?"

"Yep, my entire garage at home is practically overflowing with them."

"Have you ever thought about selling any of them to the public?"

"No, like I said before, painting serves as an outlet for me. Playing professional football pays the bills."

"If you say so," Taylor stated in amazement. "However, I'm letting you know now, if anyone asks me who's the artist or where can I go to get a picture like this, we might have to have a different kind of conversation about your artwork. We just might have to sell a few pieces right here in my boutique."

"I'll have to think about that some more. I do thank you for your enthusiasm and the offer. So how did your dance class go today?"

"We ended up having a rap session at the end. One of the girls had a boyfriend problem, and another one had home problems, so I tried to create an atmosphere where they could be supportive of each other. I'm not a therapist, as you know, but I offered some words of encouragement as well."

"That's great. I don't think you realize what a difference you are making in those girls' lives."

"I definitely plan on continuing with it next semester. The days that I conduct the classes may change, but that's it. Everything else will remain the same."

"Why will the days have to change?" Mike asked curiously.

"I'm enrolled at New York University part-time. Next semester is quickly approaching, and I haven't registered for any classes as of yet. The classes that are offered in the evenings fill up fairly fast. So I may not be able to register for classes on the same days that I have now."

"Understood. So, what's your major?"

"Business."

"I majored in business as well," Mike offered. "If you need any help, just let me know. The classes will get more challenging as you progress in your major."

"Will do," Taylor said. "So far, I'm doing pretty well. What made you major in business?"

"My father is a businessman. Actually, he is a lawyer who started his own firm. I, of course, have no interest in business. Playing football is really my thing, but you never know, majoring in business may come in handy later on in my life."

"Does your father live here in New York?"

"I'm sorry I even mentioned him. I normally don't talk about my father. Do you want another soda?"

"No thanks," Taylor replied. "I'm sorry ..."

"No, it is not your fault. I opened up the door that time," Mike returned. He got up and walked toward the back office and returned with another soda in his hand. "So what about modeling? Are you still doing it? I'm asking because you had mentioned during the interview that you recently changed your professional career."

"I'm not doing it now. All I know is that I needed a serious break away from the modeling world."

"Is it that bad?"

"Let's just say it's not as glamorous as it looks."

"What do you do for fun? Or maybe I should ask, how do you release the stress from those long and tiring days? Do you go out?"

"I rarely go out to clubs," Taylor replied. Her mind went back to the nightclub where she blew him off. "You may not remember, but we actually met briefly at that new club that opened up three months ago in lower Manhattan."

"Now I definitely remember you acting like I was some pesky fly that you wanted to kill. I wasn't aware that you were Ms. Taylor LaRue, the supermodel."

"Well, I didn't know that you were Big Mike Washington either," Taylor tossed back. "Not that it would have mattered. I wasn't trying to be mean. I was truly tired and a little tipsy that night, and the last thing I wanted to do was have a conversation with anyone."

"Talk about bruising a man's ego. I definitely got the message loud and clear."

"I apologize for my rude behavior."

"No biggie," Mike returned, trying to save face. "I was just doing the normal thing, spitting my rap game on a pretty face. I'm glad Fate arranged for us to meet each other again on a different level."

"I'm glad as well."

"Are you sure you don't want another soda? I'm thirsty."

"Yes, you can bring me another one." Taylor admired Mike's rear end as he walked to go get the sodas. He came back quickly and handed her the drink.

"So Mike, were you single that night, or were you being Mr. Mack Daddy and playing the field like so many men in your profession do?"

"I was single that night, and I'm still very much single. I must admit that I date quite a bit. However, I'm not committed to anyone seriously at this time."

"Why not?"

"As of yet, I haven't found the one woman who meets all of my requirements."

"That's what all men say."

"Hey, I guess you forgot that women have their long laundry list as well. Should I refresh your memory? Women like their men to look a certain way, have the perfect job, make a certain amount of money, shall I go on?"

"Okay, okay, you're right," Taylor told him with a smile.

"Like, I said earlier. Women, you all are just too much."

"Please, don't let me get started on you men," Taylor huffed, rolling her eyes.

"Sounds like a touchy subject for someone," Mike returned.

"No, I've been single for a while, so it's not a touchy subject. I guess I just don't understand men."

"What is it about men that you don't understand? Let's see if I can enlighten you." Mike leaned in closer while he listened to her.

"Okay, I don't understand why a man would have an affair when he is already committed to a woman. Instead of being open and honest about the situation, he will give some flimsy excuse like 'her arms are too skinny' or 'her hair is too blonde.' Whatever the flaw is, it's completely fixable. Why do men have to have a 'chick-on-the-side,' as my mother would say?"

"Well ... huh—"

"Wait, I'm not finished," Taylor interrupted. "I just don't understand men who sneak around. Wouldn't it be easier to just end the first relationship and then he can go on about his own business? Mike, why do men lie so much? Why can't men be more honest with their women?"

"Someone must have really broken your heart."

"A broken heart is not even close."

"No wonder you gave me such a hard time that night. I guess that saying is true. When a woman is fed up, she is done."

"This is so true," Taylor confirmed. "I was definitely fed up and didn't want to be bothered with another smooth-talking joker. I didn't care if he was a football player that most women would kill to date."

"Understandable," Mike said calmly. "Now, I really don't feel that bad. So it wasn't about me that night. You were just going through or getting over an earlier heartbreak."

"Exactly," Taylor agreed. "I was also tired as well."

"I know you're single, but are you currently dating anyone?"

"No."

"Still not ready, huh?"

"I've been out on a few blind dates," Taylor admitted. "My girlfriend Candace had recently set me up on one two weeks ago. For some reason, the guys she selected for me were not my type."

"Like I mentioned earlier, women have their requirements also. I'm glad to hear that you are at least dating again."

"Whatever."

"I'm serious. Some women will either try to hang on to the man, or they will never date a man again ... if you know what I mean."

"You're silly." She nudged him on the shoulder.

"If you don't mind me asking, what did your friend do that ended the relationship? If it's too difficult to talk about, I will understand."

"He was actually my fiancé, and I actually ended the relationship a week before the wedding because I found out that he was having an affair with another woman who was expecting his child. Crazy, right?"

"Sorry to hear that," Mike returned. "Well, I must admit that there are some men, or shall I say boys who live in men's bodies, who know they have the right woman but behave in a selfish and even immature manner. Believe me, I know all about those type of guys."

"You do, huh?" Taylor asked. A smirk appeared on her face. "Please enlighten me."

"I'm not that type of a guy, and I never have been. My style is to be up-front with the women I date. I don't like a lot of drama. I do know guys who are like that. My father was one of those guys, which is why I'm completely the opposite. They don't know a good thing when they see it. My father is a very wealthy man. He thinks he owns the world and the people in it, I suppose."

"I'm going to have to agree with you this time," Taylor replied. "No, seriously, my ex-fiancé was very wealthy and very selfish and very immature. I'm so very grateful that I found this out before I married the fool."

"I'm glad you did too," Mike said. He stood up and stretched. "Do you think we should continue this conversation over dinner?"

"Are you still hungry?"

"Look at me. Why do you think they call me Big Mike?"

"Sure, I don't mind."

Mike reached out his hand to help her off the floor.

"There's a small café not too far from here."

"Are you finished painting for tonight?"

"You know it's hard to redirect my mind back on painting when something else has completely captured my attention." Mike smiled and pointed his index figure at Taylor.

"I like your sense of humor."

"What? I'm serious this time," Mike stated. "I'm going to jump in the shower real quick. It will only take me five minutes."

"Take your time. I'll make sure everything is turned off." Taylor walked around the store once again. In less than fifteen minutes, Mike was out of the shower and fully dressed.

"Is everything good and in order?" Mike reached in his shirt pocket and got out the master key to lock the front door.

"I believe so," Taylor replied.

They walked out the front door. It was a brisk autumn evening. The wind swirled around as cars drove down the busy street.

"It's a bit nippy out here," Taylor exclaimed, "but I feel like walking."

"I don't mind myself," Mike said, reaching out his arm. Taylor hesitated. "I'm not going to bite." He then reached for her hand and pulled her close. "Besides, we need to be close to produce some body heat to keep us warm."

Taylor complied, moving in closer. Little did he know, she was already feeling toasty. Her body temperature was boiling over.

Chapter Twenty

Coming Out
New York

It was eight in the morning as Taylor sat up in her bed trying to decide if today should be the day to inform Candace about her little secret. Taylor was not quite sure what was going on with her as it related to Mike. She was, however, very certain that her feelings for Mike were at another level. She noticed, especially in the last two weeks, that she wanted to be around him all the time.

Before she changed her mind, she picked up the phone receiver and quickly dialed Candace's cell phone number. Then she rested back again on her silk Ophelia pillows that were still neatly arranged across her bed.

"Hello, this is Candace."

"Well, good morning, Ms. Candace," Taylor said. "Are you busy right now?"

"Not yet. My first client is due here at eight-thirty, so I have a few minutes to waste away. What has been going on with you?"

"Nothing much," Taylor returned. "I called to find out your opinion regarding a particular matter."

"Okay." Candace sat down and began to spin around in the chair that her clients normally sat in. "I'm ready. Talk."

Taylor began to laugh. She still was trying to figure out how she should break the news to her friend.

"What's so funny?" Candace asked.

"Someone asked me out on a date, and I was wondering if I should go out with him."

"Taylor!" Candace screamed. She sat up in her chair. "Are you and Mike dating?"

"Yes and no," Taylor replied. "No, we're not officially dating, meaning that we are not exclusively dating each other. Yes, we have been hanging out with each other almost every night for the past six weeks."

"I *knew* it," Candace replied. "I can't believe you are just *now* telling me!"

"I wanted to mention this to you maybe three weeks ago, but then I thought that maybe I should wait just a little bit longer. Plus, I know you will tell my mother, and I don't want her to know, at least not yet."

"Why not? You know she would be extremely delighted to know that you are seriously dating someone again."

"Yes, I know, but she'll be all up in my business, asking all types of questions. I'm not ready for all of that action right now. So please, Candace, don't mention a word to Mother," Taylor reiterated.

"Okay, I promise."

"It's not that serious anyway. We're still in the getting-to-know-you stage of the relationship."

"I like that you called it a relationship," Candace commented. "I didn't know that couples still played by those rules ... getting to know you. Like, what is that all about?"

"First of all, we're not a couple," Taylor huffed. "Second, I told him about my engagement to Stephen, and he completely understands why I want to take my time getting to know him."

"Have you all kissed?"

"Well, of course, we have." Taylor rolled over on the other side of her bed. "I'm not that slow." A big grin appeared on her face as she thought about their first kiss.

"Mike might be the one," Candace declared.

"It is a bit scary," Taylor admitted. "I was just thinking that same thought this morning, which is why I had to call you. You know I had to tell someone about *my boo*. He's so adorable, Candace. I really like him."

"Taylor, I'm so happy for you. I figured something would probably spark off between the two of you once you started working at the center. I was right as usual. How exciting!"

"Actually," Taylor replied, "I wasn't looking for anything to happen. It just kind of happened. I found out later that he was really interested in me, but he didn't know how to approach me after I had blown him off at that nightclub."

"I told you he remembered you," Candace exclaimed.

"Men usually don't forget that type of stuff, especially if they like you."

"After we talked about my engagement, he understood why I was so bitter and mean toward him that night."

"Did you tell him everything?"

"I never mentioned Stephen's name. I told him the truth that I had found out a week before my wedding date that my fiancé had been cheating on me for months. We talked about this the first night we went out to eat, and we haven't mentioned that subject again because it's simply irrelevant."

"Wonderful," Candace stated. "So how does all of this feel? I mean to be dating, and dating 'Big Mike' Washington, I might add?"

"So far, so good. Mike is a nice guy."

"*Just nice?*" Candace repeated.

"Yes, nice," Taylor confirmed. "I don't know. For some reason, dating Mike feels different. When I was dating Stephen, I always felt like I was on cloud nine … and my head was truly high up in the clouds because I really didn't have a clue nor did I want to know the truth. Dating Mike is nice because it feels *right*."

"News flash," Candace replied. "Do you know that you're dating Mr. It? The women here at the salon talk about him all the time."

"What do they say?" Taylor's interest was piqued. She gathered her pillows up behind her so that she could sit up comfortably in her bed.

"For one, every woman in the world wants a piece of him. Plus, you know he just signed a multimillion dollar contact with the Giants. This, of course, does not include his endorsements. He was also dating some white model last year, which, you know, is always a good conversation piece for us black women."

"Well, you know I don't care about his money. Been there, done that, and as for the white model, her name is Brenda Starr, and I can't stand her ... she's so sneaky. We worked together several times in Paris and here in New York."

"Brenda Starr," Candace said with an attitude. "I think I know of her. Isn't she dating some rocker right now?"

"I don't know, and I don't care," Taylor replied yawning. She stretched her arms upward and then jumped off her bed. "Mike told me that they're still friends. He also keeps in touch with this black actress named Nicole Lawson. She lives in California."

"Did Mike explain to you exactly what *still friends* means?"

"Yes, he did," Taylor stated. "They *still have sex with each other* ... it's rare, but it does happen. Like, I said earlier, we're not in an exclusive relationship. We're allowed to date or have sex with whomever we want to."

"Interesting," Candace returned. "And you're okay with this?"

"Yes, I am for now. Just for the record, since we have been *dating,* he hasn't been intimate with any of these ladies, or anyone else, for that matter. This is one of the reasons why I like him. Mike has been up-front and completely honest with me. He really doesn't believe in playing games. He is not only straightforward with me, but he is straightforward with everyone he deals with."

"I'm still stuck on him still being friends with Brenda and Nicole. Why is he adding yet another woman to this equation?"

"Candace, Mike is thirty-two years old, and he has been playing football for eleven years now. He wants to accomplish two more important goals in his life: win a Super Bowl game and find a wife."

Candace twirled around in her clients' chair while she continued to listen to Taylor.

"I'm not worried about Brenda or Nicole, not at this point. Think about it, Candace. If Mike wanted to be in an exclusive relationship, or even engaged to one of them, he would have done so already."

"That's true," Candace agreed. "So if you two finally become *an official couple,* then Brenda and this Nicole woman would be completely out of the picture … meaning no more free sex … correct?"

"Of course." Taylor began to feel a little bit annoyed with her friend. "You know Diane didn't raise a fool. Mike can continue to have his fun, especially since we're not having sex with each other. I'm simply enjoying what we have now."

"Listen to you," Candace said. She admired her friend's

self-confidence. "So does he know that you're a model, excuse me, *were* a model?"

"Of course, he knows now, but he didn't know that when he saw me at the nightclub. When I told him, he said I look like a model, but I don't act like one."

"I guess he doesn't know that side of you yet."

"You know I'm not like that," Taylor exclaimed. "Mike really likes that I'm independent, smart, and sassy. What he admires most about me is that I volunteer my services at the center helping the girls."

"That sounds sweet," Candace replied. "What have you learned about him thus far?"

"That he's not only the best Little League coach in the world, but that he is an artist. He's actually gifted in that area. When you have time, please come to the boutique. He painted an amazing mural of an African woman from Senegal on the wall in the back of the store. You can't miss it; it's absolutely breathtaking. You're going to be completely mesmerized when you see it. He could open up a gallery and sell his work for thousands of dollars if he wanted to, but because he is so down-to-earth, making a lot of money just doesn't faze him. He has also accompanied me to class and joined in on the discussion. He's an all-around real *nice* guy. I like him a lot."

"I'm sitting here and listening to you knowing that you haven't talked about a guy like this since Stephen. He *must* be the one."

"He just might be," Taylor repeated. "He does, however, have one flaw."

"Don't you mean two?" Candace teased. "Brenda and Nicole?"

"No, I don't mean those two," Taylor huffed back. "Anytime he mentions his father, he becomes extremely angry. It's really scary because he doesn't realize how angry he gets. His entire demeanor changes. His eyes become glassy, and he gets a little sweaty. I think he needs to speak to a therapist about this issue. Here I go again, sounding like my mother, but it is true. I just assume that because his father did not marry his mother, whom he absolutely adores, he just never got over it. He is definitely a mama's boy. He talks to her every single day."

"Brian is a mama's boy, too. You know those mothers can pose a problem."

"So far, he has been doing well. If I'm out with him and she calls, he will either not answer the call or tell her he is with me and he will call her at a later time. She wants to meet me, but I'm not sure about doing that at this stage in our relationship."

"You've talked to his mother?"

"Yes, and why does she remind me of my mother—all in your business? She wants to make sure Mike settles down with the right woman. I was like, another Diane LaRue. And his father is very wealthy, but as I told you earlier, they have never had a good relationship. So we have a few things in common."

"Mike gets two thumbs-up from Candace. I wouldn't worry too much about his relationship with his father. I mean, think about it, Taylor. There are probably very few African American brothers who don't have some sort of problem with their father. Look at us. My father left my mother for some young chick, and we never saw him again. You never knew your father. I wouldn't consider Mike not having a good relationship with his father ... a flaw for him. It's simply an epidemic for us black folks."

"I do agree with what you're saying, but it still concerns me when Mike becomes so angry and so quickly."

"Maybe he does need to talk to a therapist," Candace replied.

Beep ... Beep.

"Hold on a second, Candace. That's my other line ringing." Taylor clicked over to the other line. "Hello."

"Good morning, beautiful," Mike said.

"You're sweet," Taylor returned. "I'm not feeling particularly beautiful at this moment."

"Are you still in bed?" Mike inquired.

"No, I have been awake for a while now. I'm still a little tired though. You know it's hard to get a real good night's sleep when dating Mike Washington."

"I'm sorry. Did I keep you out too late last night?"

"No," Taylor replied. "After you dropped me off last night, for some reason, I couldn't sleep."

"That's good to know," Mike commented. "I thought I was the only one experiencing restless nights."

Taylor smiled.

"So what are you doing this morning?" Mike asked.

"I really didn't have anything planned. Wait a minute, Mike. I forgot I had Candace on the other line."

"I can call you back."

"No, no, no. Just hold on a second, I was just telling Candace about what a wonderful guy you are, and now you are here on the line talking to me."

"Now that's good to know."

"What's that?"

"I'm glad to hear that you're talking to your friends about me. Tell Candace I said hello and mention to her that we should all go out soon. I'm sure Brian would agree. We haven't seen each other in a while."

"Will do," Taylor said. She clicked back to the other line. "Candace, are you still there?"

"I'm here. What took you so long?" Candace barked. "I was about to hang up."

"That's my sweetie pie," Taylor said, blushing in her mirror.

"You're excused. I guess that means our conversation is ending?"

"You're correct once again."

"I can go back waiting for my client ... who is now late."

"Mike says hello. I told him I was talking to you, and he said he would like for all of us, including Brian, to go out soon."

"That sounds like a good idea. As a matter of fact, I'll call Brian now. You know I can't wait to see you two together.

Then I would be better able to tell if Mr. Mike Washington is truly the one for you."

"Whatever," Taylor replied. "I'll talk to you later." She quickly clicked back over to her second line.

"I'm back," Taylor stated. "You mentioned something about my morning plans?"

"Are you up for an early brunch?"

"Sure," Taylor returned. "Where are you thinking about eating?"

"I'll leave that up to you. I have to return a few phone calls, jump in the shower, and I should be in front of your building in about two hours."

"Sounds good," Taylor said. She hung up the phone, went into her bathroom, and turned on the shower.

Chapter Twenty-One

The Dating Game
New York

Taylor felt like a schoolgirl while she anxiously waited for Mike in the front lobby of her building. Fortunately, she was not waiting long because, as promised, Mike pulled up in front of her building in his Mercedes LX 649 exactly two hours later.

Wow, she looks great! Mike noticed Taylor in the entrance-way. He quickly hopped out of his car to greet her. He was intrigued as she wore a casual black jump suit with a plunging neckline that slightly revealed her breasts. *Just enough,* Mike continued to walk toward her, *to bring a strong man to his knees.*

"You look fantastic," Mike declared. He politely embraced and kissed Taylor on the cheek.

"Thank you," Taylor replied. Mike opened the passenger door and Taylor slid into the car. He then quickly strolled around to the driver's door, hopped back into the car, and turned down the radio.

"So have you decided where you would like to eat?"

"There are some really good places to eat in this area. Do you mind driving around to see what would interest us?"

"Indecisive," Mike stated. "That's a side of you that I didn't know exists. If that's what you would like to do, that's fine with me; we can drive around." Mike pulled away from the building and began to drive down the busy street.

"I prefer using the word *spontaneous*." Taylor giggled. She leaned over and kissed Mike on his cheek.

"Spontaneous it is," Mike repeated. "I'm just glad that I have another opportunity to be with you. You know once the playoff season begins next month, I won't have this amount of time on my hands."

"Will you still come to the Center?" Taylor asked.

"Yes, but not as often. I have not asked my mother yet, but I plan to have her fill the position of overseeing the entire operation. Hopefully, she will say yes."

"I'm sure she will."

Mike drove into the lane that led to the expressway.

I guess we're not eating in this area after all, she thought.

"Where are we going?"

"It's a surprise — or should I say, I'm being spontaneous," Mike returned with a smile.

"Wherever you go, I will follow." Taylor rested back in her seat.

"I promise you won't regret it," Mike stated. He placed his hand on Taylor's thigh.

Ring ... ring ... ring.

"Is that mine or yours?" Taylor asked. She began to dig deep in her colossal-size Gucci bag.

"That's mine," Mike returned. He pointed toward his phone. As Taylor reached to hand Mike his phone, she notice Brenda's name pop up on the front screen. She opened the phone and handed it to Mike.

"Hello, this is Mike. Hey, what's going on with you?" Mike sat up straight in his seat. "You're in New York? Now? No, I won't be able to do that, not right now. I'm in the middle of a—I can't give you a time. Stop it, stop it! You are still the same. I guess you'll never change. I don't think your rocker boyfriend or whatever his name is—Yeah him, I don't think he would appreciate Mike Washington walking his lady down the red carpet."

Red carpet, what? Attempting to keep her cool, Taylor looked out her window while Mike continued his conversation with Brenda.

"Okay, so you are denying him now, now that you are in New York. What happens when you get back to London? I guess it will be a different story ... right? You know I am teasing you ... just having a little fun."

I can't believe this man! Taylor thought to herself. She was becoming more irritated with Mike by the minute.

"Seriously, Brenda, can I call you back? I'm in the middle of a date and if I had known it was you calling, I wouldn't have even answered the call. Calm down, calm down. I was just kidding, once again. Enjoy your day, talk to you later."

"That was Brenda," Mike stated. He flipped his phone closed and looked over at Taylor. "She flew into New York to attend a movie premiere, and she needs an escort."

Brenda, her nemesis! Taylor wanted to scream. "No need to explain," Taylor returned nonchalantly. She turned her body toward the car door and continued to look out the window. Taylor wanted to say something, but she couldn't form any words to come out of her mouth. The next five minutes seemed a bit awkward, as neither one of them said a word to each other.

"We're about five minutes away from the restaurant," Mike said finally.

Taylor nodded her head and continued to look out the window. Mike turned the radio sound up. The silence in the car was aggravating him. Taylor could not believe how she was acting. She did not realize that her feelings for Mike were so strong. She actually felt herself becoming more and more upset about this entire situation.

"Taylor, Taylor," Mike repeated. Taylor continued to ignore him. "Taylor, can you please look at me." Taylor finally turned her body around to face him.

"I don't have to go to this event with Brenda if it bothers you that much. It's really not that big of a deal."

"Mike, please," Taylor returned. She tried to appear as if she had not been affected by the phone call. "You don't have to disappoint your good friend on my account. This may not be a big deal to you, but it sure is a big deal to her … she called you, didn't she?"

"Taylor, Brenda can go to that event with anyone; she has several male friends who live here in New York."

"Mike, do what you want to do," Taylor insisted sharply. "Who am I to tell you who you can or can't go out with? I'm not your woman."

"Please don't remind me," Mike sighed. He was trying not to rush their relationship, as Taylor had told him several times before she was not ready to be in a committed relationship. "Like I said, it's really not that big of a deal; really, it isn't."

"Okay, Mike," Taylor fired back. "Can I ask you question, if it's really not that big of a deal?"

"Go ahead," Mike said. He pulled the car up to the restaurant.

"If you were not here with me, would you go out with Brenda tonight?"

"Probably so," Mike admitted. Taylor turned her head away from him and began to look out the window again. "Come on, Taylor. That's a silly question." He reached over to turn her face back toward him.

"Mike, please," Taylor pleaded. "Let's just change the subject."

"I want you to know that taking Brenda to a red-carpet event is not even an option because I have something to do. I'm here on a date with you."

"Let's just change the subject," Taylor repeated.

"Fine," Mike returned. "Do you want to eat here?" He pointed at the restaurant.

"Not really," Taylor said nonchalantly. She pretended to look for something in her purse to avoid making eye contact with him.

"Okay." Mike was now past being frustrated. He pulled away from the curb. "Maybe we can eat down the street at Rick's place."

"I'm really not in the mood for burgers this early. If you don't mind, I would like to go home."

"Come on, Taylor. Don't you think you're being a bit immature about all of this?"

"Immature! You think *I'm* being immature?"

"Taylor, look at me," Mike ordered. He pulled over into an empty parking space on the street. "Let's just have an open and honest conversation about this entire situation."

"That's fine."

"Believe me, Taylor, if I wanted to go out with Brenda tonight, I would. The fact of the matter is; I don't. Do you want to know why I don't? I don't want to scare you away by saying this, but I'm falling in love with you."

"Mike you're right," Taylor said. She was stunned to hear his words ... *falling in love with her.* "I'm being very immature. I just don't think ..." Taylor stopped speaking.

"You don't think what?" Mike asked curiously.

"I just don't think I'm going to be able to deal with this open relationship thing ..."

"Keep going," Mike persisted. He was trying to figure out where Taylor was going with this conversation.

"I feel so stupid saying this," Taylor admitted. "I didn't

realize until now that I won't be able to deal with these so-called good women friends of yours, especially Brenda, who I know you casually sleep with from time to time."

"Maybe I should clarify my relationship with Brenda," Mike stated as he looked directly in Taylor's eyes. "Brenda is a friend who I do care about. I'm not going to lie to you. If we do go out tonight to that event, I probably wouldn't have sex with her because I'm more interested in becoming intimate with you."

At that moment, Taylor wanted to kiss Mike's big round lips all over. She really wanted to believe every word that came out of his mouth, but the gigantic wall she had built up held her back from showing any true emotions toward him.

"Actually," Mike said, as he smiled at her, "I'm glad Brenda called today. This gives us the opportunity to revisit where we are in our relationship and discuss where we want to go from here. Taylor, do you think you're ready to go to the next level?"

Taylor was silent. She wasn't sure she was ready to have this conversation with Mike. She wasn't sure what she really wanted from him. This was the question she had to answer, and she hoped when she answered it that he really wanted the same thing that she wanted. After all, he did say he loved her.

"Okay, I'll start," Mike declared. "I would love for us to go to the next level in this relationship. I would love for us to be committed to each other, as I told you just a minute ago. I really do care for you, Taylor ... I have fallen in love with you. Even now, you're driving me nuts, but when I look into your eyes, all I want to do is make it right with you. I don't want you feeling sad or hurt. I promise if you were any other dame, I would've made a U-turn a long time ago. You should know me by now. I'm a no-nonsense type of a guy. I don't have time for a lot of drama."

"So this is drama?"

"To be honest, yes, it is. Who am I sitting in the car with, you or Brenda?"

"Okay, Mike," Taylor said hesitantly. She decided at that very moment to be brave and go down the rocky road of love and happiness yet once again, but she hoped this time it would be better. It had to be better because this time it would be with Mike.

"Answer this question. What if I were Brenda, or even Nicole in this same situation? I'm just curious. Would you take them home or show them the curb?"

"No, I wouldn't because—"

"You don't have to explain, Mike," Taylor said, interrupting him. "You wouldn't do that because you truly care about them as well, correct?"

"Yes, but the difference between them and you is that I don't love either one of them. Honestly, Taylor, I don't know why you are focusing on these women." Mike was becoming extremely annoyed with her as he repositioned himself in his seat.

"Taylor, I asked you a specific question," Mike persisted.

"Where do we go from here? Either you want to or you don't want to take our relationship to the next level. Just a word of advice. You shouldn't base your decision on what I would or wouldn't do with other women."

"Mike," Taylor said feeling exhausted, "I would love to have a closer relationship with you. However, it bothers me that the man I believe I, too, am falling in love with ..." Taylor stopped speaking once again. She couldn't believe those words came out of her mouth.

"Continue on," Mike pleaded with a smile.

"I don't like that you care about other women just as much as you care about me. I know you said that you love me, but I'm still just a bit uneasy about all of this. I thought I had overcome my past relationship and all the hurt and pain that came with it, but maybe I haven't."

"Listen, Taylor, I will have this conversation with you one time and one time only. Brenda is a very sweet and nice young lady, but I lost interest in her a while ago. She is young, and she still wants to have fun. As for Nicole, we actually tried dating each other exclusively, but that lasted all of three months. We both agreed that it just wasn't working out. Both of those ladies are very smart young women and will probably make some man very happy one day. I have come to the conclusion that that man was not going to be me. During those few times that we did engage in sex, trust me, none of us were committed to anyone in particular. We are all consenting adults. After it was over, they went on with their lives and I carried on with mine. Now that I've been dating this amazing woman whom I am really crazy about, going out with Brenda is not an option. I promise you, neither one of us will lose any sleep over it. My mind, heart, and soul are completely focused on you ... Taylor."

"Really?" Taylor was still a bit apprehensive.

"Taylor," Mike said reaching out to take her hands. He knew she still wasn't fully convinced. "Maybe you will believe my mother."

"Your mother?"

"As I have told you several times before, my mother has been my rock, my teacher, my everything. My mother recognized early that I was gifted and I had talent, so she protected me as much as she could from dating silly girls who just wanted something from me. Yes, I dated and had my fun, but I never introduced a girl to my mother unless I was serious about our relationship. To date, my mother has met only two of my female friends. One was my high-school sweetheart who broke my heart. She decided to be with some other dude. The second one was my college sweetheart. We were both tipping and slipping in and out of the relationship until we both decided it was over. My mother may know Brenda and Nicole by name, and I say 'may,' but she has never met either one of them. Now that I have said all that ..." Mike picked up his cell phone.

"What are you doing?"

"I'm calling my mother."

"Mike, please. Stop!" Taylor demanded. "Don't involve your mother in this situation."

"Don't worry, she won't know you're sitting right here next to me. I'll put the phone on speaker. I know hearing our conversation will be helpful to you in making your final decision."

"Mike, this is ridiculous," Taylor sighed. She grabbed his phone.

"Trust me, Taylor," Mike returned. He took back his phone, dialed his mother's number, and then pressed the speaker button so Taylor could hear their conversation.

Ring ... ring ... ring.

"Hello."

"Hey."

"Well, that was quick. I thought you said you were going out with Taylor this afternoon. Is the date over already?"

Taylor raised her eyebrow. She was pleasantly surprised that Mike had told his mother about their date.

"It really never got started," Mike returned, smiling at Taylor at the same time. "Before we left her building, we had a really intense conversation and she then decided that she wasn't hungry anymore."

"Haven't I taught you anything about women??? Did you forget to save the serious conversation until *after* dinner, or even toward the end of the date? So when you all make up, you can really make up ... get my drift?"

"Well, she started the conversation, not me. There was no way of avoiding this discussion."

"I did finally see what she looks like. I ran across one of

my old *Essence* magazines and there she was on the cover. She looks kinda young, but she sure is gorgeous. I know looks are not everything, but I think you should go back and apologize to this one. There's something about her eyes ... in her picture. She seems to be at peace, the easygoing type ... you know what I mean?"

"I don't know about all of that, but she is definitely beautiful," Mike confirmed as he caressed Taylor's face.

"I thought you said you were going to bring her over to meet me. You know I will talk to her for you."

"That's quite all right. I'm a big boy now. I think I can handle my own love affairs."

"Are you sure?"

Giggle ... giggle ...

"So what exactly did she get mad about?"

"Other women."

"Other women? What other women?"

"Women I have dated in the past and we keep in touch and are very good friends even today."

"Women like who?"

"Women like Brenda."

"Brenda? Who is that? Is that someone you know at the center?"

"No, we used to date each other. I don't know if you remember her, but our entire conversation was centered on Brenda as well as Nicole, another young lady I had dated in the past."

"I remember Nicole. I'm so glad you decided to move

on. You would've been broke by now if you had continued to date that one."

"Yes, but we're still friends."

"Now I understand why Taylor wanted to stay at home. She was probably so confused. Hell, I'm confused. All of these women who you are no longer dating, but they're still in your life, *these so-called good friends*. What woman wants to deal with all that confusion, Mike?"

"What's so confusing about having good friends who happen to be women?"

"Keep on living, son. You will eventually understand what I'm trying to tell you, which is why you are sitting in your car, all alone, talking to your mother on the phone. You just might have to let the old friends go, especially if you want this new relationship to work. I can tell that you really care about this young lady, Mike."

"How can you tell?"

"First of all, you called me, didn't you? Plus, when you talk about her, there always seems to be an excitement in your voice, which is why I'm anxious to meet this Ms. Taylor. I have to meet this woman that has my son sitting in his car all alone crying to his mother."

Mike chuckled.

"You always know how to put a smile on a brother's face. I think I'm going to call her back now. If all goes well, we might come to your house next Sunday for brunch."

"That sounds great. I'll let you go take care of your business."

"Love you, Mom, and thanks."

"Anytime, sweetie. Anytime."

Mike closed his phone and turned to look at Taylor.

"Any more questions or doubts?" he asked, then waited for her to respond.

"Mike, I'm sorry. I feel really stupid—"

"Sshhhh," Mike said. He quickly put his index finger on her lips. He then held her face and passionately kissed her. Several minutes later, they came up for air.

"Can you find it in your heart to forgive me?" Taylor said as she panted for air. "I've completely ruined our brunch."

"Yes, I forgive you," Mike stated while he kissed her between each word. "I'm really not very hungry anymore." He continued to kiss Taylor on her lips and around her neck.

"Are you up for a drive?" Mike asked.

Taylor couldn't respond. She was busy pulling her clothes back into place. Mike sat up in the car, turned the engine on, and drove out of the parking lot.

"Where are we going?" Taylor asked.

"Let's finish this date at my mansion. It's just on the outside of the city in Saddle River, New Jersey."

"That's fine," Taylor returned still trying to catch her breath. She was in desperate need of an ice-cold drink to cool her hot insides down.

Chapter Twenty-Two

Friends & Lovers
New York

Taylor woke up in darkness, and just for a few seconds, she had forgotten that she was in Mike's luxurious ten-bedroom mansion until she felt his arms wrapped tightly around her body. She could smell his cologne as well as the scent of good lovemaking, which still lingered in the air.

Taylor untangled herself from his grip and slid out of his oversized bed. A sudden chill went throughout her entire body so she reached for one of the blankets on the bed and wrapped it around herself while she walked toward the balcony that was connected to Mike's master bedroom. She pushed the huge stained-glass double doors completely open and walked onto the balcony. Taylor looked up at the sky and noticed that the stars were still beaming so brightly.

This is definitely a night to remember. Taylor felt so at ease and relaxed. She knew their lovemaking was well overdue, at least for her it was. She had not had sex with anyone since Stephen. Although she vowed that she would not compare the two, she couldn't help herself. Mike seemed to be more experienced and less selfish in bed than Stephen. Mike wouldn't stop his performance until he knew for sure that Taylor was completely satisfied. She greatly appreciated his thoughtfulness and tenacity. As young as Stephen was, he should've had more stamina. Taylor knew after the first thirty minutes with Stephen, their lovemaking was pretty much a wrap. This was mostly probably due to Stephen's mind being preoccupied with himself—or another woman. Mike, on the other hand, was much more disciplined. How he controlled himself, Taylor would never know. She hoped that this wasn't just a one-time phenomenon.

Taylor had to admit, at first, she was a bit timid when she saw Mike completely nude. His brutish football figure towered over her thin frame just like a wild animal that was ready to devour his prey. Mike noticed that she was a bit nervous, so he began to caress her shivering body until she felt more relaxed. They began to engage in tantalizing foreplay, and when Taylor could no longer resist him, she voluntarily—eagerly—opened herself to him.

A warm liquid substance began to run down her leg. She wrapped the blanket more tightly around her body because just thinking about that this night made her hot and wet all over again.

"How's my favorite girl?" Mike asked. He came up behind Taylor and hugged her tightly. A smile crossed Taylor's face as she leaned back into Mike to savor his embrace.

"Aren't you cold out here? Come on, let's go back inside."

"I was just enjoying the view," Taylor said finally. "It's so peaceful and quiet out here."

"I agree," replied Mike. "That's one of the many reasons why I bought this home—for its tranquility. I usually come out to think or to just relax."

"This is lovely."

"Speaking of lovely, how would you rate our first fight and make-up session?" Mike began to nibble on her earlobe.

"It was nice."

"Just nice?" Mike replied perplexed. "I was shooting for *'fantastic,'* or *'wow, Mike, you're the best lover I've ever experienced.'*"

"Now you're reaching …"

"Ouch!" Mike chuckled. "Talk about a bruised ego. Maybe I shouldn't have asked."

Taylor turned around and moved closer into his chest. "Look at my face. Can't you tell that my evening here with you was absolutely wonderful? I mean, words can't even describe how I feel right now." Taylor opened up her blanket and pulled Mike into her.

Staring at Taylor's face, Mike said, "Your face always glows. I'm not letting you go until you say words that pacify my male ego."

"What words would these be?" Taylor asked laughing. *"Wow, Mike, you're the best lover I've ever experienced."*

Mike wasn't ready for her response. So he kissed her passionately on the lips and then picked her up in his arms. Taylor felt a chill go down her spine as the blanket fell on the balcony floor. Mike carried her back into the room and gently laid her down on his bed. He stared into her dreamy brown eyes. Eager for their dance to begin, Taylor grabbed Mike's buttocks and pushed him down onto her body. Ready to oblige, he pressed hard into her warm, wet, and intoxicating inner walls. In no time at all, they were at it again, making wild, passionate love to one another.

Two days later, Mike drove Taylor back to her place. They finally decided to come up for air after romancing each other for nearly forty-eight hours straight. Before getting out of the car, Taylor pecked Mike on the cheek and then whispered in his ear. A big grin suddenly appeared on his face.

"Are you okay?" Taylor chuckled. She let herself out of the car.

"I'm just fine," Mike declared. He sat there still smiling. Taylor turned around and walked away. When she approached the front door of her building, she looked back over her shoulder. To her surprise, Mike was still there watching her. Taylor was now smiling back at him. She finally confessed that she was in love with him too!

Chapter Twenty-Three
Ecstasy
New York

It was Taylor's 22nd birthday, and after a year of dating each other Mike decided to do something extra spectacular for her. He shut down one of New York's hottest clubs in Midtown and reserved it for 150 of their closest friends and family to celebrate Taylor's special day. Taylor was utterly amazed by Mike's thoughtfulness when he told her about his plans for the birthday party. She truly believed that this time she had found real love.

Taylor stood in front of her full-length mirror admiring her slender physique. She never dreamed that she would be back in this place in her life and so fast. She was completely over Stephen, the wedding, and all of that mess in her past. She was giving back to her community, her business was thriving, and she had acquired ten credits in college. She had also started modeling again part-time. Everything had worked itself out, like her mother and best friend said it would.

Taylor was all smiles while she changed from one outfit to the next, trying to decide on which clothes she would wear tonight. She finally narrowed the choices down to two outfits. She hoped she would choose right because she wanted to look drop-dead gorgeous.

Ding dong ...

"Candace is early," Taylor whispered. She walked toward the front door.

"You aren't ready yet?" Candace exclaimed in a playful voice.

"No, and you're early for once in your life," Taylor returned.

"I know I'm a bit early. I guess I'm a little anxious about getting the night started. It's your birthday, it's your birthday, it's your birthday," Candace exclaimed.

"I just need a few more minutes, and then I'll be ready to go," Taylor told her rushing off into her bedroom to put on the finishing touches.

Two hours later, Taylor and Candace arrived in front of the club in a limousine. They knew they looked absolutely fabulous. They slowly stepped out of their ride and walked toward the entranceway. Taylor decided on a sleek yet elegant short black Calvin Klein dress which bared her back and revealed her sexy, long legs. Candace went with a sexy yet sophisticated look as she sported a Valentino red swing dress that accentuated and enhanced her slim and toned figure.

"I wonder where the guys are," Candace inquired curiously while she scanned the room with her eyes. Being old high-school buddies, it didn't take Mike and Brian long to become reacquainted with one another. Besides being professional athletes, they had a lot in common. They both went back to the 'hood to visit with old friends and relatives who still resided there. Taylor spotted them talking away at a table, giving each other high fives and gulping down beers, doing, as they call it, "the typical male thing."

"Don't worry about them," Taylor told her. "Come with me to the bar. I'm ready for a birthday drink." They continued to walk the opposite way until they found two empty chairs at the bar area. "Tantalizing" was the word that jumped out as Taylor sat down and scanned over the place. Many of their friends had already arrived. Some of them chatted effortlessly away in the oversized yet stylish couches and chairs that encircled the entire club. Others danced on the open-air dance floor that led to a magnificent 50-foot waterfall that cascaded into a secluded outdoor patio.

"Here you are, ladies," the bartender said. He handed them their drinks. Candace slipped him a tip, and they got up to look for the guys. When Mike laid eyes on Taylor, she knew the dress she had decided to wear was a winner. His mouth gaped open until they finally walked over to their table.

"Happy birthday, Taylor!" screamed everyone boisterously at the table.

"Thank you, thank you," Taylor replied excitedly.

"Happy birthday, baby," Mike repeated. He embraced her and kissed her on the cheek. "You look absolutely amazing. If it was up to me, I would vote to leave right now. You know later we're having our own private party back at the house."

"We can talk about that later." Taylor kissed him back on his cheek. "Thank you for all of this. It's fantastic."

"You deserve this and much more."

"You're so sweet." She pecked Mike on his lips and began to inspect the room. "Did you invite my mother?"

"You know I did. But she said she didn't want to upstage you on your special night."

"She's such a tease," Taylor said while she waved at a few of her friends who were sitting on the other side of the club.

"She told me to tell you to call her later on after the festivities are over."

One of Mike's friends came over and whispered in his ear. Before Taylor knew it, Mike was on top of one of the tables with a microphone in his hand.

"Can I please have everyone's attention? Our guest of honor, the lovely Ms. Taylor LaRue, has graced us with her presence. Baby, I just want you to know that I love you and I hope this will be a night you'll never forget. Now, let the party begin!"

The music began to flow throughout the entire place. Taylor blew Mike a kiss, jumped up on the table, and began to dance with him.

When it was time, several of Taylor's guests began the parade of happy birthday speeches. This was followed by Taylor opening up her presents.

Before she could finish, Mike jumped on top of one of the tables once again.

"Babe, I'm sorry, but I can't wait any longer. Pause the music, please. I need everyone's full attention as I present my girl, the love of my life, her birthday gift." Mike pulled an elongated box from his jacket pocket.

Okay, so he bought me a piece of jewelry, possibly a necklace, Taylor thought to herself. Mike then reached his hand out to Taylor so that she could join him up on the table.

"This is for you." Mike pulled her close and kissed her on the cheek. Out of nowhere, Taylor began to feel nervous.

What is this man up to? She opened the box, but she didn't see any jewelry. She looked at Mike.

"Keep looking," he ordered with an oversized smile on his face.

Taylor was speechless as she saw an elegant 5 carat princess cut solitaire ring pop up and out of the box. She looked at Mike as he picked up the ring.

"Is he serious?!" she screamed to herself. "An engagement ring?" Taylor knew she loved Mike and felt that he was the one, but she wasn't sure if she was ready to be engaged again. As Mike got down on his left knee in front of all of their guests, Taylor knew as she looked into his eyes, ready or not, she had to say yes.

Taylor heard no words while Mike's mouth continued to open and close. She looked at the ring and thought it was definitely not the one-of-a-kind 10 carat pink emerald cut that Stephen had given her two years ago. She knew, however, that Mike wasn't the flashy type. He's the only person that she knew who has made millions and it hadn't gone to his head. She should've known her engagement ring would look like this ... simple and sweet.

Taylor didn't hear Mike's words, nor did she hear the words that came out of her own mouth. From the crowd's expression, however, she must have said YES. Mike got up, and they kissed each other passionately until someone said, "I guess we should start up the music again."

As they both came up for air, Mike told Taylor it was time to go. "I'll have one of my partners drop your other gifts at your condo tonight."

"Okay," Taylor returned. "Here comes Candace. I want to say good-bye."

"I'll meet you at the front," he said, walking away.

Unbelievable, Taylor thought. *Is this real? Is this happening again? A ring, planning a wedding, and being married to Mike Washington?*

Candace came over and gave Taylor a bear hug. "Congratulations, girl! You are truly the luckiest person I know." Candace picked up Taylor's ring finger and showed it off to a few of her girlfriends that were sitting nearby.

"Stop it," Taylor demanded, pulling her hand down. "Did you know about this?"

"I must confess," Candace admitted, "yes, I did. You truly deserve it. I'm so happy for you."

"You got me. This was a complete surprise. Mike usually would've given me a hint or something, but I didn't have a clue."

"Girl, you know how hard it was for me to say nothing. Mike threatened me. He told me he would kill me personally if I said anything to you."

Taylor chuckled.

"Yeah, you're laughing, but he was serious."

"Candace, you know he was joking. Mike wouldn't hurt a fly." Taylor hugged Candace good-bye and walked to where Mike was waiting for her.

"I'm ready to go." He seemed impatient. "We're late for our own party."

"Are you sure, babe?" Taylor asked. Mike continued to lead her toward the front door. "It's still kind of early. We don't want to be rude to our guests."

"I don't know about your friends, but my boys completely understand. They told me to go ahead and take care of my business. Believe me, babe, I plan to do just that." Mike ushered Taylor out of the doors and into his personal limousine.

As soon as they closed the front door to his mansion, Mike wasted no time trying to pull off Taylor's dress.

"Babe," Taylor murmured. She unlocked her lips from his, gasping for air. "Let's slow down and savor the moment."

"I don't know about you, but as you can see," Mike leaned back to show Taylor his erection, "you have my full attention. I'm ready."

"You know I don't like it when you're in such a rush."

"You win, Taylor," Mike attempted to appease her. "We can take it slow." He slowly pulled the dress over her head and took off her bra. He didn't have to worry about removing her panties. She left them in the limo where they had begun their escapade. Mike picked Taylor up and carried her up the stairs to the master bedroom.

Taylor sat up in bed while she watched the darkness of the night slip away and the break of day sluggishly unfold. For some reason, she could not go to sleep. It was probably due to all the excitement. Soon, this would be her new home. She looked from one end of Mike's bedroom to the other. He had the classic masculine décor going on in his room. The color scheme was beige, black, and dark brown. She loved the traditional leather chairs that he had in front of his fireplace. The browns and deep dark espresso finish on the furniture that was placed perfectly throughout the entire space was also a nice added touch. Taylor made a mental note to herself. One of the first things on her "to-do list" after she moved in would be to remodel this room. It desperately needed a female touch. She leaned over to peek at Mike's face. He was, of course, knocked out, completely unaware that he was snoring like a grizzly bear. She eased out of the bed to look for her purse. She decided to call her mother. Maybe that's why she hadn't been able to fall asleep. She hadn't told her about the good news.

Ring … ring … ring.

"She must be in a deep sleep," Taylor whispered. She thought to hang up the phone.

"Hello." Her mother's voice sounded drowsy.

"Sorry, Mom. I know it's early, but I couldn't sleep," Taylor said, yawning on the phone.

"Don't worry; I'm up," Diane replied. She sat up and looked at the alarm clock. "So, how was your big birthday bash?"

"Did you know about the ring, Mom?"

"Yes, I did. Mike was a complete gentleman. He invited both me and his mother out for dinner two weeks ago and asked if he could marry you. Even though I'm not one hundred percent sure about all of this, I do believe that Mike will treat you well. You know that's what matters to me the most."

"That's funny, I was feeling the same way. When he asked me to marry him, I think I was having an out-of-body experience. I didn't hear a word. I didn't even hear myself say 'yes, Mike, I would love to marry you.' According to Candace, that's what I said."

"Do you love him, Taylor?" Diane inquired curiously.

"Yes, but I'm a little scared that something may happen and we won't get married."

"Taylor, Mike adores you. You shouldn't think such negative thoughts."

"I know, but you never know; anything could happen."

"Like what? Like Mike having a chick-on-the-side too?"

"Talk about negative thinking." Taylor felt herself getting annoyed. "Mom, I really don't think I'll have to worry about that issue with Mike. He's in the bed right now, sleeping, snoring, and feeling very satisfied. You know what Candace and I always say—a woman ain't a real woman unless she can put the 3 S's on them."

"Now, that's just too much information."

"Come on, Mom. Your little girl is all grown up and in six months, I'm going to be Mrs. Michael Washington."

"Six months?" Diane sounded shocked. "That's not a lot of time."

"We've already discussed some of the details on the way home tonight. Mike wants to get married after the football season is over. We're going to have an intimate yet unforgettable ceremony. We only plan to have about a hundred guests."

"Six months is still a very short amount of time, especially if you all are planning to have an elegant event."

"Mom, I've become a pro at planning a wedding," Taylor chuckled. "I can even do it in my sleep."

"Speaking of sleep, you better go check on your husband-to-be. He might be ready for round two."

"Try round five. After my third body spasm, I simply stopped counting."

"Here we go again, too much information."

"You started it. I was just finishing it. Good night, Mother."

"Good night, sweet pea. Love you."

"I love you more," Taylor replied. She closed her cell phone and threw it down on one of Mike's lounge chairs. Crawling back into bed, she thought about her mother and gently rubbed her body up against Mike.

To her surprise, Mike rolled over and embraced her tightly. "Are you ready to put me to sleep again? I'm a big boy. So you know it's going to take a lot to knock me out."

"Were you listening in on my conversation?" Taylor asked. She playfully hit him on the head.

"No, I just woke up when you said something about putting the 3 S's on me."

"So, you *were* listening in on my conversation I had with my mother."

"What conversation?" Mike teased. "I, however, would love if you could put those 3 Z's or 3 T's on me again."

"The phrase I think you're searching for is the 3 S's."

"Right, those three little letters," Mike said as he began to kiss Taylor softly all over her entire body. Although Taylor was extremely tired, as soon as she felt Mike's lips gulp up her skin so seductively, she eagerly submitted herself to him yet again.

Chapter Twenty-Four
THE COLLISION
Miami

Taylor woke up to the music of Mary J. Blige. She remembered that she was too lazy to get out of bed last night to turn off her stereo. "**Just Fine, Fine, Fine, Fine, Fine, Fine, Fine, Whoa ...**" The words in that song resembled Taylor's life right about now. Even though Mike was miles away and she had not seen him for seven days, her life was just fine, fine, fine, fine ... whoa. Taylor jumped out of bed and began to dance around the room. She was gearing herself up to face another day.

No voice mail messages, Taylor thought as she looked at her cell phone. "I'd better hurry up and get into the shower before Mike calls."

Mike was in Miami with his team preparing for the Super Bowl game. Fortunately for him, his team was the favorite to win. Still, the coach wanted the players to stay focused, therefore limiting their phone calls, especially to significant others, wives, and family members. In her attempt to comply with the rules, Taylor opted to fly into Miami on the day of the game as opposed to arriving on Friday, two days before the game. She knew there was no way she would be able to just receive a phone call from Mike and not be able to be with him in the same city. This was Mike's time to shine. He was a few days away from completing one of his two lifelong goals.

Ring ... ring ... ring.

"Hello." Taylor answered the phone and flopped back down on the side of her bed.

"Hey, girl. It's me, K.T."

"Hey."

"Just calling to make sure we're still going to fly down to Miami together."

"Most definitely. I haven't bought my ticket yet, but I didn't forget. You better not 'go ghost' on me."

"Girl, please, I wouldn't miss this for the world. I'm going to be right there by your side handing out my business cards."

"You're too much!" Taylor laughed.

"I know you think I'm joking, but I'm completely serious. This trip is all about building up my clientele, and speaking of clientele, guess who else is going to be down there in Miami ... your—"

Beep ... beep ... beep.

"That's my other line," K.T. grumbled. "I hate when that happens. Right when I'm about to divulge some juicy news, I get interrupted. Hold on, it will only take a second."

"She so crazy," Taylor mumbled. Then a weird feeling came over her, a feeling that she had felt before. She quickly sat down on her bed. *What in the world was going on with her?* Suddenly, Taylor began to think about the time she was sitting at Stephen's desk in his villa, frantically looking through all of Dena Anderson's medical records.

"Why in the world am I thinking about that horrible day?" Taylor said out loud while she waited for her friend to return to the phone.

"Sorry, about that. It's an emergency. Gotta go."

"What about the juicy news? You were saying something about … *your … your what?*"

"I can't get into it right now. One of my clients is having a crisis. I'll talk to you later."

Click

"Oh, well." Taylor hung up the phone, popped up off her bed once again, and turned up her stereo volume to its maximum.

I won't trade my life … it's just fine, fine, fine, fine, fine, fine, fine, whoa …

"Whoa … whoa," Taylor sang walking into the bathroom. She turned on the water in the shower and continued to dance to the music.

Ring … ring … ring.

"You have reached 212-445-4444. Please leave a message after the beep."

"Where are you, babe? This may be the only time I'll be able to call you today. I thought you said you were going to keep your cell phone tucked in your bra. You know I like to hear your voice when I'm not able to touch those luscious lips of yours. I guess I will have to tell you about my special guests after the game. It will just have to be a surprise for you because I don't think I will be able to call you back today. I have to tell you, I'm feeling just a little nervous about all of this, but I know for sure that you won't. You are going to be completely thrilled about our reunion. Anyway, I gotta go. Can't wait to see you babe ... love you."

Taylor walked out of the bathroom wrapped up from head to toe in a bathrobe and towel that her mom bought her for Christmas. Thinking about her mother, Taylor knew she'd better call her to find out if she changed her mind about accompanying her to the game. She picked up her cell phone from the nightstand and immediately noticed someone had left a voice mail message.

"I hope Mike didn't call," Taylor moaned. She quickly pressed the button to retrieve the message. "Darn. It was Mike," Taylor murmured. She knew she wouldn't be able to return his phone call.

"Special guest, surprise, reunion," Taylor pondered. She continued to listen to his message. "What in the world is Mike planning now? He did say that I would be thrilled about these guests. So I'm sure it's really nothing for me to worry about."

It was Super Bowl Sunday. Taylor and K.T. walked out of the airport, located their private limousine, and headed to their hotel. Taylor finally spoke to Pamela, Mike's mother, before leaving New York. As usual, she knew exactly what was going on. She told her about Mike's big party plans and how he decided to reach out to his father one last time. Mike had invited him as well as his half brother, to his game. Taylor was shocked to find out that Mike had a half brother — she actually thought he was an only child because there weren't any pictures of the half brother anywhere in Mike's home or in his office at the center. Whatever the case, Mike told Pamela that he wanted to introduce Taylor to his family before they officially kicked off the events that would lead up to their wedding day. Taylor quickly updated K.T. on all the details of Mike's post party plans.

"You're the luckiest woman I know," K.T. said. She pulled off her oversize shades and placed them in a designer eyeglass case. "You know, I live my life vicariously through yours. Hell, I experience this 'imaginary life' with all my clients."

"Girl, please. I know several people who would pay to have your life." K.T. nodded at Taylor instructing her to keep going. "You know *everybody* who is *anybody*. Plus, you know all the 411 on everybody, including their mommas. Shall I go on?"

"You're right. I do have a fabulous life."

"Speaking of your fabulous life and insider knowledge, you never did tell me about this person that was going to be down here." K.T. wore an "I-can't-remember-what-you-are-talking-about" look on her face. "You know … the juicy gossip you had to tell me?"

"Oh, yeah." K.T. recalled what she had planned to tell Taylor after hearing about Mike's big plans. She decided it was unnecessary to divulge that type of information at this point. "Let's stay focused on what really matters: Mike, your fiancé." K.T. then pulled out her Blackberry and began to scan through her text messages.

Taylor lay back in her seat and relaxed. She thought about Mike's last attempt to revive his relationship with his father. Taylor applauded his effort. She felt that this "reunion" was a great idea. She hoped that Mike would finally find it in his heart to release the bitterness and forgive his father so they could begin their new life together on a positive note.

Taylor looked out the window while K.T. called several clients, checked her appointment book, and returned text messages, all at the same time. She really did have a fast paced and exciting life.

Taylor moved closer to the window to get a better view. Miami was steaming, and it wasn't all due to the heat. This hustling and bustling city was teeming with a wide variety of cultures, languages, and cuisines. It seemed as if the National Football League had selected the right city to host this event. The streets were electric; excitement was in the air. People were busily preparing for the main event while others were already engaged in the pre-game festivities.

As the limousine pulled up to the entrance of the hotel, her phone rang.

"Where are you? You should be here already!" She paused while listening to her mother. Taylor finally snapped her phone closed. "Diane told us to enjoy ourselves. She's not going to be able to make it down here."

"Let me guess ... the workload?"

"You know she's a workaholic. Her excuse was that she's swamped with trying to meet deadlines."

"Yeah, yeah, yeah, that's what they all say." K.T. put on her shades and stepped out of the limousine. "I'm not mad at her. I know she's making mad money behind that decision ... to stay in New York."

"I'm not mad at her either." Taylor glided out the car and slipped on her shades. "She's the one that's going to miss out on all the fun." Taylor looked at her watch. She only had two hours left before she would have to meet Mike's mother in the lobby. K.T. had no time to spare. After they checked in, she went to locate a client who was staying in a hotel down the street.

Taylor went to her room, swiped her key card, and opened the door. She walked over to a full-length mirror and admired her figure while she waited for her luggage to arrive. After she had posed a few times in front of the mirror, she decided that she wouldn't make a major production out of what she was going to wear to the game. She wanted to make a good first impression when she met Mike's father and brother, but she also wanted to be comfortable.

"Maybe I'll wear something casual, yet sporty," Taylor whispered. She glanced at her watch again as she slipped it off her wrist. Then she took off her diamond-studded earrings, put them on the bureau, and headed for the shower.

Two hours later, Taylor arrived in the lobby and was immediately informed by one of the doormen that Pamela Washington was waiting for her outside in her private car. Taylor walked toward the glass entrance and began to look around. There were several limousines waiting outside of the hotel.

"Taylor, darling, I'm over here," Pamela shouted, waving her hand indicating for Taylor to come over. Not wanting to delay any of Pamela's pre-game plans, Taylor quickly walked over to the car. She hugged and kissed her soon-to-be mother-in-law when she got into the car.

"You look gorgeous as usual," Pamela commented. She continued to sip her glass of wine.

"Thank you," Taylor returned. "You look magnificent yourself."

"Well, of course I do," Pamela replied.

Taylor smiled.

"Join me," Pamela pleaded. She handed Taylor a wine glass. "Today is my son's big day. He will finally get what he has been working so hard for his entire career, a Super Bowl ring. I know I'm talking as if they have already won, but we all know who is going to win, don't we, Taylor?"

"The New York Giants, of course," Taylor confirmed, reaching out to take the glass. "Just a little, please. You know we'll be drinking champagne all night."

"You're absolutely correct," Pamela smiled as she filled Taylor's glass to the top. "Everything seems to be falling right into place. All I need now are some grandchildren. Do you think you two can hurry up and make that happen for me?"

"Can we get married first?" Taylor teased.

"Well, of course, you can," Pamela replied. She gulped down another glass of wine. "Mike reserved the perfect skybox for us. It's located right above the fifty-yard line. I wanted to be the bigger person and invite Stephen to join us so that we would look like we were somewhat of a family unit, but I simply couldn't bring myself to do it. After all of these years, I guess I'm still a little bitter as well."

"Did she say Stephen?" Taylor wondered. She watched Pamela pour another glass of wine. "Pamela, Mike's father's name is Stephen?"

"Yes, his name is Stephen."

"That's interesting," Taylor said, not realizing that she had said those words aloud.

"Interesting?" Pamela replied. "How so?"

"Mike never mentioned the name of his father," Taylor replied. She knew that this was not the time or the place to bring up Stephen, her ex-fiancé. "He has also never told me that he had a half brother. Isn't that amazing?"

"Yes, that's amazing," Pamela laughed. "Mike and

Stephen were never close. Mike may have met him once ... or twice. I'm not sure because I was never around."

What! Taylor screamed inwardly. *Why did she call Mike's brother Stephen?*

It was obvious Pamela had a bit too much to drink.

"Pamela," Taylor said again to get her attention, "were you referring to Mike's father or his brother? I'm asking because Mike told me that he has had contact with his father on more than one occasion."

"No, darling," Pamela returned. She put down her wine glass. "I was referring to his half brother not his father. Mike's brother's name is Stephen as well. Maybe I *have* had too much wine. I'd better slow down like you suggested."

"That's weird," Taylor continued to ponder.

"I guess there is still time to invite them to join us at our skybox, but knowing how they are, I'm sure they have already reserved one for themselves. Don't let me start talking about those Blake men ... I told myself I was going to be positive today."

"Did you say those—" Taylor blurted out.

"Wait, just one minute," Pamela rambled on. "If that idiot brings that wife of his with him, then Taylor, I will have to apologize to you right now because you will *definitely* see a side of me that you have never seen before."

Taylor chuckled, thinking about her mother, so she completely understood what Pamela was alluding to.

"Pamela, did you say those—" Taylor said attempting to speak.

"Taylor, you know, I'm not a petty or a mean woman. I don't like that woman because she always hated Mike. Look at me, I'm getting upset. I don't want to spoil my son's big day by talking negatively about his side of the family. This conversation is officially over."

Taylor wanted to quickly ask her about what she said previously. But Pamela had already flipped open her cell phone to call someone. Taylor couldn't stop thinking about what she'd heard ... "those Blake men." Maybe she said those Tate men. Pamela was, after all, a little tipsy.

Taylor sat there and watched Pamela talk on the phone. Every bone in her body began to ache with pain. She wanted to find out Mike's father's last name.

The limousine pulled up to the stadium. Taylor's mind was still on Mike's father. Could they be the same men she had known in Paris? "What are the odds of that occurring? Zero to none?" Taylor said quietly.

To calm herself down, she began to breathe deeply, in and out. *Taylor, there is no way that these people are the same people. Same names, maybe, but same people, impossible. Enough of this rubbish! I have to think positive. This is Mike's big day. I will focus on my man, his game, winning his Super Bowl ring, our engagement, our wedding, and giving Pamela what she wants so badly; grandchildren.*

Pamela snapped her fingers to gain Taylor's attention while she continued to talk on the phone. When Taylor looked directly at her, Pamela told her to tell the driver to drop them off as close as he could to Gate Number Nine.

"I don't want to walk more than I have to in this place," Pamela grumbled. She still seemed a bit upset. Taylor did as she was told. She pressed the button that allowed her to speak to their driver.

It was fourth quarter with a minute and thirty seconds to go. As predicted, the Giants were favored to win and at this point, they were up by fourteen points.

"Do you want to start toward the media area where the team will meet their family members?" Taylor asked anxiously.

"Well, even though the game will soon be over, it will be a while before we will be able to interact with Mike. It'll take time for the team to gather in the media area to speak to the press."

"Yes, Mike told me all about the post game events," Taylor returned. They left the skybox and began to walk toward a long corridor that would lead them to the locker room area. Pamela and Taylor somehow ended up in the press area as several reporters flocked to interview Mike's mother.

Taylor decided to walk around the lobby. No one seemed interested in interviewing her, which was actually a relief. She no longer wanted to be on the front page of a magazine or the newspapers, in this case. Those days were over for her, as difficult as it might be, considering that she would soon be Mike's wife. She had already decided that she was going to do everything in her power to keep it that way.

Taylor walked into the ladies' restroom to freshen up. She figured that Mike and the rest of the team would be arriving in the pressroom soon.

When Taylor came out of the bathroom, she could hardly make her way back into the pressroom. It was now flooded with the entire team, the coaches, and all of their family members. Taylor looked up. She began to hear Mike's voice through the room. She could not see him at the podium. The room was too crowded, so she decided to push her way to one of the oversized flat screen televisions that were mounted up throughout the corridor.

"There he is!" Taylor whispered excited. Not satisfied with the view, she tried to squeeze her way inside the room. She heard Mike as he introduced his mother. He mentioned how she, of course, played a major role in helping him become the person and player that he is today. Taylor somehow found herself stuck within a pool of people. She gave up trying to move forward toward the podium where Mike and Pamela were standing. Taylor then heard Mike introduce his father. She really wanted to get a glimpse of Mike's father. She began to move backwards, hoping to get out of the traffic of people. Taylor finally moved back far enough to see the full view of one of the television screens, but in doing so, she accidentally rammed herself into a man, who promptly fell to the floor.

"Oh my goodness. I'm so very sorry," Taylor said. She turned around and tried to help the man get up from the floor.

"Taylor?" The stranger sounded stunned. She looked at him.

"Stephen! What in the world are you doing here?" Taylor asked shocked.

Stephen pointed toward one of the flat screens. Taylor thought to herself, *No way could this be happening to me. What are the odds? Not here, not now.*

Taylor looked up at the screen, and sure enough, there were Mr. Blake and Pamela hugging Mike. As the star quarterback continued to talk, Taylor's mind was telling her to run but her body would not comply. Instead, she stood frozen, staring at Stephen.

All of a sudden, Mike's voice became very loud as he said, "I would also like to say thank you to my lovely and soon-to-be better half. She is actually somewhere here in this room today. Taylor LaRue, if you can hear me, please know that I love you very much and can't wait to start our new life together."

As the crowd applauded, a stunned Stephen, who was by now standing next to Taylor, looked directly at her and mouthed, "What? Are you and my brother Mike engaged to be married?"

Taylor couldn't move, nor could she hear the words that were coming out of Stephen's mouth.

Déjà vu, Taylor thought as everything around her suddenly faded to black.

Chapter Twenty-Five

Impasse Miami

Dazed, Taylor woke up to what looked like five people huddled around her. As her vision became clearer, she first noticed Mike, Pamela, another person who was probably a medical attendant, Stephen's father, and Stephen. They all still had that shocked, frantic look on their faces. Other people had begun to crowd around her to find out what was going on. Taylor felt like she was suffocating as the jumbo flat screen televisions hanging on the walls everywhere were now spinning all around above her head. She closed her eyes and began to pray. She wanted to get out of this building as soon as possible.

God, if you're really out there ... please perform one of your miracles ... make me disappear ... right here and right now. Taylor opened her eyes. The flat screen televisions were now back in their places, but she was, unfortunately, still lying on the floor.

"Taylor, can you hear me? Are you okay?" Mike asked in a panic.

Taylor's prayer went unanswered. She saw everyone was still fixed in their same positions, staring down at her.

"Babe, are you okay?" Mike asked again.

"No," Taylor lied. Since God was unable to perform a miracle, she quickly decided that she wasn't getting up off this floor.

"We need an ambulance," Mike demanded, looking at the medical attendant. The attendant quickly pulled out what looked like a walkie-talkie and made the request. Before Taylor knew it, two men had lifted her off the floor, placed her onto a stretcher, and pushed her into the ambulance. Mike hopped into the ambulance and kissed her on her forehead. When the vehicle began to move, she drifted off to a troubled sleep.

Taylor woke up once again, but this time she was in a hospital. She noticed Mike out of the corner of her eye, reading a magazine near the window.

"Are you feeling better?" Mike asked. He closed the magazine and walked toward the bed.

"Yes," Taylor replied. "How long have I been in here?"

"Not too long. The doctor said that you're dehydrated."

"Mike, I'm sorry. I hope I didn't ruin your big day."

"Please, Taylor, you sound ridiculous. You didn't ruin

my day. The doctor said you were dehydrated, which is why you fainted back at the stadium. They are putting more fluid in your system via the IV. When that bag is empty, you'll be free to leave."

"I know, but ..." Taylor reluctantly agreed looking at the IV connected to her arm.

"But nothing," Mike returned. "We'll probably be leaving here soon. Please don't worry about me or my big day. The game is over, and we won."

Taylor smiled at Mike. He leaned over, kissed her, and sat back down to read his magazine. Turning her head, Taylor noticed the phone in her room. It reminded her that she desperately needed to call her mother and Candace. She wanted to let them know what had happened today at the game, but she knew she couldn't have that conversation now, not with Mike in the room.

Although Mike had his cell phone on vibrate, Taylor could tell that someone was trying to call him. It continued to make a rumbling sound from the inside of his pocket.

"Aren't you going to answer your phone?" she finally asked.

"No, I'm not," Mike stated calmly, pulling the phone from his pocket to find out who was calling. "I don't recognize the number, so whoever it is will find out how you're doing when we get back to the hotel."

"That's actually a good idea," Taylor mused quietly. She began to think Mike being at the hospital with her wasn't such a bad thing after all. If he was back at the hotel, he would've already found out that his half brother, Stephen, was a previous love interest of hers.

Taylor cringed at the thought of Mike finding out. If this standing-by-your-woman-while-she-fainted-right-in-the middle-of-the-pressroom-on-one-of-the-most-important-days-of-your-life is a precursor of what was to come…well, Taylor really didn't have anything to worry about. However, for some reason, she was terrified, for she knew Mike would not handle the news well.

"Mike," she started. In that split second, she decided that she should be the first to tell him about Stephen.

"Yeah, babe," he replied casually, still occupied by the magazine.

"This is going to sound … crazy."

He stopped reading and looked directly at Taylor. Feeling as if he could see right through her, Taylor quickly jumped to Plan B. She would call her mother or Candace first. Hopefully, they would be able to tell her what to do.

"What do you mean, *sound crazy?*" Mike asked studying Taylor's confused face.

"I'm hungry. Can you go get me something to eat … please?"

"Sure, babe."

"Outside the hospital. I really don't want to eat anything from this place."

"That's not crazy," Mike chuckled. "You forget that I have a mother who acts just like you."

"Whatever," Taylor uttered, rolling her eyes.

"What do you want to eat?"

"A garden salad with sliced grilled chicken strips on top."

"Ranch dressing on the side … correct?"

"We are *so* ready to walk down the aisle," she teased.

"You're tripping. I'll be right back."

Taylor watched him intently until he closed the door to her room. She waited for a few minutes and then reached for the phone. She quickly dialed Candace's number, but there was no answer. Taylor hung up and called her mother.

"Taylor!" Diane frantically yelled.

"Mom, what's wrong?"

"Hold on for one second and do not—I repeat—do not hang up this phone." Diane clicked over to the other line.

"Mother, please, hurry up," Taylor mumbled. She sat up in her bed.

A moment later, she heard a voice. "Sweetie, are you okay? I heard that you were taken to the emergency room."

"I'm okay; I was just dehydrated," Taylor insisted. "Who told you that I was in the hospital?"

"Pamela Washington called and told me. She also told me about Stephen and his father being there. Taylor, they have talked and they know that you've dated both men. They're having a discussion about all of this as we speak. Pamela is trying to figure out the best way to inform Mike about this travesty. I just got off the phone with her."

"Travesty!" Taylor exclaimed. "How in the world was I supposed to know that Mike and Stephen are brothers? Mike never talked about his father, and he never even mentioned that he has a brother. Mike doesn't even have a photograph of his father anywhere in his home, office, or at the center. Before the game, Pamela was babbling on about Stephen and the Blake men, but I thought she just had too much to drink. I simply came to the conclusion that she couldn't be talking about the same Stephen Blake. Think about it, Mom, what are the odds that all of this could be happening to me?"

"Lord Jesus, I don't know what to say," Diane sighed. "I'm beginning to sound like *my mother* because this situation is absolutely ludicrous. This all sounds like a scene right out of a horror flick."

"Please, don't remind me."

"Where's Mike?"

"I sent him to get me some food so that I could call you."

"You better tell him, Taylor." Diane commanded. "You must tell him now before he hears it from anyone else."

"I tried just a moment ago, but the words would *not* come out of my mouth."

"If Mike's mother tells him about Stephen ..." Diane said hesitantly. "I don't know, Taylor ... Pamela seems to believe that Mike will not be able to handle this well."

Taylor's body began to stiffen as she looked at Mike, who returned to the room empty-handed. His had an icy-cold look on his face. Taylor continued to talk to her mother. He flopped in one of the chairs and began to stare directly at her. She knew it was time to get off the phone and deal with the situation at hand.

"Mother, Mike just stepped back into my room. I will call you later."

Hanging up the phone, Taylor didn't know where to start. They both continued to stare at each other.

Breaking the silence, Mike furiously demanded, "Taylor, my mother told me that Stephen, my estranged brother, was once your lover, or should I say, your ex-fiancé. Is this true?"

"Yes, Mike, that is true," Taylor replied calmly.

"So, if that is true, I can safely assume that you two had sex. Am I correct?"

"Mike, first of all, I'm just as shocked as you are right now. I was sitting here trying to figure out how I was going to talk to you about all of this."

"Taylor, just answer my question," Mike demanded. "There is no need to explain. I understand that you were not aware of our biological connection."

"Mike, this is so unfair."

"JUST ANSWER THE QUESTION!"

"Yes, Mike, yes. After all, we were engaged to be married," Taylor returned, stunned. She couldn't believe Mike had yelled at her in that manner.

"That's all I need to know." Mike got up out of the chair and headed toward the door.

"Where are you going?" Taylor inquired frantically.

"To be honest, I really don't know."

"Mike, this is a difficult time for you, but this is a difficult time for me, as well. What we need to do is go back to the hotel and figure out how we can all have an open and honest conversation about this situation."

"Open and honest conversation?" Mike chuckled, feeling very irritated. "I don't know about you, but I don't want to talk to anyone about this mess. I'm so humiliated. It's like I got slapped in the face yet again."

"Mike, this is not a good time to be by yourself. We can, and we will, get through this chaos together."

"Taylor, think about what you're saying," Mike fumed. "The woman that I love, my pride and joy, the woman I planned to parade around my father and brother as my proudest accomplishment yet ... instead, look what happened: the joke was on me. They're probably both laughing uncontrollably at some upscale bar and club, feeling so very sorry for me *yet again.*"

"Mike, I doubt that they're laughing at you," Taylor finally interjected. "*I left Stephen!* I walked away from his family, from the wedding, from it all. If they are feeling anything, it is humiliation. Mike, babe ... this is just an awkward situation for us all."

"You got that right, Taylor!" Mike hollered as he hit the wall.

Taylor looked at Mike in shock. She knew he still had anger and bitter feelings toward his father, but she had never seen this side of Mike manifested.

"Taylor, I need a serious time-out," Mike stated calmly.

"I need to go somewhere *by myself* and think. Can you respect my request, please?"

"Fine, Mike," Taylor sighed, feeling helpless. Tears began to stream down her face. "Just tell me where I can reach you; I want to make sure you're okay."

"I don't know," Mike said. His eyes became watery. "I don't know ... I just don't know." He had a lost look on his face. Without looking back, Mike opened the door and walked away.

Chapter Twenty-Six
Time-Out
Jamaica

Two days later, Big Mike and his best buddy, Chuck, were lying on oversized Cape Cod chairs, highly intoxicated, at one of Blue Lagoon's finest private villas in Port Antonio, Jamaica. The sun was setting, and an easy pulse of reggae was playing in the background.

"This is just what the doctor ordered," Mike told his friend feeling relaxed and at ease. Admiring the scenery, he sat up to view the shoreline on the beach that seemed to stretch on forever. This was the perfect location for a getaway. Their villa was nestled directly on the clear turquoise water of the Caribbean Sea right between lush tropical palm trees and the magnificent backdrop of the Blue Mountain. Mike was glad he had made the decision to lease a villa. He needed to recuperate and remove himself physically and emotionally from the chaos he had been experiencing.

"I know you're missing Taylor right about now, man," Chuck commented. He rolled on his back and gulped down another can of beer.

"This may sound crazy, but I'm still mad about this entire situation." Mike pounded his fist in the white burning hot sand.

"Mad about what? Who could've known that—"

"Think, man," Mike interrupted. "I'm mad that my plan did not work out. The joke was on me."

"What joke?" Chuck asked looking at Mike feeling clueless.

"Man, you're drunk. Why am I trying to explain this situation to you anyway?"

"Because I asked you," Chuck responded, clearing his throat, "if you missed Taylor, your fiancée. It's obvious I'm not the only one drunk around here."

"I haven't even had time to think about Taylor, let alone miss her. Is that okay with you?" Mike attempted to get out of his chair. He was, however, unable to do so. "Our engagement and the wedding are off."

"Permanently?"

"Yes, man! Do you have a hearing problem?"

"Mike, you're kidding, right?" Chuck sat up in his chair in shock.

"I knew you would take this hard because, after all, you were responsible for hooking us up."

"Dude, I would understand you more if you said you needed some time. Maybe a few months to find a counselor.

Who wouldn't want to talk to a shrink after all of this, but to end it all … *forever?*"

"Yes, forever."

"*Forever, forever, ever,*" Chuck sang, mocking the popular Outkast song.

"Yeah, man. I'm truly sorry, but like I said, at the end of the day, the joke was on me."

"There you go again, talking about *the joke.*"

"Let me explain my life to you once again," Mike said. He repositioned himself in his chair to look directly at Chuck. "The plan was to rub Taylor, my leading lady, in both my father's and my brother's faces. I wanted to show them that not only have I acquired the American dream but also much more than that: the stellar career, the mansions, the expensive cars, world travel … shall I go on?"

"I get the point," Chuck said. He sank back down in the beach chair.

"The Blake men have acquired all these things and more, but I was going to introduce them to something they had not yet acquired: true love. Taylor was supposed to be the cherry on top. The gorgeous, savvy, rich ex-model turned entrepreneur. My fiancée. *My one and only lady,* something neither my father nor my brother know anything about due to their excessive, self-indulgent, self-absorbed, and serpent natures. Then, to find out that Taylor has slept with one of those bastards—well, that news just hits me right in the gut. Please, will someone just kill me and take me out of my misery?"

"Since you mentioned the words 'true love,' the better question to ask is, are you in love with Taylor?"

"Of course, I love her," Mike stated sheepishly. He grabbed another beer and began to gulp it down furiously. After he finished the beer, Mike threw the can in a box that was beginning to overflow with other empty cans. "Like I was saying, I know I will never be able to get over this. Think about it, man — every time I look at Taylor, especially during our private moments, I will see Stephen."

"Yeah, but true love conquers all," Chuck pleaded with his friend. "If you love her like you say you do, then eventually the two of you will get over this unfortunate situation."

"So what are you trying to say, Chuck?" Mike asked while attempting to sit up in his chair. "Do you think I don't love her?"

"It doesn't matter what I think. You're the only person that can answer that question." A smirk appeared on Chuck's face.

"I know what you're thinking. You think I don't love her because I'm calling the engagement off. Don't you, Chuck? Don't you?"

"Man, you know what I think? After hearing your side of the story, I think you fell in love with 'the idea' of finally being able to get even with your father. Taylor was simply a part of the equation of your great big idea. That's what all of this sounds like to me."

Mike couldn't believe his buddy's words. All he could do was lie back down in the lawn chair. Could Chuck be right?

Was *he* in love with Taylor? Right now, he was stewing in the anger that he felt from his father not being there for him for so many years.

"Mike, man, you have to let all of that childhood stuff go. That hatred and bitterness can only harm a person."

"I have to admit, Chuck," Mike said, reluctantly, "you just might be right." Mike managed to get out of his chair this time with success. "With that being said, I'm going to walk my tired, drunk butt inside. I'm tired of talking about Taylor, my father, and Stephen."

"I didn't mean to get you upset," Chuck persisted. He got up and followed behind his friend.

"My decision is still the same. Our engagement and the wedding are off … permanently."

"When are you going to break the news to Taylor?"

"I don't know. I might invite her up here and have a helicopter whirl us to Strawberry Hill."

"Strawberry Hill?" Chuck stated curiously.

"It's a Georgian-style hotel in the Blue Mountains. I'll take her up there for a champagne brunch. Once we get back here at the villa, I'm sure we'll both be in the mood. I'll have sex with her one last time, and then break the news."

"That's so cold-blooded!" Chuck exclaimed, shaking his head with disappointment.

"Look at me," Mike told him. "When was the last time you saw me like this? Out here babbling like a drunk fool with you. This situation upsets me as well. I have to end our relationship like this … cold-blooded."

"Suit yourself," Chuck mumbled, shuffling his feet in the sand. They had reached the back entrance way of the villa. "If this was me, I would definitely take the high road. You know?—the dignified way out. Just be honest with her and tell her the truth. YOU'RE THE ONE THAT'S JACKED UP IN THE HEAD, ESPECIALLY WHEN IT COMES TO YOUR FATHER."

Mike laughed. He knew Taylor had already figured that one out.

"Thank you, my friend." Mike patted Chuck on the back. "Thank you once again for reminding me about my harsh realities. It's me, THE MAN IN THE MIRROR, that needs to make that change."

They both began to sing that song in unison while they walked through the sliding doors into the cool room.

"Well, just to let you know," Chuck announced, "I'll be out of here by tomorrow. I don't want to be anywhere around here when you drop that bomb."

As promised, Chuck left Jamaica the following day. Mike walked into his bedroom and flopped on the bed after his morning run. Thinking about what Chuck said the day before, Mike decided that he was not going to invite Taylor down to the villa. Taylor was not at fault, so he didn't have to end the relationship in a mean-spirited way. As he got up off the bed and headed toward the bathroom, he noticed that his cell phone was lying on his bed.

I don't remember placing my phone here. Mike picked up the phone and began to listen to his voice messages. As he predicted, he had what seemed like a million messages to listen to. Scanning through a few of them, his mother had called him several times. She wanted to know if he was okay. Taylor called several times as well. Mike decided that he could no longer hide here in Jamaica. He was going home to meet with Taylor, face-to-face. He was going to end their relationship the dignified way as his friend instructed him to do. As Mike attempted to flip his cell phone closed he did not realize that he accidentally pressed that button which dialed Taylor's cell phone number.

Ring ... ring ... ring.

"Hello?"

Click

Mike quickly closed the phone to end the call.

Ring ... ring ... ring.

"Darn," Mike whispered as he saw Taylor's number pop up on the front screen of his cell phone.

"Hello," Mike answered his phone. He knew he would later regret this conversation.

"Finally, you thought to call me," Taylor said sarcastically.

"I told you I needed time to think," Mike returned sharply.

"Well, I heard you and Chuck had a great time relaxing on the beach."

"You spoke with Chuck?"

"You know Chuck would never divulge your little secrets. I have my sources."

"I'm sure my mother probably told you."

"No, she did not. You know your mother hates me now."

"Taylor, you know my mother doesn't hate you," Mike returned, defending his mother. He knew his mother was even more upset than he was at this point.

"It really doesn't matter who told you about where I am. I was going to call you anyway. We need to talk ... seriously."

"So, let's talk," Taylor said sharply. She could tell by the way he spoke that this conversation was not going to be in her favor.

"I would prefer to speak with you when I return to New York."

"Whatever you have to say, you can say it now on the phone," Taylor told him. She was anxious to hear what he had to say.

"This conversation will be about our future. I think it would be best—"

"Mike, spare me the details," Taylor rudely interrupted. "If you want to take a break, you don't have to beat around the bush with me. Just tell me the truth. I will not get upset."

"No, that's not what I want to say to you, Taylor. Let's just wait to discuss this when I get back home."

"Well, if you don't want to take a break, then what do

we have to talk about, Mike?" Taylor was feeling a sense of relief, but still she was very confused. Where was Mike going with this conversation? "I think we should talk to Dr. Davis, the psychologist who helped me out previously. She offers counseling services to couples twice a month."

"Taylor, please, don't make this harder than it already is for me." Mike had begun to sweat profusely.

"Mike, whatever you have to say, just say it now. I can handle whatever it is you have to say to me." Taylor sat down on her sofa and crossed her legs. She had already prepared herself for whatever it was Mike was going to tell her today.

"All right, if you insist," Mike said reluctantly. He did, however, want to get this all out in the open ASAP. "I'm calling everything off. No engagement, no wedding, no marriage, no nothing. There, I said it. Are you satisfied?"

Silence

Taylor was completely stunned.

"Mike, I can completely understand if you need a break to figure everything all out. I know you will need more than a week or even a month. I could even understand if you wanted to push back the wedding date to next year, but to call off our engagement ... I'm baffled ... I'm not really understanding how you could come to that conclusion."

"Taylor, I told you I didn't want to talk about this over the phone."

"What's the difference, Mike?" Taylor asked. She felt tears streaming down her face. "Did you want to see what my face would look like when you put the dagger in my heart, or what?"

"Now you're being unfair," Mike said angrily. "I never got into this relationship with the intention to hurt you."

"I thought you loved me. You claimed that you have never loved another woman the way you love me. Was that all a lie?"

"You can say that I'm being childish, immature, or whatever. But there is no way I would be able to marry a woman who has been sexually intimate with my brother. Think about it, Taylor. Every time I would lie down with you, I would think how he held you or touched you. I would be constantly reminded of this fact, about my father, and about this mess all over again."

"Mike, with counseling, we can overcome all of this, especially if we truly love one another. I promise you, with time, you will heal. You will be able to forgive everyone and forget this entire situation."

Silence

Mike wanted this conversation to come to an end.

"I was actually glad that Chuck did come down here with me because after a few nights of us drinking and talking, I realized that I ... that I ..."

"That you what, Mike?" Taylor asked curiously.

"That what I was most upset about was that I was not able to parade you around my father and brother. Chuck helped me see that I never once took the time out to think about how you were feeling about all of this."

"Well, at least someone was thinking about me."

"Taylor, in all honesty, you're the lucky one."

"*I'm* the lucky one? How so, Mike?" Taylor asked furiously.

"God, in his infinite mercy, allowed you to escape—yet again—from making the mistake of being united in matrimony to a man who would have married you for all the wrong reasons. Yes, Taylor, I know for a fact that you are, indeed, the lucky one. As for me and my brother, we're still trapped. Trapped in our past, trapped in all this bitterness and misery, which for me continues to surface itself in unspeakable pain—"

Click

Mike suddenly stopped talking when he heard the dial tone. He was now sitting on the edge of his bed with his head hung low. He knew their relationship was officially over.

Chapter Twenty-Seven
Delirious & Dazed
New York

Even though Taylor knew that Mike was correct when he said that she was "the lucky one," she still couldn't stop herself from hyperventilating. For just a second, she thought about going to the top of her building and jumping off it. Instead, she went hysterical, knocking over and smashing everything that wasn't nailed down in her condo.

"Trapped?" Taylor screamed. "What the hell is he talking about? I'm the one who is trapped. I'm trapped in this wretched nightmare that I can't seem to wake up from."

Walking into her kitchen, Taylor looked around to see what else she could destroy. "Why is all of this happening to me?" Taylor picked up a crystal bowl that she bought two years ago in Italy and threw it against the wall, shattering it. She went on for hours, ranting and raving, until her body could no longer take it. She ended her rampage in the living room, flopped down on her plush carpet, and cried herself to sleep.

Ring ... ring ... ring.

Taylor woke up in the dark. She heard her phone ringing. She lay there trying to figure out how long she had been sleeping on the floor. The phone continued to ring, but Taylor didn't bother to answer it.

Ring ... ring ... ring.

"Ouch," Taylor moaned. Her entire body ached as she finally got up off the floor. Walking around her apartment, the pain in her joints jogged her memory back to her episode. She completely lost it. Her condo looked like a tornado had destroyed it. Everything was in complete disarray. Broken pieces of glass covered the floor. Her dining room chairs and kitchen bar stools were turned over.

Ring ... ring ... ring.

"Hello," Taylor whispered.

"Are you okay?" Diane inquired hysterically. "You told me this morning that you were going to be here way before your scheduled time. Did something happen? I have been calling you for hours. Is Mike back in town?"

"Yes, I'm okay, and no, Mike is not back in town," Taylor replied, rolling her eyes. She did not feel like discussing what Mike had told her earlier today with her mother. "Are you still waiting for me?"

"Yes, Taylor! This production is costing the company close to half a million dollars, and you're holding us up. You know how all this works. Time is money, and you've wasted a lot of it today. Can you get here within the next thirty minutes?"

"Yes, I'm on my way, and this time I mean it." Taylor hung up the phone and went into the bathroom. She looked at herself in the mirror and was mortified. She looked like a chick from a horror flick.

The makeup artist will definitely need to work a miracle. She knew she looked absolutely dreadful. She went in the bathroom to get ready for her shoot.

Taylor still felt numb while she instructed the taxi driver to drop her off in front of her mother's building. No matter how she felt now, Taylor knew she would have to "work it" when she got in front of that camera. She was very late and knowing her mother, she probably had already substituted as much as she could for the day. The company specifically asked for her to represent their product, not second-rate models. After this was over, Taylor knew she would have to make it up to her mother big time.

When she got out of the taxi, she began to regret accepting this job and returning to the modeling industry altogether. As Taylor walked toward the building, the Starbucks coffee shop at the corner of the block caught her eye. She desperately needed a shot of caffeine, for she knew she would have to work well into the night. As she headed toward the coffee shop, she figured they could wait another five minutes for her.

She stepped into the Starbucks, got in line, and began to look at the menu. Not sure what to order, Taylor stepped back, unaware that she had gotten out of line. Suddenly, Stephen Blake III rudely stepped in front of her and ordered a Venti Chai Latte.

"Excuse me," Taylor said sternly. "I *am* in line."

"I'm sorry," he said as he whirled around.

"Stephen … what in the world …" Taylor gasped. "I'm beginning to think you're following me."

"This is scary, isn't it?" Stephen agreed.

"It's beyond scary, it's insane," Taylor answered, moving completely out of the line. "What are you doing here in New York?"

"I'm here on business. My father was here also but he left a week ago. As usual, he left me here to tie up the loose ends."

"I remember," Taylor smiled.

"You still look great."

"You don't have to be polite, Stephen. I know I look like death."

Stephen chuckled and asked, "How is everything going with you … and Mike?"

"Well, our engagement and wedding are off, permanently."

"What?" Stephen said in amazement.

"Mike can't deal with the fact that his woman has been intimate with his half brother, a brother whom he despises."

"Thanks for that information."

"Like you didn't know."

"I *didn't* know. I haven't seen or heard from Mike in years. Can you please tell me why you would agree to date him?"

"Do you think I would've dated Mike if I knew you all were *brothers* ... are you crazy?"

"I told my father that you couldn't have known," Stephen admitted. He picked up his tea from the countertop. "I never told you about Mike, so why would he tell you about us?"

"Exactly!" Taylor confirmed. "That's how this entire situation happened ... poor communication!"

"Do you have time to sit down?"

"Only for a second," Taylor returned. They went and sat down at one of the small round tables.

"Mike talked about his father to me maybe twice," Taylor continued to explain. "I knew his father was wealthy, but Mike never mentioned his name nor did he say his father lived in Paris. Just like you all, Mike never displayed any pictures of his father in his home or at the office. Mike also never mentioned, not even once, that he had a brother. I figured all this out the same time you did ... *right there after the Super Bowl game.*"

"You're kidding!" Stephen said, shocked.

"I really wish I was kidding, Stephen," Taylor stated as her eyes began to well with tears. "I really have to go. I'm super late for this job that was scheduled for hours ago." Taylor stood up to leave.

"I'll be here for another two days," Stephen pressed. "Can we at least finish this conversation somewhere else? I'm staying not too far from here, at the Trump Towers."

"I don't know," Taylor said reluctantly. "You can imagine how I'm feeling right now."

"You're right," Stephen agreed. "I can only imagine, which is why I want to finish this conversation. Give me your cell phone and I'll put my number in it." Taylor dug into her purse and placed her phone into Stephen's hand.

"Call me later tonight, Taylor," Stephen pleaded. He gave her back her phone. "You know I'll be up."

"I'll call you, but not tonight," Taylor replied. She waved good-bye and walked away from the table.

As she walked up the stairs to her mother's building, she wasn't sure why, but she felt a whole lot better. As predicted, as soon as she arrived on set, she was mobbed by the hair stylist and makeup person. They began to prep her for the task at hand: getting ready for her project.

It was one o'clock in the morning when Taylor walked into her condo. She was still wide awake, so she thought to call Stephen. As he had said, she knew he would be up. She remembered how he could stay up all night reviewing documents for meetings that were scheduled for the following day. Taylor sat in her living room in the dark, contemplating whether she should or shouldn't call. She ended her mental battle by following through with her first thought. She picked up her cell phone and looked for his number.

"You changed your mind," Stephen said. He knew Taylor would be the only person calling him at this late hour.

"Yes, I'm wide awake."

"Actually, I'm glad you called. I now have a viable excuse to put aside all this work."

Taylor sat in her living room and talked to Stephen until sunrise. As she peeked out her window, the warm sun's rays felt good shining on her. They continued to beam down on her face while she stood there for a few minutes.

"Can you believe it's morning?" Taylor asked. She stretched her hands in the air. "We managed to talk all night without falling asleep."

"Yeah, can you believe it?"

"What time is it?"

"Let's see," Stephen yawned. He glanced at the desk clock. "It's six-thirty. I'm sure you'll be able to fall asleep right now with little effort."

"You're probably right about that one. What are you going to do after your meeting?"

"I plan to come back here to the hotel and go to sleep. I have an early flight out tomorrow, but I'd like to do something together ... maybe a late dinner?"

"That sounds nice," Taylor said. "Call me when you leave your meeting or, better yet, when you wake up from your nap."

"All right, I'll talk to you soon."

Taylor flipped her phone closed and walked slowly to her bedroom. As she lay down on her bed fully dressed, she thought about her mother. She was right when she said that life becomes less complex as one matures. Who would have thought that she and Stephen would meet up again? She was also surprised at how open and honest Stephen was about everything: Dena, the abortion, and his life in general. Even though what Stephen had done to her was inexcusable, Taylor was glad that she had a better understanding about why he behaved the way he did while they lived together in Paris. Her mother would've called it generational curses, but Taylor called it a lack of understanding, living in the past, harboring hurtful and bitter feelings inside, and last but not least, not forgetting or forgiving others. Whatever the case, she knew that they were both at a vulnerable stage in their lives. Taylor was elated when they vowed to support each other throughout these unpredictable and turbulent times.

Taylor's bed never felt so good as she lay there snuggled up in her warm blankets. It took no time before she drifted off to sleep.

Chapter Twenty-Eight

Reminiscence
New York

*R*ing ... *ring* ... *ring*.

"Hello," Taylor mumbled.

"You sound horrible," Diane stated.

"Am I late for another job?"

"Very funny, Ms. Taylor. You know you owe me one."

"Mom, I worked until one in the morning. Isn't that enough?"

"Everyone received overtime for working that late. Sorry, honey, you still owe me."

"Just keep my check."

"Girl, don't have me jump through this phone. You know this is not about money. There is no excuse for arriving six hours late to a job. Not only is it inconsiderate, it's unprofessional."

"Mom, I'm sorry. I was just joking."

"What happened? You still haven't told me why you

were late. I know something happened."

Taylor paused. "If you must know, Mike and I are no longer a couple."

"What?"

"Yes, Mother. The wedding and the engagement are off … for good. Mike kindly informed me about this shortly after we had talked that morning."

"I figured something like this would happen sooner or later."

"Well, I didn't. I knew he would be upset for a while but to call everything off … I just didn't handle that news well."

"Oh, Lord."

"Don't worry, Mom. I plan to meet with Dr. Davis next week. That's if she's available."

"Good!"

"I just don't get it. With Stephen, I'll have to admit I knew something just wasn't quite right when we were engaged. But because he was my first love, I was going to marry him anyway. I know that sounds crazy, but it's true. With Mike, I guess I was completely delusional. I really thought Mike was the real thing. He seemed so genuine and honest. I now know the truth. He was never in love with me."

"How do you know that, Taylor? You have to consider your situation. You dated two brothers."

"Mother, he told me himself that he was more infatuated with getting even with his father and his brother than moving forward to work on our relationship. The bottom line is Mike has unresolved issues with his past and he was never truly in love with me."

Silence

"Just saying those words makes me hurt all over again."

"Sweetie, I wish I could bear all of this for you. You're a beautiful young lady who deserves so much more than what both of those fools gave you."

"Mom, you know as well as I do that this is all a part of life. I believe it's called growing pains. Hopefully, next time, I will be much stronger and wiser."

"I blame your good-for-nothing father for all of this."

"Mother, please!!" Taylor laughed.

"His absence has caused you to feel like you need a man to make you whole."

"There you go again, Dr. LaRue ... but this time you're wrong! For your information, I'm already a complete woman ... lacking nothing. Well, I'm far from being perfect, but I don't need a man to make me whole. My life experiences have caused me to be a bit more mature than your average twenty-two-year-old woman. Being engaged twice within the last two years may be disturbing for your normal, all-American girl, but not for women like us. You know our lifestyle. Even though my father walked out on us, you can't blame him for what has happened to me these past few years."

"You're forgiven."

"For what?"

"For yesterday. Your debt is paid. I think you have suffered enough. I had actually called to demand that you take me to the spa and salon and then later on, out to lunch. However, since you've been forgiven, I think you should go and get some much-needed rest instead."

"Thanks, Mom."

"I'll call you later on to discuss the next assignment that I think would be perfect for you."

"No, Mother!"

"I haven't even given you all the details."

"I don't care about the details."

"It's in the Greek islands."

"My answer is still no!"

"Just think about it some more before you make your final decision. You can take a two-day vacation after the shoot. I'll make sure to include those details in your contract."

"No! No! No! Bye, Mother. I'll talk to you tomorrow."

"Taylor, come on … you're becoming way too sensitive."

"I love you, too, Mom."

Click

Taylor hung up the phone and lay back in her bed.

Ring … ring … ring.

She put her pillow over her head and rolled over. The phone eventually stopped ringing.

Ring … ring … ring.

"What do you want, Diane?" Taylor decided to answer the phone.

"Taylor, this is Stephen."

"Stephen, I'm sorry. I thought you were my mother."

"Just hearing you say your mother's name sent chills down my spine. You know she scares me. The last time I saw her, she told me that she was going to kill me, and here I am in New York."

"You are too funny!"

"Are we still on for tonight?"

"Of course."

"Great, I'll have a car pick you up at seven this evening."

"That's fine."

"I'll see you soon."

Click

It felt like old times as Taylor and Stephen strolled through Central Park arm in arm. Neither one of them was ready to say good-bye. They decided to continue the night at Taylor's pad. Stephen was eager to check out her new place. For the rest of the night, they sipped tea, discussed their plans for the future, and occasionally glanced at a late-night sitcom on television. Before either of them knew it, they were stretched out across the sofa, sound asleep.

Taylor was awakened by the sound of her alarm going off in her bedroom.

"Is it five in the morning already?" she asked herself as she rushed into her room to turn it off. She brought back a blanket to place over Stephen. As she kneeled down to make sure the blanket covered his chest and shoulders, he woke up. At that moment, their eyes locked. Reading each other's eyes, they seemed to know exactly what the other one wanted to do. Not saying a word, Stephen sat up and kissed Taylor softly on the lips. Taylor thrust her tongue deep into his mouth. Her mind was saying "take it slow" but her body was saying "don't stop now." They continued to kiss each other passionately until their body heat ascended into the atmosphere and soon forced them apart.

"I've missed you so much," Stephen whispered in her ear.

"Shhh," Taylor whispered putting her finger to his mouth. She didn't want to hear any words. She only wanted Stephen to make her pain go away. Taking off his shirt, Taylor began to gently kiss Stephen's chest and stomach. She finally made her way down to his jeans. Feeling the heat of her breath on his stomach, Stephen quickly unbuttoned his pants. Helping him out, Taylor unzipped and pulled down his pants. She then proceeded to give him pleasure over and over again.

"Ooooh" Stephen moaned, pulling Taylor off of him. "Let's finish this in your room."

"What about your flight?" Taylor remembered.

"There are always other flights," Stephen mumbled. He planted another kiss on her lips. They walked into Taylor's bedroom. Stephen kicked the door closed behind them. They stayed in her condo for the next few days making up for lost time. Taylor knew she would have to set up an appointment to talk with Dr. Davis after this little love affair. But she had no regrets. Being with Stephen felt like therapy. He was helping her ease the pain after her breakup with Mike.

"Dr. Davis, are you suggesting that I tell my mother about Stephen?" Taylor asked, trying to understand her initial statement.

"No, Taylor. I'm merely helping you to revisit all your options as they relate to your support system," Dr. Davis confirmed.

"As awkward as this may sound, Stephen is now a part of my support system. I know what we have agreed to may be considered by others as destructive behavior. However, we perceive it differently. We're both consenting adults, and we both completely understand what has happened in our lives."

"Please, remember, Taylor, I'm not here to judge you."

"I know, but my mother and Candace would think I've gone crazy."

"Like you said, you're consenting adults. The better thoughts to process are about the choices that you're making. Are they healthy for you and everyone else who is involved? Second, are your decisions enhancing or improving your immediate situation?"

"Yes, yes, and yes," Taylor reassured her. "The only thing

I regret is that I stopped volunteering at the center. It's been well over a month since the breakup, but I'm still not ready to be around Mike again. All I feel for him now is hatred. I know that isn't a good sign in terms of me moving forward with my life, but this is how I truly feel."

"You can always volunteer at another facility."

"Now, why didn't I think of that idea? I guess my mind has been consumed with so many different thoughts that I didn't think about the obvious thing to do."

Ding ... ding ... ding.

Dr. Davis walked over to her desk to turn off the timer which indicated that the session was coming to an end.

"We can continue, if you like," Dr. Davis offered politely as she returned to her chair. "I have approximately forty minutes before my next patient is due to arrive here at the office."

"Unfortunately, I have another appointment across town. I would love to meet with you next week, if that's feasible."

"Let's see," Dr. Davis quickly glanced at her schedule on her Palm Pilot. "This time next week works for me. I'll see you then."

As soon as Taylor left Dr. Davis' office, she flipped her cell phone open to call Stephen. For about a month and a half now, they had been flying back and forth from Paris to New York, from New York to Paris, in secrecy, to see each other. They both knew what they wanted out of this relationship: absolutely nothing. In Taylor's eyes, Stephen was her savior. He was helping her heal as she went through her own personal grieving process. There wasn't any pressure, no hidden agendas, nor were there any strings attached. It was just a simple agreement between old friends. A devilish smirk appeared on Taylor's face. She wondered how long their little escapade would last.

Chapter Twenty-Nine
Meilleur Ami
Paris

"Mmmm," Stephen moaned. He woke up entangled in Taylor's arms. They were both lying buck-naked and uncovered on his bedroom floor in his apartment in downtown Paris. He slowly freed himself from Taylor's soft grip and reached for his bedspread to cover her up. He then sat up and glanced over at her as she continued to sleep peacefully.

"What a magnificent gem," he whispered, ashamed. "She should've been respected, honored, and protected." Unfortunately for Stephen, he figured this out much too late. He knew Taylor was still very much in love with his brother, Michael. However, at this point, he didn't care. Stephen knew he was behaving more like a groveling dog that ate the breadcrumbs that fell off the table onto the floor. He was just glad Taylor allowed him back into her life. Instead of leaving on an early flight after her photo shoot, she decided to stay in Paris another day to spend some more time with him.

"Good morning, sleepyhead," Stephen said when he noticed Taylor's eyes open. "Do you know what time it is?"

"You don't have to tell me," Taylor sighed. "I know it's late."

"Did you have a good time last night?"

"You know I did," she said with a big grin. Attempting to get up, Taylor flopped back down on the plush carpet. "But it doesn't feel like I've slept at all after partying all night."

"I'm sure once you get into the shower, you'll start feeling better." Stephen leaned over to massage her back. "So what's on your agenda today?"

"It all depends on whether or not you're going into the office."

"Taylor, you know I have to go into the office today. If I miss another day, my father will begin to wonder what in the world is wrong with me. You know he thinks I'm a workaholic."

"No problem, Stephen," Taylor said, yawning. She couldn't complain. This was her third time this month flying up to Paris to visit him. This time with success, she sat up. "Okay, so while you're at the office, I can go downtown and pick up a few items for Mother. We can meet up later at your office."

"Sounds like a plan."

Taylor slowly got up off the floor and walked toward

the bedroom. Stephen admired her slender body. But he noticed that she looked a bit thinner than usual.

"Are you losing weight?" he asked.

"I don't think so," she said over her shoulder.

Taylor decided to search for the scale that she remembered Stephen kept in his bathroom closet. "Oh my goodness!"

"What wrong?"

"I can't believe it."

"You can't believe what?"

"I've lost ten pounds."

"Is that a lot?"

"For me it is. I don't need to lose any weight at all."

"I'm sure it's due to your travels. Think about it. You've been flying here quite frequently, which interrupts your eating and sleeping schedule."

"You may be right," Taylor confirmed, putting the scale away. She walked over to the shower, opened the oversize glass door, and turned on the water.

"Have you told anyone about us?" Stephen called out from the bedroom.

"No," Taylor shouted back. She quickly jumped into the shower when she saw Stephen walking toward the bathroom. She really wasn't sure where he was going with this conversation, and she didn't want to find out.

"I was wondering," Stephen said, as he opened the shower door, "maybe, we should start letting others in on our little secret. My father just might give me the green light to work out of our New York location. I'm only thinking about you. Think about it. This would definitely decrease much of your travel time."

"I'm not ready to disclose our relationship to anyone, at least not right now." Taylor sighed and put her head underneath the running water. The water cascaded over her entire body like a waterfall. Stephen's words gripped her mind. The truth of the matter was she wasn't going to tell anyone because she knew what everyone would say ... that she was acting like a desperate housewife, being superficial and weak. Taylor wasn't ready to hear all the flack that Candace or her mother would dish out.

"Okay, moving on to a lighter subject, would you like me to order us brunch before you go shopping?"

"I should be famished after last night. We hardly ate anything, but for some reason, I'm not hungry at all."

"That's strike two," Stephen said as he held up two fingers.

"I have a question for you," Taylor said stepping out from under the trio showerhead. "Would you like to join me in the shower before you head off to another busy and stress-filled day at the office?"

"That's not fair," Stephen replied. He joined her under the water. "You already know the answer to that question." Stephen then began to wash Taylor's back.

"Should I call Tracey and let her know that I won't be in for another hour or so?" Stephen whispered in her ear.

Turning around to face Stephen, Taylor said, looking

directly in his eyes, "I think you know the answer to that question, too."

"Mr. Blake, your three o'clock appointment is on the phone," Tracey announced over the speakerphone. "He wants to know if he could meet at four o'clock instead of three today."

"Did he mention why he wanted to change our meeting time?"

"Yes, he said something about being behind schedule."

"Aren't we all?" Stephen replied sarcastically. "My time is valuable as well … I thought he, of all people, would know that."

"I'm reviewing your schedule as we speak, and it looks like that four o'clock time frame is open."

"Let's see," Stephen mumbled. He looked at his schedule on his desk. She was right. He was available at that hour. Stephen hit the speaker button and picked up the receiver to talk with Tracey. "Please, tell Mr. Wright that I'll call him back momentarily with an answer."

"Will do, sir," Tracey replied.

"Tracey, one more thing before you go."

"Yes, Mr. Blake."

"No more interruptions. I really need to focus all my attention on McFarlane's account." Stephen hung up the phone, whirled around in his chair, and began to reexamine the file on his conference table.

Ten minutes later, Taylor walked off the elevator and strolled into the reception area of Stephen's department. "Hello," Taylor said. She placed her shopping bags down. "Is Stephen available?"

"He's in his office. However, he has instructed me not to interrupt him—"

"He's such a workaholic," Taylor said interrupting Tracey. She walked past Tracey's desk and headed toward Stephen's office.

Tracey quickly picked up the phone, "Mr. Blake."

"Yes, Tracey," Stephen replied irritably.

"Sorry for the interruption, sir. Ms. LaRue is on her way to your office."

"Great," Stephen returned. "Please, bring us some hot tea."

"Right away, Mr. Blake," Tracey returned, sounding frustrated. She went to fulfill her boss's request.

When Taylor arrived at Stephen's door, she knocked twice, waited for a second, and then walked in.

"Why are you giving my assistant such a hard time?" Stephen asked jokingly. "I told her no more interruptions."

"Stephen, please," Taylor said with a smirk on her face. "I'm sure Tracey knows that your request did not include *me*." She sat down on one of Stephen's Italian leather sofas and unraveled her shawl from her body. Stephen chuckled and smiled back at Taylor. They both knew that Tracey was the only person who knew about their secret reunion.

"You're early. I wasn't expecting to see you for

another three hours or so. I thought you said you were going shopping."

"I bought a few things, and then I got bored."

"Bored while going shopping? That's not the Taylor I know. The Taylor I know could go shopping for an entire week ... nonstop."

"I do remember those days, especially here in Paris," Taylor smiled as her mind flashed back to those earlier years. "Fortunately for me, those days are long gone." She got up and walked toward Stephen while he sat at his conference table. "Working hard, huh?"

"Yeah, I was just reviewing one of my accounts."

"Isn't life funny?" Taylor stated, picking up one of Stephen's files and placing it back down again after a quick glance. "As your fiancée, I never could build up the courage to come down here to visit you at the office. Now that I'm your mistress or whatever it is we call ourselves, I have all the audacity to walk in and disrupt your day."

"For one, you're not a disruption. I'm glad you're here. And two, you're not my mistress. I'm a single man ... remember?"

Knock ... knock

"Come in," Stephen ordered.

"Here is your tea," Tracey announced, placing the tray on Stephen's desk. "Do you think you will need anything else?"

"No, I believe we're okay," Stephen returned.

"Thank you, Tracey," Taylor added while she watched

her walk out of the room. Taylor then sashayed over to Stephen's desk. "Hot tea is exactly what I need," she exclaimed, pouring the brew into the teacups. "I have been feeling queasy all day."

"I'm sure that's because you only shopped for an hour."

"Stop being silly, I'm serious. I haven't been feeling my best."

"Please excuse the interruption, Mr. Blake," Tracey chimed in. "Mr. Wright is on line three."

"Please reschedule him for another day," Stephen returned, as he sipped his tea.

"Excuse me, sir?"

"Tell him his three o'clock slot has been filled." Stephen sounded irritated as he began to move papers around on his desk. "After all, he did say he was running late. Correct?"

"That's correct, sir."

"Mr. Wright should know," Stephen said grunting, "when you snooze you lose." He then placed his documents in a pile that was labeled work-in-progress and pushed away from his desk.

"Mr. Blake, your schedule is booked solid for the next three months."

"Thanks for your concern, Tracey. However, my response is still the same. Reschedule him. Mr. Wright will definitely understand."

"All right," Tracey said. She then switched the phone line back to line three.

"Now, why couldn't you have done that when we were

engaged?" Taylor asked teasing. Stephen walked over to her and held her gently.

"You still don't believe that I'm a changed man," Stephen sighed.

A strange look appeared on Taylor's face. "Are you okay?" he asked.

"I don't know what's wrong with me," Taylor murmured while her face continued to turn bright red. "I need to go to your restroom, *now*." Stephen sensed the urgency in her voice so he quickly led her to his private bathroom.

I hope she's okay, he thought inwardly. He walked back over to his desk and sat down.

Moments later, Taylor walked out of the bathroom as if nothing had happened, and sat down again at the conference table.

"Well, how do you feel?" Stephen asked.

"I feel much better."

"That's good to know."

"You know, this same thing happened to me today right after you left your flat to go to the office. One minute, I was feeling fine and the next minute my stomach began to feel queasy. Before I knew it, my lunch was all over your deck. You know, the one that is connected to the kitchen."

"Taylor, please. I don't need to hear all the details," Stephen said with a frown.

"It's gross, I know. I felt really bad for your new housekeeper. She was not a happy camper when she learned that she had to clean up the mess. She continued to give me the evil eye until I decided to get out of her way and go shopping. Within seconds, I felt better … just like now."

"Well, I apologize. It was, after all, my idea to have brunch at that time."

"It's not your fault. This nausea started about a week ago, after I eat or drink anything."

"No wonder you've lost weight. You can't keep any food in your stomach."

"I know."

"You might be pregnant," Stephen said chuckling. "The symptoms that you've described sounds like a woman in her first trimester of pregnancy."

Taylor frowned.

"I'm just kidding. We both know that would be impossible … right?"

"You're absolutely right about that one. I don't take my pink little pills every day for nothing. Plus, you always wear your *latex gloves,* so we're doubly protected."

"I have learned, over the past few years, never say never. Maybe you should take a pregnancy test, just to rule it out."

"Pregnancy test? Are you kidding," Taylor exclaimed. "Stephen, we both know I'm not pregnant."

"I think taking a pregnancy test whether you are or are not pregnant is not such a bad idea," Stephen persisted.

"You might be right, but I have to catch an early flight out of here tomorrow." Taylor put her teacup down and went to the sofa to gather up her purse and shawl.

"It was just a suggestion, sweetie. No need to rush off."

"Stephen, I'm fine. I think it's time to let you get back to work." Taylor walked over to Stephen and kissed him on the cheek. "I'll see you later."

"Tracey," Stephen said after he picked up the phone.

"Yes, Mr. Blake."

"Please call for a driver to take Ms. LaRue back to my estate."

"Right away, sir," Tracey replied. "Ms. LaRue's shopping bags are in front by my desk."

"Oh, yeah. I forgot that I had left my bags there," Taylor whispered.

"Have one of your assistants take her bags downstairs to the car."

"Will do."

Stephen hung up the phone and quickly moved away from his desk to walk Taylor to the door.

"Stephen, you know I could've carried my own bags downstairs. I brought them up here."

"You need your rest," Stephen said, opening the door. "I'll see you back at home." He pecked her on the lips and watched her walked down the hallway until she disappeared around the corridor.

Later on that evening, Stephen scooped Taylor up from his villa. He decided to take her out to eat since this was her last night in Paris. He knew she wasn't feeling well, so he planned a relaxing yet enjoyable evening.

As they walked in the door, the restaurant manager greeted them and directed them to their usual spot. It was a private area outside on the balcony where the view of the city's skyline was simply spectacular.

Stephen added a surprising touch by hiring a chamber orchestra to entertain them while they enjoyed their conversation and their private feast. He knew Taylor was pleased, as a smile appeared on her face. He signaled to the waiter, ordered their meals, and turned his attention back to Taylor. They continued to engage in causal conversation. Moments later, a server rolled out a cart that displayed a variety of their favorite appetizers.

"My mother would be in heaven right now," Taylor said picking up the plate that held the blue cheese walnut toast. "This is also one of her favorite places to dine."

"That doesn't surprise me. Look at this place. It looks like a castle. And the food is excellent. What more can a person ask for?"

Several minutes later, the waiter brought out their main course, smoked lobster.

"This looks simply divine," Taylor exclaimed while the waiter placed a plate in front of her. "I can't wait to dig in."

"I'm glad to hear that your appetite is back."

"I am too," Taylor smiled. They spent the duration of the evening talking, laughing, and dancing.

While driving home, Stephen put in one of his contemporary jazz CDs. He put the car into cruise and sat back to relax. They were almost near his home when Taylor ordered him to pull the car to the side of the road. Stephen looked over at her. He saw the same expression on her face as when she became ill at his office earlier.

"What's wrong?" Stephen asked, pulling his car over to the curb. Saying nothing, Taylor quickly jumped out of the car. Stephen turned his head when he realized that Taylor was spewing her dinner all over the sidewalk.

"Hand me a tissue," Taylor gasped. Stephen went into his jacket side pocket and handed her one of his personalized handkerchiefs.

"This is insane!" Taylor said. She slowly slid back into the car. Stephen made a sharp U-turn.

"Where are you going?"

"To one of those 24-hour pharmacies."

"Why?"

"To buy you a pregnancy test."

"Stephen, I told you that I'm not pregnant."

"And I told you … you should just take the test to rule out the notion that you might be pregnant."

"This is ridiculous," Taylor huffed, folding her arms.

"Stop giving me a hard time and help me look for the store." Ignoring his words, Taylor turned her head to look out her side of the window.

"Taylor, please look down the streets. If you see a flashing neon green cross that's when you know you're near one."

Silence

"Think about it? When was the last time you had … you know … your girly thingy?"

"You mean my menstrual cycle."

"Yes, that thing … when was the last time?"

Silence

"Well, isn't that another sign?"

"No, it isn't. It simply means that I have a poor memory."

"Like I said before," Stephen persisted, "taking this will only rule out the suspicion." Stephen continued to drive looking up and down the streets. "There's one."

"You're crazy," Taylor murmured, rolling her eyes at him. "I'm not going in."

"You don't have to. I will." He put his car in park and hopped out of the driver's seat. Minutes later, he returned with a small white plastic bag in his hand. He got back in the car, tossed the bag in the backseat, and drove off down the dark, narrow street.

"I can't believe you."

"We'll put this issue to rest once and for all tonight."

"I'm not taking the test tonight. Everyone knows that an early morning urine sample yield the best results."

"Whatever the case, morning or night, we *will* have the results."

Chapter Thirty

Another Bun In The Oven
Paris

Taylor's eyes suddenly popped open. It felt like she was having a nightmare. Her nightgown was drenched with sweat. She attempted to recall her dream, but she couldn't remember anything. So she lay there for a while rubbing the sweat off her face. Then she turned over to face Stephen. He was still sound asleep. She flipped over and lay there quietly for another minute looking up at the ceiling. When she realized that she wasn't going to be able to remember the dream, her thoughts went to the pregnancy test Stephen had purchased last night.

"The very thought of me being pregnant is ridiculous," she chuckled inwardly. To appease Stephen, she slipped out of bed to find the bag he brought to their room last night.

"There it is," she uttered, grabbing it. She walked into the bathroom, pulled the box out of the bag, and threw the bag on the floor. Carefully, she opened the box while reading the directions.

This can't be too difficult to do. Taylor continued to read the 1-2-3 instructions. Then she pulled out one of the strips, placed the box down, and walked to the toilet. Taylor followed the instructions exactly. Just like Stephen, she, too, wanted results. After she was done, Taylor kept her eyes fixed on the small window on the front of the strip. Nervously, she walked over to the light near the mirror so that she could see better. Taylor looked up into the mirror when she heard Stephen push open the bathroom door.

"So you decided to take the test?" he said yawning. "It's negative, right?"

"I don't know," she replied irritated.

"What do you mean you don't know?"

"I don't know," Taylor repeated. "I've never had to take one of these tests before."

Stephen walked over to Taylor and looked at the window on the strip. He saw two red lines. "What does that mean?"

"I don't know."

"Where's the box?" he asked. Taylor pointed at the countertop. "What did the directions say?" Stephen picked up the box and began to read the backside. "According to this information, two red lines means positive."

"No way," Taylor sighed, grabbing at the box. She must have missed that information.

"Here you go, read it yourself," Stephen said. He handed her the box.

"There has to be some kind of mistake." Taylor stood there reading the instructions over and over again. "This can't be right."

"It's right there written in black and white."

"I just don't think I'm pregnant."

"Taylor, these tests are pretty accurate, which means that there is probably a ninety-nine percent chance that you're pregnant." Reaching for the box, he noticed that there was another test inside. "Do it again."

"What?"

"Look, there's another strip in the box." Stephen pulled out the strip and handed it to Taylor. "I guess this is why the company has two tests in the box. For this very reason, just in case the person is not sure about the first results."

Taylor snatched the strip from his hand, walked back to the toilet and performed the steps again. When she flushed the toilet, Stephen walked over to her and they both stared at the small window anxiously waiting for the lines to appear.

"It's positive," Taylor mumbled underneath her breath. "I still don't believe it."

"Taylor, don't panic. Go to your doctor. He will either confirm or dismiss these results."

Now he tells me not panic, she thought while she stood there staring at him. "Wasn't this your crazy idea in the first place … to take a home pregnancy test?"

"Babe, I'm here for you—"

"Stephen, please. I'm not pregnant. Think about it. For

the past two months you have been the only person I have been intimate with and you always wear a condom."

Stephen began to look at her with a doubtful smirk on his face.

"Don't look at me that way, Stephen. You know I always take my birth control pills."

"Always?"

Silence

"I'm not trying to be difficult," Stephen said. He walked over to Taylor and wrapped his arms around her. "It's just that ... Dena wasn't very careful either."

"Yes, *always!*" Taylor confirmed, pushing Stephen's arm from around her. "It's time to get ready to go. I don't want to miss my flight."

"Sure thing, babe."

Taylor stepped into the shower and turned the water on. Although the frigid water sent chills down her spine as it splashed over her face and body, she didn't react. She was still stunned about the possibility of her being pregnant.

"This can't be true," she continued to tell herself until her mind went back to the day after she and Michael broke up. That day, she threw her birth control pills away. Thinking back, Taylor couldn't recall when she had started using them again. *Maybe it was right after the first night she and Stephen started having sex again.*

"Oh, no," she mumbled. Taylor began to think about their *"reunion night" and the next day and the next day and the next day.* She didn't remember taking a pill during that entire time. She wouldn't dare mention this to Stephen, at least not now. Taylor knew one thing for sure: she was going straight to her doctor's office as soon as her plane landed in New York.

Stephen pulled his Porsche up to the international entranceway of the airport. He leaned over to kiss Taylor. Anticipating his gesture, Taylor turned away.

"I'm sorry, Stephen. I'm just ..."

"No need to explain, I completely understand. Just do me a favor ... call me when you get back to New York. I don't care what the results reveal. I want to make sure you're okay. Remember what I said earlier today ... whatever you decide ... I'm here for you."

"Thank you, Stephen," Taylor said with a smile. It was nice to be reminded that she had such a supportive friend during this time. "You're such a sweetheart." She then leaned over to kiss him. Still in a daze, Taylor stepped out of the car after the airport attendant opened the passenger door. Stephen rushed out of the car to tip the attendant. He also told the attendant to check her luggage in right there at the curbside. Taylor kissed Stephen good-bye once again, walked into the airport, and waited for the announcement to board her plane. She was relieved that Stephen wasn't able to stay to see her off. He had an urgent meeting to attend which worked out nicely for her because she really wanted to be alone.

"Now boarding at Gate 53, Flight 2064 from Paris, France, to New York City," a voice announced loudly over the intercom.

Taylor moved quickly to the line that was forming where she and other passengers would soon board the plane. Once on the plane, she found her seat. Taylor generally flew first class and she always had to have a seat by the window. As the plane engine started to roar, she glanced out the window. She began to think about the conversation she had with Stephen while they drove to the airport. His words lingered in the back of her mind ... *Marry me, Taylor.*

I will support you and this unborn child ... regardless of whether the child is mine or not.

He's such a gentleman, she thought. A tear rolled down her cheek. "He always wants to do the honorable thing." Unfortunately, her heart and mind were still stuck in the same place: in love with Mike. Taylor sat back in her seat and tilted her head toward the window. Her thoughts returned to the first time she met Mike at the club. She then thought about their first date, their first fight, and their passionate make-up session. *It was a nice ride,* she thought. Soon, she looked away from the window and drifted off into a troubled sleep.

Chapter Thirty-One

The Disclosure
New York

As soon as the plane touched down at JFK Airport, Taylor wasted no time contacting her doctor to set up an appointment. The receptionist told her that someone from Dr. Goldberg's office would call her back. He was not available at that time to speak with her. Taylor knew Dr. Goldberg probably wouldn't have any available time slots, but she hoped he would finagle his schedule to accommodate her. Minutes later, Dr. Goldberg's assistant called Taylor to inform her that he would be able to see her today.

As Taylor walked outside of the airport terminal, she quickly put her oversize shades on and flipped open her cell phone again. This time she decided to call Candace.

"Hey, it's me. Are you busy?" Taylor closed her handbag and placed it on her other arm.

"Where have you been?" Candace said with an attitude. "For two days, I've been trying to get in touch with you.

I even called K.T. looking for you. I couldn't believe she didn't know where you were."

"I went to Paris for a few days," Taylor said attempting to flag down a taxi. "Can you get away from the shop for an hour or two? I might need your shoulder to cry on."

"Uh ... I don't know about that ..." Candace looked at her watch. Her two o'clock appointment should've been at her shop fifteen minutes ago.

"Please, it's an emergency!"

"Are you okay?"

"I need you to meet me as soon as you can uptown in front of my doctor's office."

"Your *doctor's* office? Okay, now you *are* scaring me."

"I'll tell you everything when you get here. If I am not in front of the building, just come on up to the office. Suite 8751. I'll text you the address momentarily."

"Today must be your lucky day." Candace closed the magazine she was thumbing through and walked over to her coworker's booth. "Stephanie is here today, and my clients only trust her to do their hair when I'm not available or out of town."

"So, you'll meet me over there?"

"Yep, I'm on my way."

Click

Taylor closed her phone and tossed it back into her purse. Although she was still in denial about her pregnancy, she knew that she needed Candace by her side when the doctor told her the official results. She was now more than ever appreciative of Candace's friendship. Her willingness to drop everything without knowing what was really going on to support her friend in distress was just amazing.

For just a second, Taylor thought about calling Mike. Instead, she called her mother's office and instructed one of her personal assistants to arrange for someone to pick up her luggage from the airport.

Taylor went to the curb and attempted to flag down a taxi again. This time, a cab immediately pulled up to her. She hopped in and rattled off the doctor's office address.

When Taylor arrived at the doctor's office, she checked in and sat down near the front door. She was anxiously waiting for Candace because Taylor still wasn't sure how she was going to break the news to her. One of the nurses, instead, walked over to Taylor to escort her through the doorway to one of the exam rooms in the back area of the doctor's suite.

"Please remove all of your clothes," instructed the nurse. She handed Taylor a white garment and walked out of the room. Taylor moaned inwardly while she sat down to disrobe. She was just not in the mood to be in a doctor's office right now. But she had to know if she was pregnant or not so she did what she was told. A few minutes later, the nurse returned and took Taylor's blood pressure. She then asked Taylor to stand on the scale that was in the room. The nurse recorded her weight and blood pressure. The nurse was clearly on a mission. She said few words in between directing Taylor from one task to another. Lastly, she handed Taylor a sealed plastic cup and a form which she told her to complete after she had provided a sample of urine in the cup.

"The bathrooms are down this corridor to the left," the nurse told her. She opened the door and pointed down the hallway. Taylor placed the sheet down and walked out of the room with the plastic cup in hand. When she had returned to the room, Candace was there waiting for her with a panicked look on her face.

"I got here as fast as I could," Candace told her. She got up and hugged her friend. "What exactly is going on? Why are you here?"

"It's such a long story—" Taylor began.

"Long story?" Candace interrupted.

Before Taylor could fully explain why she had told Candace to meet her here, Dr. Goldberg walked into the room.

After all these years, he still looks the same, Taylor thought as he sat down in front of her. He looked like one of Taylor's stern professors at NYU. His black, round, wire-rimmed glasses sat perfectly on his nose.

"Well, hello, Ms. Taylor. It's nice to see you again."

"The feeling is mutual," Taylor said with a big grin on her face. She pointed to Candace. "This is my best friend, Candace."

"Hello, Candace."

"Hello."

"Should we go ahead and complete your yearly physical? Last month, you had cancelled your appointment without rescheduling … remember?"

"Yes, we might as well get that over with today."

"Great, I'll have one of the nurses come in to prep you before we proceed with the exam. Let's see, we have your urine sample. Did the nurse draw any blood yet?"

"No, not yet."

"Okay, I'll have her come back in to draw your blood as well. I shall return shortly with the results from your urine sample. As you know, the results from the blood test will take longer … perhaps three days or so." Dr. Goldberg stood up, closed Taylor's chart, and walked out of the room.

"What in the world is going on?" Candace pleaded. "Why did you have to give a urine sample, and why are you taking a blood test?"

Before Taylor could say a word, the nurse walked in the room. Searching for visible veins, she looked at Taylor's arms. The nurse decided on Taylor's left arm. She quickly pricked a needle into the vein. The blood flowed into the tubes fairly quickly. When the second glass tube was completely filled, the nurse secured the lid and left the room.

"Don't ask another question," Taylor quickly said to her friend. "I'll tell you everything in just a second … let's just wait for Dr. Goldberg to come back with the results." Dr. Goldberg returned just as soon as Taylor finished her sentence.

"It's okay to discuss your results in front of your guest?"

"Yes," Taylor sighed. "She is here to support."

"I figured that might be the case. Well, your urine sample is positive. I suspect that your blood will be the same. You told the nurse that your two over-the-counter pregnancy tests were positive as well."

"Yes, I did."

What! Candace screamed inwardly but outwardly, she remained cool, calm, and collected.

"At this point, I'll have to ask that your friend wait for you in the reception area while I conduct the rest of the exam." Dr. Goldberg pointed at Taylor's chart showing her the various components: the Pap smear, breast exam, and the pelvic and rectal exam. "When we're done, she may return."

"Okay, that's fine," Taylor said. Candace got up and left the room while Taylor got up and walked over to the examination table.

Taylor and Candace remained silent while they walked out of the medical facility onto the busy street.

"I'm parked over there across the street," Candace finally said pointing to a black hummer.

"Whose truck is that?" Taylor asked curiously.

"It's Brian's," Candace replied hitting the remote button which started the engine and unlocked the doors simultaneously. "My car is in the shop. My brakes went out yesterday."

After they got into the truck, Candace immediately turned to Taylor and began staring at her.

"What?" Taylor asked, irritated.

"Please, start explaining because I don't know if I should be jumping up and down or feeling like I am right now: still in shock."

Silence

"How did this happen?" Candace continued to press. "Was this pregnancy planned? I mean, it had to be, right? I mean, we've been popping our little pink pills since we were teenagers. Okay … let me stop. I'm sorry, Taylor. I'm not trying to be mean, but … I'm just confused."

Taylor continued to look at her friend without uttering a word. She knew she had to let Candace get all of her thoughts and questions out of her system before she would allow Taylor to speak.

"Okay, forget about answering those questions. The better question to answer is: who is the father?"

"Are you finished?"

"Yes, so start talking."

"Start driving, please. I'll answer all of your questions on the way to my place."

As Candace pulled up to the front of Taylor's building, she continued to listen to her friend with amazement.

"That's it," Taylor said. She then looked at Candace hoping to gain her sympathy. "That's the entire story."

"Okay, let me get this straight," Candace said, pausing for a moment. "After you and Mike decided to call it quits, you and Stephen hooked back up again."

"Correct."

"You stopped taking your birth control pills after the breakup, but because you and Stephen realized fairly soon after the first date that you would probably be having sex on a regular basis, you decided to start taking the pills again, but this did not occur for another week or so."

"That sounds about right."

"This is why you don't know who your baby's daddy is … it could be either Michael or Stephen at this point."

"Exactly. Now do you feel my pain?"

"No … not exactly. Taylor, help me understand. What in the world did Stephen do, or better yet, say, to you to make you want to immediately jump into the sack with him again? Especially after everything he put you through when you all were together in Paris."

"Candace, please don't focus on Stephen … this is hard."

"Taylor, the fact of the matter is, you're pregnant and you do not know who the father is. If Mike is the father, you were pregnant during the entire time you were going back and forth to Paris just to screw Stephen for the past two months. If Stephen is the father, your mother is going to kill you. She still refuses to say his name. Plus, we can't forget that both of these men are brothers. Taylor, you know I love you, but even I have to ask you: WHAT were you thinking?"

"Candace, everyone makes mistakes. Maybe, I wasn't thinking … my gosh, I'm only human."

"I'm sorry, Taylor. I know I'm being kinda harsh asking you all of these questions. But … I'm envisioning your mother right now, and she is going to kill you … no … us. I can just hear her right now. '*Candace, why didn't you tell me?*'"

"Hello, Candace … news flash. My mother will never know about Stephen, this pregnancy, or the abortion."

"What are you talking about, the abortion?"

"I'm terminating this pregnancy. I have already discussed this with Dr. Goldberg. He referred me to another doctor in his building that will be performing the surgery. A tentative date has already been set."

"Taylor, are you sure you want to have an abortion?"

Ring … ring … ring.

"It's Stephen," Taylor murmured, as she answered the call. "Yes, it's positive. I'm fine, Stephen. There is no need … because I'm having an abortion. Stephen, I really can't talk about this now. Yes, Candace is right here with me. I told her everything. She was with me when I was at the doctor's office. Okay, Stephen. If that's going to make you feel better, then it is fine with me." Taylor slapped her phone closed. "Stephen's on his way to New York."

"Well, I would hope so," Candace replied with an attitude.

"Candace, Stephen has been completely wonderful throughout this entire ordeal. He would like for us to give our relationship another try. He wants me to marry him."

"Taylor, it's time for you to get out my car. This is all just too much … this is just too much information for me to digest in one day."

"Candace, just for the record, I do not plan on marrying Stephen. My only reason for this is because I do not love him. You do need to know and understand that Stephen is not the man I was engaged to two years ago. He has changed … for the better."

"That's wonderful, Taylor."

"Candace!"

"What? I'm serious. I'm happy for Stephen."

"Did you forget that you're not a good liar?"

"Enough about Stephen. What about your mother? I think you should tell your mother. Don't you think she has a right to know?"

"I am not a child … this is my business."

"Taylor, your mother loves you so much. She would be devastated to know that you made such an important decision without seeking her advice."

Silence

Taylor knew her friend was right. She felt so miserable. "Thanks for everything." She leaned over to hug Candace good-bye. "I'll call you tomorrow."

"Promise?"

"Yeah, I promise." Taylor sighed. She got out of the car and strolled slowly to her building. Taylor was surprised at Candace's reaction. She wasn't as empathetic as Taylor thought she should've been. *Oh, well. C'est la vie!*

Chapter Thirty-Two

More Drama
New York

Taking Candace's advice, Taylor decided to invite her mother over for dinner to tell her about the pregnancy and her plans to have an abortion. She also told Candace to come over to act as the referee. This was, after all, her bright idea. Taylor knew she wouldn't be able to eat. Just thinking about her mother's response to the news made her lose her appetite.

Mother is going to be outraged! She walked into her dining room and admired the spread. How did she let Candace talk her into having this little gathering? She would never know.

Ding dong ...

"It's showtime," Taylor whispered walking into the kitchen to peek at the clock on the wall. She then walked back to the front door.

"Well, hello, sweetie," Diane said. She kissed Taylor on

the cheek. Taylor and Candace greeted each other with a smirk. It was obvious by her mother's tone that Candace had kept her promise to not say a word.

"Let's eat," Taylor announced. "The dinner is hot and ready to be served."

After finishing their meal, the women walked over to the living room and sat down.

"Taylor, are you okay?" Diane asked. "You've barely eaten, and you've been talking a mile a minute since we've stepped through the door. What's wrong?"

"Well, Mom, it's kind of a long story. To be honest, I don't even know where to start."

"I can tell already that I'm going to need a drink. What alcoholic beverages do you have here to drink?"

"Mother, I'm serious!"

"Taylor, I am too." Diane got up and returned momentarily with a cocktail in her hand. "Okay, *now* I'm ready. Whatever it is that you want to tell me … just say it."

"Well … huh," Taylor said, looking to Candace for assistance.

"Why are you looking at Candace?" Diane asked, turning to look at Candace.

Silence

"Candace," Diane continued, "I thought you told me that you didn't know why Taylor wanted us to come over here for dinner."

"I lied. Taylor made me promise not to say a word."

"Taylor, is it *that* bad that you can't even—"

"Mother, I'm pregnant," Taylor blurted out.

Diane stared at both of them in astonishment.

"Say something, Mother. Anything. Just don't sit there and say nothing."

"What do you want me to say: the sins of the parents will someday fall on their offspring? I'm in shock. I really don't know what to say." They sat there for another silent moment looking at each other.

"Who?" Diane finally asked, breaking the silence. "No … what? … Better yet, how … how did all of this come about?"

"Mom, I didn't bring you over here to discuss those details. I simply wanted you to know that I made a mistake. Yes, I'm pregnant, and I plan to terminate the pregnancy."

"You plan to have an abortion?" Diane asked.

"Yes, I do."

"I'm sure you know that I wouldn't be in agreement with this. You know my views when it comes to that subject. Do you know how many people told me that I should've 'terminated the pregnancy' when I was pregnant with you? I could have done just that, but I didn't."

"Mom, you don't know all the details. My situation is completely different from your situation, which happened two decades ago."

"Your situation … what's so different about your situation?"

"What if I was going to die ... or what if I was raped?"

"Is either of these cases your situation?"

"No ... not exactly."

"Even if they were, I believe that God would have made a way out for you. I'm glad to hear that death and rape are not involved here. So what *is* your reason?"

"I'm not getting into all of that, Mother. You wouldn't understand."

Diane put her drink down and started pacing back and forth in Taylor's living room. "Where did I go wrong with you?" she finally said. Tears began to flow down her face. "Your good-for-nothing father lied to me for two years straight. When I told him I was expecting his child, I actually thought this man was going to divorce his wife and marry me. Instead, he told me that this was my problem and that I would never see him again."

"Oh God, here she goes again!" Taylor folded her arms across her chest and turned toward Candace.

"Taylor, I wanted to die. I lost my job. I had no money. No one wanted to hire a pregnant woman. Your father did not start paying me child support until after you were born. That is ... *after* the DNA test had confirmed that you were, in fact, his child. That bastard! He knew I was a virgin. Yes, Taylor. Your father was my very first lover. Talk about heartbreak hotel ... I was the originator of that song. I was surprised when the doctor told me that you weighed seven pounds and six ounces, because all I ate during the nine months I carried you was crackers. I remember drinking lots of water during that time too and it wasn't because I was trying to be healthy, either. So, please, Taylor, spare me the baby mama drama."

Taylor said nothing as she continued to look at her mother revisiting her past yet once again.

"Sweetie, you have enough money in the bank to support a family of six for ten years. You have dedicated friends and a supportive family. These days, women who are on your level are doing this on their own with no problem. So what's your excuse? Please explain to your mother your reason for wanting to terminate the pregnancy."

Taylor still couldn't say anything. She continued to stare at her mother while she stood there in the middle of her living room.

"You can't say that I wasn't there for you," Diane continued. She finally decided to sit down. "I talked to you and Candace about all the various birth control methods. You made your bed, Taylor. Why won't you make the right decision and lie in it?"

Silence

At that moment, the front door swung open. Their heads turned at the same time toward the door as Stephen walked in.

"I *see*," Diane huffed, irritated.

"Hello," Stephen said reluctantly. He wasn't sure what he was walking into, but he could feel the chill in the air. It was ice cold.

No one said a word.

"It seems like I have come at a bad time. Maybe I should go back downstairs and wait—"

"No, Stephen, it's okay," Taylor said quickly. "Come on in and sit down. We were just talking about my issue."

"Is *he* the father?" Diane asked sternly. "One can only assume that since he walked right in here with his own set of keys …" Diane began to shake her head in disgust when both Taylor and Stephen quickly responded with a "No" and "Yes" respectively.

"Which one is it?" Diane asked again.

"Yes, he is the father," Taylor said, feeling ashamed.

"Why did you just say no a few seconds ago?"

"Diane, this is a very complicated situation," Candace finally chimed in.

"Would someone please tell me what in the world is going on?"

"Mother," Taylor replied as she began to cry, "I don't know who the father is … are you happy now?"

Diane stared down at her daughter in disbelief. Her initial thought was to go over to where she was sitting and slap some sense into her, but she went ahead with her second thought.

"Stephen!"

Candace and Taylor were stunned. They couldn't believe Diane said his name.

"Yes, Ms. LaRue?"

"Maybe you can shed some light on this situation. Was it your idea for Taylor to have an abortion?"

"No! Absolutely not! Taylor knows where I stand when

it comes to that subject. I told her that I am willing to do the honorable thing. I've asked her to marry me. She still has not given me an answer. She seems to be determined to have this abortion. I came here today to see if I could talk her out of making another mistake."

"Okay, let me get this straight," Diane said, surprised. "You have asked Taylor to marry you? Aren't you married already? Where is your wife ... and your child, for that matter?"

"Diane, I never got married, and as for the child ..." Stephen said, as he tried to hold back tears.

"Mother, Stephen never married that woman," Taylor explained.

"What!?" Candace returned in amazement.

"She left Paris and had an abortion a few days after we left."

"I apologize, Stephen," Diane said sympathetically. "It wasn't my intention to be mean-spirited when I asked you those questions."

"No problem," Stephen returned, catching his breath. "I assumed you didn't know about that part of my life."

Diane immediately turned her attention back to Taylor.

"Taylor, I'm completely baffled. You have a wealthy suitor who not only wants to marry you but also says he is the father of your unborn child. He's here to put a glass slipper on your foot and take you far, far, far away to the land of Happily Ever After. Please, explain to me what the problem is, because I'm confused."

"Mother LaRue," Candace chimed in again, "Taylor really doesn't know who the father is. It could be either Stephen's or Mike's child."

"I got that. I understood that fact ten minutes ago. Who cares if we don't know who the father is *right now*! I do know one thing: we will definitely find out when the baby is born." Diane got up and began walking toward Taylor. "This still doesn't explain why my daughter wants to terminate this pregnancy."

"Mother, please …"

"'Mother, please *what?*" Diane repeated annoyed.

"This conversation is over!" Taylor stated sternly. "I'm terminating this pregnancy, and that is final! You can stay here if you like, but I'm going to my room."

Taylor got up and stormed toward her bedroom.

"TAYLOR ANN LARUE!" Diane scolded. "You come back here *right now*."

Taylor stopped suddenly.

"Turn around and look at me," Diane ordered.

Taylor reluctantly followed her mother's command.

"I know your grandfather is turning over in his grave right about now. To know that I have raised such a ruthless, coldhearted … I don't even know who this person is that is standing before me right now. You still have yet to give me one sound reason why you have chosen to murder an innocent, unborn child. HEAR ME AND HEAR ME GOOD, MS. TAYLOR. IF YOU GO AHEAD WITH YOUR PLANS TO TERMINATE THIS PREGNANCY …" Diane paused.

"I DON'T EVEN HAVE TO TELL YOU BECAUSE I KNOW YOU KNOW WHAT THE CONSEQUENCE WILL BE OF THAT FOOLISH DECISION." Diane went to get her coat and other belongings. Candace continued to look at Diane, dumbfounded.

"She knows, Candace," Diane reiterated in an attempt to help her friend understand the meaning behind her words. "Taylor knows that I will *never* speak to her again." Diane glared at Taylor once again before storming out the door. Taylor cried as she ran to her room. Candace and Stephen did not move. They stood there in the middle of the room with their mouths open looking at each other in disbelief.

Chapter Thirty-Three
Double Trouble
New York

The clinic where Taylor had scheduled the abortion was part of the medical center where her doctor's office was located. Dr. Goldberg promised that he would walk over to check on Taylor. He reassured her that she was in very good hands. He was very familiar with the doctor who was performing the surgery. Stephen and Candace agreed to accompany Taylor. They arrived an hour early before the appointed time. They were both nervous and anxious about the procedure. Although Taylor was early, a nurse soon escorted her into a private room where she was given a robe and a plastic bag to put all of her belongings in. The nurse informed Taylor that her friends would have to stay in the waiting room during the surgery.

Taylor was then escorted into the operating room. She was told to lie on what looked like an examination table. As promised, Dr. Goldberg came with the operating surgeon to greet her. Dr. Goldberg introduced the surgeon and mentioned that they were still not exactly sure how many weeks along Taylor was. The nurse began to prep Taylor for the ultrasound.

For just a second, Taylor thought about getting up to leave when she heard her mother's words echo in her head. *I will never speak to her again ...*

The technician came in and interrupted her thought as he introduced himself. Taylor's body jerked a bit while the nurse spread the cold gel all around her belly.

"I'm sorry. I know the gel is cold," the technician said. "This will only take a few minutes." He purposely turned the monitoring screen away from Taylor's view, then picked up the instrument and began to press and roll the hand-held scanner all over her belly.

"There it is," the technician said to the nurse. They both looked at the screen. He then looked at Taylor. "This means that you're far enough along to perform the surgery."

He then turned to the nurse and instructed her to go get the doctor. The technician continued to roll the device around on Taylor's belly.

"Uh, that's interesting. Okay, there are two."

What is he talking about?

"I'm all done. I'm waiting for the doctor to return to make sure we're all in agreement about the time factor."

"I heard you say there are two ... what did you mean when you said that?"

"Let's just wait for the doctor to return. You can direct

all your questions to him."

Moments later, the surgeon returned to the room with the nurse.

"Let's see what we have here. I was told that it looks like we have the green light to move ahead."

The nurse put some more gel on Taylor's belly. The doctor picked up the scanner and rolled it across her belly once again.

"Do you see two fetuses?" Taylor asked.

"Do you really want to know that kind of information? I wouldn't want to encourage it if you plan to move forward with the procedure."

"Please, just tell me. What do you see?"

"There are definitely two fetuses in this sack. You're about ten weeks pregnant."

"I'm having twins?" Taylor said shocked.

"Yes, you're pregnant with twins," the doctor confirmed.

"I can't go through with this ..."

"I thought that might be the case," the doctor replied. "As always, the choice is yours." He then instructed the nurse to take Taylor to the aftercare room. She told Taylor that she would get her personal belongings and have her friends come back to meet her here as well. Taylor was completely dressed when Stephen and Candace walked into her room.

"That was fast," Candace said, reaching out to hug her friend.

"I couldn't go through with it," Taylor told them.

"What?" Stephen said.

"Thank goodness," Candace sighed.

"I'm glad, too," Stephen said. He hugged Taylor tightly. "What made you change your mind?"

"Let's just get out of here," Taylor replied. "I feel awful. You all were right. If I would have gone through with this … I would've made *another* terrible mistake. We can talk more about this in the car."

While in the backseat of Stephen's rental car, Taylor began to cry.

"It's okay, sweetie," Stephen said.

"I can't believe I almost—"

"It's over," Candace said, attempting to console her friend.

"While I was on the operating table, I found out by accident that I am having twins."

"Twins!?" Stephen and Candace repeated in unison.

"Yes, twins. Can you believe it? My mother was right. I was behaving like such a selfish, spoiled brat. What if I would have had the abortion?"

"Taylor, don't go beating yourself up," Stephen replied. "God allowed all of this to happen for a reason. Look at the positive side of this entire ordeal."

"You're right, Stephen," Taylor said adjusting in her seat. "You all know what this means? I have to tell Mike about the pregnancy."

"For what?" Stephen asked in amazement. "I can't believe you're even thinking about him right now."

"Stephen, I'm so grateful that you and Candace are here supporting me, but it's only fair. Mike has a right to know also."

"Babe, the ball is in your court," Stephen said as his jaw tightened and the words turned sour in his stomach. "If you feel that Mike should know about the pregnancy ... then I'm all for it," Stephen lied. He looked out his side of the window. The truth of the matter was that he didn't want Mike involved in the situation at all. He was trying to build a solid foundation with Taylor, but he knew he couldn't discuss his future plans with her at this time. He continued to look out the window and envision himself in Paris as a family man with Taylor and their twins relaxing on the patio near the pool. He turned back to look at Taylor while she leaned on Candace's shoulder staring into space. He knew he was right. Now was not the time to talk to Taylor. She needed her rest.

Chapter Thirty-Four
Busted & Disgusted
New York

"Are you ready?" Stephen asked. Taylor was lying across her bed talking on the phone to her mother. He quickly made a U-turn and walked out of the room when she indicated to him with her index finger to wait one more minute. Stephen was more than ready to go. After all, they had been cooped up in Taylor's apartment for the past two days. Despite his many efforts to get her to go outside, Taylor continued to tell him that she simply was not in the mood. So when she asked Stephen this morning if he wanted to go out and get a bite to eat with her, he jumped at the opportunity.

As Stephen walked into the kitchen, he looked at the time on the oven. It was now four o'clock and he was still waiting to get outside to breathe the city's air. He was becoming more impatient as the seconds ticked by; so much so that he began to pace back and forth on the kitchen floor.

Now, looking at his watch, he hoped her "one more minute" meant just that … ONE more minute.

"Mom, I better get off this phone," Taylor said. She repositioned herself on the bed. "Stephen is waiting for me." As she hung up her home phone, she thought about what her mother told her. They both felt that Mike should be informed about the pregnancy. She reached for her purse and began to search for her cell phone.

"Stephen!" Taylor called out. When Stephen did not respond, Taylor began to scroll through her cell phone contact list. She wasn't sure if she had deleted Mike's number from her address book or not.

"Here it is," she whispered. She paused for a second to rethink her decision. Taylor then pressed the "call" button to quick-dial Mike. She knew she was doing what was right.

"Taylor!" Stephen called sharply. Taylor quickly pressed the end button which disconnected the call.

"I'm ready," Taylor yelled back, hopping off her bed. Even though she knew she was doing the right thing, she had to do it at another time.

Maybe, I'll call him later on tonight, she thought. She picked up her purse and rushed out of her room.

Mike felt his cell phone rumble in his hand. He had just put it on vibrate a few seconds ago. He would soon be in front of the hotel where he was going to pick up his dinner date, Brenda Starr. She had come into town and asked Mike if he would spend some time with her. After Mike pulled up in front of the hotel, he checked his phone to see who was trying to contact him.

"Taylor," Mike said inwardly while he switched the gear into parking mode. "I wonder what she wants." Mike had to admit that he missed Taylor ... a lot. The last time he had spoken to her was when he was in Jamaica.

I'll give her a call back tomorrow, he thought. He got out his car and refocused his thoughts back on the reason why he was at this hotel in the first place ... Brenda. Mike knew she wanted to get something to eat. He probably would take her to one of his favorite spots down the street. He wanted to remain in the vicinity. After experiencing a grueling practice, he really wasn't up for driving around the busy New York streets. He was looking forward to the massage Brenda promised to give him later on in the evening.

Twenty minutes later, Mike and Brenda walked into one of his teammates' restaurant. They both agreed that it was the perfect place to eat. And it was only a few blocks away from the hotel Brenda was staying at. One of the managers immediately greeted Mike at the door and escorted them to their table.

"Big Mike, you know your money is no good here," the manager teased, offering Brenda a chair to sit in. He then turned to the waiter and told him whatever they ordered was on the house.

"Is Russell in the back?" Mike asked. He knew his

teammate enjoyed cooking and preparing a few of the main courses in the kitchen.

"He's not here right now, but I'll tell him that you asked for him," the manager replied, placing a menu in front of each one of them.

"Thanks," Mike told him.

"Enjoy your meal," he said, looking at both of them. He then turned his attention to another table where another high-profile couple was seated. "Can I get you all anything?" The man shook his head no, the manager smiled, and walked away. Shortly afterwards, the waiter approached Mike's table again.

"Do you know what you would like to drink or do you need another minute to decide?"

"Give us another minute, please," Mike instructed picking up his menu. As Mike scanned the menu, he noticed a couple to the right of him holding each other's hands. He continued to stare at them. They looked very familiar to him.

"What ... the ..." Mike mumbled.

"Did you say something?" Brenda questioned.

"No, just reading the menu," Mike said, trying to remain cool.

"What do you want to eat?"

"I'm not sure," Mike said calmly. Inwardly, he was fuming. He could actually feel his body temperature going up.

"Well, I know what I want," Brenda told him putting her menu down.

"I want to go," Mike finally said. He could no longer deal with Taylor and Stephen staring into each other's eyes like they were two lovesick teenagers.

"You're kidding, I know," Brenda said, looking at him in disbelief.

"No, I'm actually serious."

"Mike, I'm starving," Brenda moaned. "Plus, you know we picked this place for a reason." Brenda kicked off one of her shoes, navigated her foot up Mike's pants, and began to rub his legs seductively.

"We can always eat somewhere else around here."

"What is it?" she asked confused. "You don't see what you want to eat? You know Russell would have them fly in whatever food you want to eat."

"He's not here, remember? We're leaving."

"Mike!"

"Brenda, don't give me a hard time about this," Mike told her looking serious. "Put your shoe back on and meet me out front." He then reached inside his jacket and pulled out his valet parking ticket.

"Fine," Brenda huffed, putting on her shoe. She snatched the ticket from his hand and stormed out of the restaurant.

Mike stayed in his seat for another moment. He wanted to make sure that Brenda went out the front door. Then he unfolded his napkin and wiped the sweat that had now formed a puddle around his forehead and mouth. Seething, he threw down the napkin and continued to watch the lovebirds for another second. He wanted to get hold of his emotions before he approached their table. Mike finally made his move. He got up and walked toward the table.

"Well, hello," Mike said with a grin. By the way their mouths dropped open, he knew he had caught them off guard. "Now, this is an interesting sight to see."

"Mi ... Mi ... Mike," Taylor stuttered. "What a surprise ... a pleasant surprise, that is ..."

"No need to be polite," Mike replied. "I was just as surprised as you are, which is why I had to come over here to say hello."

"Mike, it's nice to see you again. How have you been?" Stephen asked.

"I'm doing well — but as usual, not as well as you are ..."

"It's funny that you're here," Taylor interrupted. "We were just talking about you."

"You'll never get me to believe that lie," Mike said smiling. "Not the way the two of you were gazing at each other."

"Mike, do you have time to—" Taylor said, ignoring his previous comment.

"Time for what?" Mike rudely interrupted.

"Mike, tone it down," Stephen said. He was becoming annoyed with his demeanor.

"Excuse me ... brother dearest," Mike replied looking directly at Stephen.

"Stephen, don't ..." Taylor chimed in.

"Taylor, you don't have to tell Stephen to stop," Mike

continued. "He is the one that has all the brains in the family ... and smart men don't make foolish mistakes."

"Mike, I'm serious. Can you speak in a more respectful manner, especially when you're talking to Taylor?"

"You're funny, little brother."

Stephen attempted to get up. Taylor quickly grabbed him and pulled him back down.

"Mike, we're not here to fight," Taylor pleaded. "All we want is to have a civil conversation with you."

"Let the man go," Mike said, laughing. "I've been dreaming about this day for years. I'll finally get a chance to knock out one of the Blake men."

"Taylor, as you can see, it's time to go," Stephen said.

"Fine," Taylor said throwing her napkin on her plate. "If not today, when? We're going to have to tell him sooner or later."

"Tell me *what?*" Mike said with a smirk on his face. "I noticed that you called me earlier today."

"You called him?" Stephen asked surprised.

"Now, that's not a good look, little brother," Mike said teasing. He wanted Stephen to feel just as outraged as he was feeling. "Your girl is keeping secrets this early in the relationship?"

"It's not a secret," Taylor replied quickly.

"Why didn't you mention it to me?" Stephen persisted. "We've been sitting here for well over an hour."

"Stephen, don't get sidetracked. Now is not the time to discuss this."

"So, what is it?" Mike looked back and forth at the two of them. "What do you have to tell me?"

"Let's just drop it!" Stephen said angrily.

"No. Taylor, tell me," Mike said mischievously. He was enjoying every minute of this situation. "Seriously, I want to know."

"We'd better get out of here," Taylor said. She could tell Stephen was becoming more furious by the moment.

"Well, can I take a guess?" Mike asked tauntingly. "Once again ... the two lovebirds are getting married and you would like my approval. Was I right? Please, don't let me stand in your way ... by all means ... I say yes, yes. Taylor of all people knows that I'm all for true love and happiness."

"Mike, this is not a joke!" Taylor snapped at him. "What we have to say is very important."

"That's not it?" Mike continued. "What could be more important than marriage? Let's see ... something that's serious and important ... not like your cars, or your penthouses, or your millions, huh?" Mike then thought about one of his friends and jokingly said, "Don't tell me you're pregnant ... because you know—"

Taylor almost fainted when she heard the word "pregnant." Stephen had had enough as he stood up and hit Mike directly in the mouth. Mike's big body flew backward onto another table.

"Stephen, please! No!" Taylor shouted getting up out of her seat. But she quickly sat back down when Mike got back up and tackled Stephen to the floor. At this point, Taylor knew there was nothing she could do as she sat helplessly watching both men tussling on the floor. Within minutes, the police arrived and separated them. Brenda rushed back in to get Mike and to find out what was going on. She soon learned that he was, in fact, a part of the commotion. Taylor figured out that Mike and Brenda were seeing each other again after the police interviewed everyone. Their celebrity status cushioned the situation. The police gave everyone warnings and strongly suggested that both parties leave the restaurant as soon as possible.

Chapter Thirty-Five

Generational Curses
New York

A week later, Mike called Taylor to apologize. He also agreed to meet with her at the boutique alone. Taylor was in the back of the store counting inventory when Mike arrived at her store. One of her salespersons came to the back to tell her that a very good-looking man was waiting for her in the front.

"I'm closing the shop early today," Taylor told the clerk. She got up and brushed the dust off her clothes. The clerk's brow went up.

"Don't worry," Taylor assured. "You'll still receive a full day's pay. I'm sorry. I decided to do this at the last minute."

"No need to apologize, boss. I don't think anyone will have a problem with leaving early today."

"Stop it!! I'm not *that* much of a slave driver, am I?"

"No, actually I like working for you," the clerk replied.

"It's the whole notion that I have to get up every single day and work at another person's establishment ... that's what I despise the most."

"Talk about being pessimistic," Taylor teased. "Seriously, you should think more positively about your situation. You never know, maybe one day you'll be able to have your very own shop."

"Yeah, yeah ... that's what everyone always says ... one day. You never had to beg or plead your case to these financial institutions only to be told no a trillion times."

"Believe it or not, I have experienced rejection ... just in a different way. It probably wasn't a trillion times though ..." Both women began to laugh.

"You're so silly."

"I know," Taylor confirmed. "All I'm trying to say is ... don't give up on your dream. A door will eventually open up for you."

"Thanks, Taylor. Do you need us to do anything else before we leave?"

"No, I'm good," Taylor told her. "I'll close up just the way you all like it."

"Oh, my goodness, we all know what that means ... clothes not hung up or folded properly."

"Hey, you know I'm always in a rush." Taylor laughed while her two employees prepared to leave the store. Both of her workers were smart, savvy businesswomen who had a strong passion for the fashion industry. Working with Taylor was definitely a good starting point for them. She not only had them work in the store, but she also introduced them to key people in the industry: people who not only worked in the forefront of the fashion industry, but behind the scenes as well. For a while now, they had been running the entire operation by themselves. Taylor was very impressed when she came back to work at the shop. They had added an entire health, healing, and wellness line which worked amazingly well with her concept and the clothes and jewelry she had in the shop for sale.

"Would you like anything to drink?" Taylor asked Mike. She walked past him and clicked the switch that turned on the "close" sign hanging in the shop front window.

"No, I'm fine," Mike replied. "Is it okay if we sit here?" Mike pointed at one of her sofas.

"Yeah, that's fine," Taylor said, walking back over to him.

"Well, I'm all ears."

Taylor sat down beside him. "Where do I start?" She paused and looked down at the floor.

"Okay," Mike sighed. He was now anxiously waiting for her to speak.

"Wow ... this is harder than I thought it would be," Taylor confessed.

"Maybe I can make it easier for you by first apologizing to you once again for joking about your being pregnant. At that moment, I was thinking about one of my buddies on the team who was already going through a lot of problems and his woman hit him with that news ... that she was pregnant. We teased him for weeks. After a while, he thought it was funny too. The ongoing joke between us was … what's next? Don't tell me you're pregnant. I was stupid when I said that to you and Stephen because, of course, you all were not in on the joke. It was very rude of me. I'm sorry."

"Mike, like I told you on the phone," Taylor said, sitting down beside him, "I accept your apology. Explaining why you said what you said has been helpful. I actually thought you were serious because my being pregnant was exactly what we wanted to talk to you about."

"You're kidding?"

"No, I'm actually not. I'm very serious."

Silence

"Mike, it's true. I'm pregnant."

"So, you're telling me this because …"

"Because you're the father."

"Wow, talk about not being ready for this type of news," Mike said, leaning back on the sofa. For some reason, Mike didn't feel as bad as his friend felt when he heard the news. At that moment, he decided that he would do the right thing. He thought about his mother. She was going to be ecstatic. She had wanted a grandchild for a while now.

"Are you okay?" Taylor asked him. In her attempt to comfort him, she put her hand on his thigh.

"I'm shocked, but overall, I'm okay," Mike told her. He wanted to move her hand from his thigh. It had been a while since he felt her touch. He couldn't believe it was actually turning him on. "What about Stephen?" Mike asked. "What's going on between the two of you?"

"We're good friends, and—"

"Good friends?" Mike said interrupting her. "Taylor, he's still in love with you. I still have the bruise on my face to prove it. Don't lie to me. Tell me the truth. Are you and Stephen dating each other again?"

"Are you and Brenda dating each other again?"

"Taylor, you know Brenda and I are just friends."

"Which means you're screwing her."

"Now, I wouldn't assume that you're *screwing* Stephen just because the two of you are good friends again."

"Anyway ..." Taylor huffed, getting up from the sofa. She wanted to end this conversation now, and leave.

"Look, Taylor," Mike said. He walked over and hugged her from behind. "I know I wasn't the best person or friend during our breakup. I wish I could make all of this right—" he stopped speaking as he began to choke up.

Mike's next thought was to tell her how he truly felt about her. How he had been feeling for the past few weeks. How he thought about her nonstop since they had broken up. He was ready to spill his guts and put everything on the table. He wanted to tell her that he was wrong for leaving her; that he should've tried to work it out, and that he did, in fact, love her.

"Now is the time," he mumbled squeezing Taylor more tightly. "Now is the time to make everything right."

Ring ... ring ... ring.

"The phone," Taylor said, releasing herself from Mike's comforting grip. She walked behind the countertop to answer the phone. It was Stephen. He wanted to know when she was coming home.

"I should be there in a little bit," Taylor said, feeling guilty. She had not told him about her plans to meet Mike today. Taylor hung up the phone and directed her attention back to Mike.

"Who was that? Your mother?" Mike asked.

"No," Taylor replied. She couldn't believe that she had just said what she said. She wanted to tell a lie, but since Mike said he was willing to make everything right, she felt that she should do the same. "That was Stephen."

"Stephen? He's still in New York?"

"Yeah."

"Does he know we're meeting right now?"

"No, but I plan on telling him tonight."

"What hotel is he staying at?" Mike asked curiously. "I guess I need to apologize to him, too."

Silence

"He's staying at your place, huh?"

"Yes, Mike, he is," she finally admitted.

"Are you *screwing* him?"

"Mike ..."

"Sorry to be so crass. Let me rephrase my words."

"Yes, we have recently been intimate with one another."

"So what does he think about all of this?" Mike asked. He couldn't believe what Taylor had just said to him. Was

she that desperate, or what? Mike wanted to end this conversation now, and leave.

"He is actually very much invested in this entire
situation."

"Why is he so invested?"

A frown appeared on Taylor's face.

"Taylor, I'm not trying to be difficult. Is Stephen going to be okay with everything? This includes me being in
frequent contact with you and coming around your place.
He's going to be totally cool with me being the baby's
father?"

"Well, there is a small chance that he may be the baby's
father also."

"What do you mean a 'small chance'?"

"I did say that we were having sex."

"You said *recently*," Mike said irritated. "To me, 'recently' means 'recently.' Like maybe a day or even a week ago."

"Well, recently can also mean a month ago."

"Taylor, you're confusing me. Just speak plain English
to me."

"What's so confusing about what I've just said?"

"Just so that I'm clear, you're telling me that you don't
know who the father is?"

"Yes, I do."

"Have you been intimate with anyone *else* recently?"

"Okay, now you're being mean."

"What? That's a fair question to ask. First, you tell me
that I was the father, and then you turn around and say that

there is a small chance Stephen may be the father as well. What am I supposed to think, Taylor?"

"I'm almost ninety percent sure that this baby is yours."

"Ninety percent sure? You're joking, right?" Mike laughed sarcastically. "Why are you not one hundred percent sure? Were you sleeping with Stephen while we were engaged, or what?"

"Mike, you know I was faithful to you!"

"Taylor, I haven't touched you in almost two and a half months."

"And my ultrasound showed that I am about ten weeks pregnant ... do the math."

"So, tell me how is Stephen even in this equation? Did you jump in the sack with him right after we broke up?"

"Not directly after—"

"You're such a slut—"

Before Mike could complete his sentence, Taylor walked over to him and slapped him across the face.

"Don't you *ever* say that to me again!"

"I guess I deserved that one," Mike murmured as he rubbed his face. "Are you satisfied? We finally had our little talk. I now know that you're screwing my brother once again and the best part of it all is that *you two* are expecting a child. What can I say but ... I wish you the best." Mike turned around and began to walk toward the front door.

"Don't forget that you could be the father, too."

"I'm giving you permission to erase my name from this

equation. Now *you* do the math." Mike continued to stride toward the door.

"Are you going to walk out of your child's life … just like that?"

"Keep watching," Mike yelled back.

"And I thought you were a *real* man!"

Mike stopped and turned around. "And I thought you were a decent woman," Mike said with smirk on his face. Inwardly, however, he was heartbroken. "I guess we were both wrong. Don't worry, Taylor, your baby will be all right. Look at me. My father was never around, and I made it. Look at you. You didn't even know your father, and you made it. Just pray that you don't have a girl, and I truly believe that everything will work out just fine."

"You disgust me!" Taylor screamed. She quickly picked up one of the glass vases that was on the countertop and tossed it at him.

"The feeling is mutual, babe," he said as he swiftly ducked. The vase missed his head by an inch, hit the wall, and shattered into numerous pieces. "The feeling is completely mutual." Mike then turned back around and walked out of the door.

Taylor ran to the door and slammed it closed. Fortunately for her, the glass that was inserted in the middle of the door was thick and sturdy; otherwise, it would have shattered all over the pavement. She turned around, slid down the door, and sat on the floor. Still in shock, Taylor began to cry uncontrollably. *How in the world could I have allowed myself to end up like this? Without a man and knocked up.* She shook her head in disbelief because she couldn't blame anyone but herself. Not wanting to get up, Taylor continued to sit there, wiping away her tears now mixing with the mucus running from her nose.

"That bastard!" she screamed, hitting the floor. Her mind went back to Mike walking out the store. "I just can't believe him … I can't believe he left us." Her body was racked with sobs. After a few minutes had passed, Taylor finally pushed herself up off the floor. She walked over to the front counter looking for her handbag. *Maybe it's in the back office.* She started walking toward the back but stopped suddenly in her tracks. She remembered that she had left it up front. As she walked back up to the front of the store, her mother's voice spoke two words to her mind: *generational curses*.

"What?" she murmured and stood still for a moment. She began to think about her mother and her biological father, whom she still had never met. She longed to meet him, but what in the world would she do or say to him? She didn't know if she would hug him or slap him across the face. Mixed feelings always manifested when she thought about him. She thought about the notorious trio: Stephen, Mike, their father, and how they all met. Taylor wasn't sure if it was coincidental, miscommunication, or just plain ole Fate interfering. Whatever the case, here she stood in the same place where her mother stood twenty some-odd years ago, feeling rejected, dejected, miserable, and empty. She touched her stomach and thought about Mike's last words *… just pray that you don't have a girl, and I truly believe that everything will work out just fine.*

Through it all, Taylor wasn't sure if she had learned one single thing. All her insecurities and flaws were still there … masking themselves behind her pretentious smile and the need to want to help others. She looked up and there it was: her purse. It was lying right in the place where she had left it this morning. As she walked over to retrieve her bag, Taylor thought about how she was going to right all the wrongs of her past and regain control over her life, which now resembled a bona fide train wreck. She grabbed her bag and strode toward the front door. As she turned off the lights and locked the door, she decided at that very moment that one way or another … *this curse was coming to an end!*

Will Taylor's search come to an end?

The saga continues as a **brokenhearted** Taylor LaRue says good-bye to family, friends, and her glamorous lifestyle in New York City for better days in Atlanta, Georgia.

Mother LaRue, Taylor's beloved grandmother, and newfound friend Pastor Alex Gee attempt to restore her wounded soul and nurse her back to life. While spring cleaning one day, Taylor **unexpectedly stumbles** upon information that has been hidden for years — **secret information** that leads her directly to her long-lost father: Carlson Ellis Jackson, Attorney at Law.

Climb aboard and hold on tight while **untold truths are revealed** ... deception and lies are uncovered. This train ride is running full speed ahead and promises to leave the readers on the edge of their seat *STILL* craving for more ... **drama!!**

BREAKING THE CURSE ... the saga continues!!

Runway Collision Discussion Questions

1. What is true love? Does it exist?

2. Are you currently in a relationship where your thoughts frequently find themselves in the DANGER ZONE?

3. What do you think about Dena, Stephen's chick-on-the-side?

4. Are you or have you ever been in a relationship where you were the chick-on-the-side?

5. Do you think most men or men with power think like Stephen's father and grandfather that all men should marry a trophy wife but have at least one or even two blue ribbons within their reach at all times?

6. Do you agree with Diane when she told Taylor that a woman should never confront a man about an alleged affair, especially if the woman is not prepared to leave the relationship immediately?

7. As a wife or a significant other do you think it's ever okay to overlook infidelity?

8. What do you think about Taylor LaRue? Is she a strong woman?

9. Did you empathize with Stephen in Chapter Ten when he told Taylor he thought he was doing the right thing not wanting to make the same mistake as his father did thirty years ago?

10. Is Diane too involved in Taylor's life?

11. What are your views/opinions on receiving therapy? Do you think it works and/or is helpful?

12. Do you agree with Candace when she told Taylor that absent fathers is an epidemic in African American communities?

13. Do you think Mike was in love with Taylor?

14. Did you agree with Mike's decision to call off the wedding and end his relationship with Taylor?

15. If you were in a similar situation as Mike and Taylor, could you have the "true love conquers all" attitude and get over it?

16. Is Black men dating White women still a good or important conversation topic with Black women?

17. Do you think Taylor was foolish when she hooked back up with Stephen?

18. Do you believe Stephen was a changed man in Chapter Twenty-Nine?

19. What are your views on abortion? Was Taylor's initial decision to have an abortion the right decision?

20. What do Diane, Stephen William Blake III, Stephen's mother, Mike Washington, Mike's mother, and Taylor have in common?

21. What can women learn from Taylor?

22. What can men learn from Stephen and Mike?

23. What does a generational curse mean?

24. Do you believe in generational curses?

LaVergne, TN USA
28 May 2010
184295LV00003B/18/P